Beach Nights

Rehoboth Beach Reads

Short Stories by Local Writers

Edited by Nancy Sakaduski

A Playful Publisher

Cat & Mouse Press
Lewes, DE 19958
www.catandmousepress.com

PERMISSION AND ACKNOWLEDGMENTS

Cover illustration/book design by Emory Au. © 2016 Emory Au.

Copy editing by Katherine Pickett, POP Editorial Services, LLC

"Benny," Joey Masiello. © 2016 Joseph P. Masiello. Reprinted with permission.

"Burning for Rehoboth," Tom Minder. © 2016 Thomas Minder. Reprinted with permission.

"Cooking Lard and Candle Wax," Rich Barnett. © 2016 James Richard Barnett. Reprinted with permission.

"Fifty-Five," Mark Polo. © 2016 Mark A. Polo. Reprinted with permission.

"Finding Poe," MaryAlice Meli. © 2016 MaryAlice Meli. Reprinted with permission.

"Flight of the Songbird," Kathleen Martens. © 2016 Kathleen Langmaack Martens. Reprinted with permission.

"Good Vibrations," Kristin Norton. © 2016 Kristin Norton. Reprinted with permission.

"I Remember It Was Fun," Catherine Reed. © 2016 Catherine Reed-Fink. Reprinted with permission.

"Jazzed," Connie L. McDowell. © 2016 Connie L. McDowell. Reprinted with permission.

"Melvin and the Haunted Mansion," Weldon Burge. © 2016 F. Weldon Burge. Reprinted with permission.

"Mermaid's Moon," Jeanie P. Blair. © 2016 Jean Pitrizzi Blair. Reprinted with permission.

"Nudge," Cay Cutright. © 2016 Camille C. Cutright. Reprinted with permission.

"Partners in Crime," Joseph Crossen. © 2016 Joseph L. Crossen. Reprinted with permission.

"Salt Air Evenings," Mady Wechsler Segal. © 2016 Mady Wechsler Segal. Reprinted with permission.

"Senior Dance," Shelley Johnson Carey. © 2016 Shelley Johnson Carey. Reprinted with permission.

"Stacy Fischer Can Dance the Tango," Lonn Braender. © 2016 Lonn Braender. Reprinted with permission.

"Storm Surge," Terri Clifton. © 2016 Terri Clifton. Reprinted with permission.

"The Attitude of Gratitude List," Robin Hill-Page Glanden. © 2016 Robin Page Glanden. Reprinted with permission.

"The Last Day of Summer," David Yurkovich. © 2016 David Yurkovich. Reprinted with permission.

"The Portrait," Robin Hill-Page Glanden. © 2016 Robin Page Glanden. Reprinted with permission.

"The Triple Mary," Maria Masington. © 2016 Maria Masington. Reprinted with permission.

"The Vampire Surf Club," David Strauss. © 2016 David Strauss. Reprinted with permission.

"Tower Sixteen," Phil Giunta. © 2016 Philip Giunta. Reprinted with permission.

Table of Contents

PREFACE

These are the winning stories from the 2016 Rehoboth Beach Reads Short Story Contest, sponsored by Browseabout Books. Writers were asked to create a story—fiction or nonfiction—that fit the theme "Beach Nights" and had a connection to Rehoboth Beach. A panel of judges selected the best stories and those selections have been printed here for your enjoyment. Like *The Beach House, The Boardwalk,* and *Beach Days* (other books in this series), this book contains more than just "they went down to the beach and had a picnic" stories. The quality and diversity of the stories is simply amazing.

For contest information or other Cat & Mouse Press publications, go to: www.catandmousepress.com.

ACKNOWLEDGEMENTS

Thanks to Browseabout Books for their continued outstanding support. We are so lucky to have this great store in the heart of our community. They have supported the Rehoboth Beach Reads Short Story Contest from day one and continue to be the go-to place for books, gifts, and other fun stuff.

I thank both the Rehoboth Beach Writers' Guild and the Eastern Shore Writers Association for their support and service to the writing community. These two organizations provide an amazing array of educational programming, and many of the writers whose stories appear in this book benefitted from their classes, meetings, and events.

I thank this year's judges, Denise Camacho, Laurel Marshfield, John Nieves, Mary Pauer, Judith Reveal, and Billie Travalini, who gave generously of their time. They asked me to express how difficult their job was and how hard it was to choose from the many great stories that were submitted.

Special thanks to Emory Au, who so beautifully captured a spectacular Rehoboth Beach night for the cover illustration and who designed this book cover to cover.

I also thank Cindy Myers for her continued loyalty and support.

An extra-special thank-you to my husband, Joe, who continues to support and cheer for me.

I would also like to thank the writers—those whose work is in this book and those whose work was not chosen. Putting a piece of writing up for judging takes courage. Thank you for being brave. Keep writing and submitting your work!

—*Nancy Sakaduski*

Good Vibrations

By Kristin Norton

"I still don't get it." I threw the car into park. "No one actually *wants* to go to prom."

"Mom, yes, they do. There are, like, three types of people in the world who *don't* go to prom. You, serial killers, and people who spend more time at their PO boxes than at home. That's it."

My son, Ben. He's a puffy-haired angel, and also a complete smart-ass.

"I should've made you watch *Carrie*."

"It's not a big deal," he groaned. "They'll play terrible music, we'll take some pictures, we'll go home. No pig blood involved."

Apparently, he'd already seen it. Netflix ruins everything.

"Besides, there's only so much fun anyone can have at a prom when their mom is driving them there *and* chaperoning."

He had a point. But in my defense, I only planned on the chaperoning part. How could I know the limo driver would take a Dogfish Head detour and not show up?

I decided to chaperone because I wanted to make sure his prom went better than my own, which was a legendary disaster. Two decades later, I still suffered from post-traumatic prom disorder. (I'm sure that's a real thing. Everything is a real thing now.)

"Just do me a favor and don't do or say anything weird," he begged, as we approached his date's front door. *He should have grown up with my mother,* I thought. *Then he'd really know weird.*

A young boy, maybe seven, answered the door wearing a crab costume. After my brain caught up with my eyes, I introduced us in my perky, kid-friendly voice. "I'm Frankie and this is Ben. Is your mom home?"

Crab boy spontaneously burst into tears and ran into the back of the house, claws flailing. I reactively ran in the house to apologize and Ben followed to stop me.

"Way to go, Mom. Ten seconds. A new record."

"What did I say?"

"Their mom left a few years ago."

"Don't you think that qualifies as information you should have given me before I meet these people?"

We'd argued about this for weeks. He assured me that he and this girl Maggie were just going as friends, so there was no need for a formal family introduction. I was dumb enough to listen. Now look at us. Two fools, breaking and entering, making children cry. And yes, if I was going down, I was taking Ben down with me. Maybe next time he'll listen when I tell him nothing good ever happens at prom.

"Don't worry." I turned him toward the door. "Just go back outside and I'll explain—"

Expensive things make a distinctive sound when they break, reminding you just how many hours you'll have to work to pay to replace them. That's the sound we heard just then.

I looked down and realized that my purse had snagged a houseplant in a ceramic vase, pulling it from the table next to us and tossing it across the floor.

"Mom!" Ben yelled, officially done with me.

"It's OK," I lied. "I'm sure with a little superglue—" As I bent over to pick up the vase, the entire contents of my purse spilled, my humiliation along with my expired birth control on full display.

And that was the moment *I* was officially done with me.

"I'm leaving," Ben said, walking toward the door.

"Just wait." I scooped fists full of lip gloss, half-empty bottles of hand sanitizers, and houseplant soil into my purse to hide the evidence. It was no use. The footsteps of someone much heavier than a kid-sized crab radiated across the hardwood.

I think I began rapid-fire apologizing, the way any mumbling moron would. I don't really remember because when I stood up, everything else went foggy.

"Don't mind Max, he cries over—" The voice stopped as our eyes met. "Frankie?"

"Logan?" My throat closed so tight, I was surprised any words came out at all. "What are you doing here?"

"Well, I live here." He glanced down at the mess with a furrowed brow. "What are *you* doing here? Besides breaking my grandmother's vase. I thought you were in Seattle?"

"I moved back last fall," I half-explained, still trying to believe my eyes. "Last I heard, you were living in your van in Mexico. But now you have a house…and kids…and nice things…" I looked down at the broken vase and flinched. "I'll replace that."

"It's been twenty years, Frankie," he said.

"Twenty-one," I corrected.

"Exactly. Things change."

You'd never know from looking at him, though. His hair was in the early stages of graying but his dimples and crooked smile were just as charming as ever. How obnoxious.

"So you're—" The pieces fell together as I realized my son was going to prom with Logan Green's daughter. It had to be winning-the-lottery-on-the-day-you-get-struck-by-lightning odds.

"Can someone explain what's happening?" Ben asked.

But just then, Maggie made her entrance. She was the kind of beautiful you don't mind being distracted by, with waist-long red curls draped over one shoulder, and wearing a shimmering, champagne-colored dress. We showered her in compliments, but she was clearly distracted and by then, no one could blame her.

"What's with the dirt and tampons?" she asked.

Yes, it was as awkward as it seems.

"Just an accident," Logan said in an attempt to brush it off.

"But—" Maggie had a lot of questions. We all did.

Logan reassured her and called for Max, who emerged, still in his crab getup. Logan then turned to Ben and Maggie. "We have to get going; we're already late."

"It's OK," I said. "I'll drive them."

"It's no problem," Logan said. "I'm heading there anyway."

"Well, I'm chaperoning." As if that made me more important.

"Well, I'm chaperoning, too. Since I'm the vice principal."

Dammit. I knew I should have paid more attention to those papers the school sent home.

"He's at the top of the dad pool, too," Max said proudly.

"Oh, really?" My kid-friendly voice was struggling. "What's a dad pool?"

Logan tried to interrupt, but Max was faster. "It's a list that Madison Mahoney's mom made with some other moms. I saw it in their minivan when they drove me home from soccer once. Madison said the moms talk about who the hottest dads are when they think we're not listening. My dad's number one." He smiled. "We're always listening."

"Well, that's just great." I turned to Logan and gritted through my best fake smile. "If you think I'm sending my kid to prom of all places with the Dad Pool MVP, you're crazy."

"So..." Maggie's finger wagged between her dad and me. "You two know each other?"

Just say no, I thought.

"Really well, actually," Logan answered.

"Gross." Maggie cringed.

"So gross." Ben agreed, whole-heartedly.

"That's not what he meant." I hoped, anyway.

He insisted it wasn't, then reminded everyone how late we were and ushered us around the dirt pile and out the door.

"You're welcome to join us if it makes you feel better, Frankie."

I wanted to argue, but I knew that look of humiliation and resentment on Ben's face well. I made the same expression when my own mother was ruining my life. So, I swallowed the irony of how trying to shield my son from having the worst prom night ever was actually creating the worst prom night ever and went along.

Parenthood in a nutshell.

* * * * * *

In the garage sat the same 1972 faded green Volkswagen bus Logan drove around in high school. Sitting in it made me feel eighteen again, despite the side mirror, which revealed the aging truth.

"I can't believe you still have this," I said as we pulled out of the driveway.

"It's the only thing I got to keep out of the div—." He stopped short, glancing in the rear-view mirror. "This and the kids." He didn't sound bitter at all. Just the opposite.

"It looks exactly the same," I said, touching the dashboard.

"I replaced the engine last year. And I completely redid the back—you should see it."

"We're still here," Ben yelled, throwing one hand up and using the other to wave a crab claw from Max's costume.

Logan tried to clarify but Ben pleaded for him to stop. "We know what you meant!"

"So, you two dated?" Maggie wanted answers.

I was fine with lying, but...

"Junior and senior year," Logan confirmed.

Brilliant.

"Wow," Maggie said. "That's so..."

"Weird," Ben finished.

"It's not *that* weird." Logan tried diffusing the awkwardness. "Coincidentally, we went to prom together."

"Even weirder."

Despite Ben's protests, Maggie wasn't done digging. "If you went to prom together, how come I've never seen pictures?"

"Frankie burned them all."

"Why would you burn your prom pictures?"

"Well, for starters, I was wearing a wedding dress."

Logan winced, realizing the can of worms he'd just opened.

"Why would you wear a wedding dress to prom?"

"Funny you should ask." I turned to them, pleased to have an audience. "After picking me up an hour late…"

"Twenty minutes!" Logan protested.

"Twenty minutes that turned into an hour because you threw up on my four-hundred-dollar dress."

"Dad!"

"It was an accident," he conceded.

"How does that even happen?"

The question loomed in the dead silence.

I could say her dad got smashed on blueberry schnapps and Zima with Jeff Holtz in the limo on the way to my house and he got sick after the two of them decided to show my nana what goes on in a mosh pit. Instead, I lied and said he had the flu. Maggie thought it was so brave of him to take me even though he was sick. *Yeah,* I thought. *What a prince.*

He shot me a look from the corner of his eye and mouthed the words "thank you."

But I was quick to extinguish the sympathy. "Well, we didn't exactly have twenty-four-hour prom dress stores then and everyone I knew with a decent dress was going to prom, too. So, the only fancy dress available—"

"Nooo." Maggie gasped as Ben rolled his eyes into the back of his head, hoping to escape the hundredth time hearing this story.

"My mother's wedding dress," I said. "And this wasn't some vintage dream dress. We're talking full satin sleeves, a lace turtleneck, and a ten-foot train."

"NO!" It was the kind of horror only another girl could understand.

"I was sobbing, my makeup was running, and I broke out in head-to-toe hives. I looked like the bride of Chuckie."

"It wasn't that bad," Logan lied.

"You spent the whole prom with my best friend!"

"Cindy Bowman was *not* your best friend. She wasn't even your *friend*!"

"Yes, she was. We did the finale from *Dirty Dancing* in the eighth-grade talent show. We practiced the lift in her pool all summer. It was incredibly strange but that's not the point. That's best-friend cred."

"You hated her."

"Only because she made me cut my hair to be Swayze while she got to be Baby even though *my* name is Frances. She was a horrible person."

"I tried getting rid of her. She was just always there, talking about getting a role on that show *Blossom*."

"Oh my God," I huffed. "It was one episode for, like, seven seconds. She acted like she married Joey Lawrence."

"Well, she definitely wasn't worth the bloody nose."

"Whose bloody nose?" Maggie asked.

"*My* bloody nose," Logan said, as if he finally had something against me.

"I had nothing to do with that," I huffed. "He thought he could cheer me up by dancing along to Marky Mark and the Funky Bunch, but he slipped on my train and fell into the bleachers."

"What's a Marky Mark's Funky Bunch?" Ben asked.

I thought explaining trigonometry to my kid was hard. But explaining Mark Wahlberg's rap career? Even harder.

"Wait," Ben said, choking through laughter. "Mark Wahlberg was actually a rapper?"

"And you actually danced to it?" Maggie asked. "I thought you don't dance, Dad?"

"I was trying to impress Frankie!" he deflected. "*She* liked him, not me."

"Oh, please. You had the whole dance memorized."

I heard Ben say to Maggie under his breath, "It's like watching the worst reality show ever but I can't change the channel."

He was right. As much as I enjoyed a good train wreck, I didn't want to be in one. Besides, it was their night and we were sucking up all the oxygen. So, I rolled my window down manually—I couldn't remember the last time I did that—and took a deep breath. The smell of salt grew stronger as we neared the ocean, hugging me like an old friend, reminding me why I moved back here.

My mom used to always say no matter where you go in life, Rehoboth always has a way of pulling you back. She was right. It just never gets old.

* * * * * *

The kids gathered at the bandstand for their formal announcement and photos—the first stop before moving to the convention center. As the sun began to set behind the Dolle's sign, creating the perfect photo op, I realized that in all the chaos we hadn't gotten any of the traditionally forced pictures regular moms take. I didn't even bring a camera with me. This is why I'd never win at Facebook.

Normally I wouldn't care much, but not having a way to capture Ben's last school event (besides graduation, and I couldn't even *think* about that) caused my anxiety to take me from "I forgot the camera" to "what kind of mother am I" in under ten seconds flat. That's talent.

Logan reached for my jeans, stopping me mid-meltdown, and carefully pulled out the phone that was nestled in my front pocket.

"They put cameras on these things now, you know," he said.

It was a simple gesture, but it felt mildly intimate. Maybe I was reading too much into it.

We took photos of the kids and watched as they were announced. I was plagued by the phenomenon of seeing my grown child as the little kid he once was. But the photos on my screen refused to lie, reminding me that the boy who seemed like he was just six years old was now suddenly seventeen and leaving for Georgetown in the fall. I swore I wouldn't get emotional, but it was everything I could do to choke back a blubbering mess of emotions that would leave me looking like a washed-up jellyfish.

Luckily, I was distracted just enough by a group of women who kept looking our way. I guess you could call them attractive. You know, if you like the tiny-waisted, big-boobed, perfectly polished type. But how much of a market is there for that, really?

One of them, let's call her Barbie, approached us.

"Hi, Logan," she said, with a long, drawn-out croon. "I need your help over there for a second. I promise to give you back in one piece." Her face dropped to a subtle scowl as she looked at me.

Logan excused himself to run off with Barbie. It was typical, but no matter. I found a friend from high school—one who didn't make me cut my hair or steal my boyfriend—and we ducked out early to make our way to the convention center where the dancing part of the evening would be taking place. When we arrived, someone who took their prom responsibilities very seriously directed me to run the table filled with fudge and salt water taffy—easily the best location for miles.

As the kids poured into a room lit by hundreds of globe lights, I watched as they mingled and danced. It was familiar but somehow different. I was struck by how they seemed so much more mature than any of my friends and I were at that age. I still struggled accepting that Ben was ready to be off on his own. That's when it occurred to me that maybe *I* was the one who wasn't ready. It had been just him and me for so long now, I was terrified of letting go. I was pretending that I chaperoned because I was worried about his night without me when really, I was worried about mine without him.

I lost myself in waves of nostalgia and before I knew it, the night was winding down. The music slowed and nearly every student was comfortable enough to be on the dance floor at that point. That's when I felt a subtle tap on my shoulder. Logan held his arm out toward the dance floor and said, "Nobody puts Baby at the fudge table."

I held back a full smile but didn't hesitate to make eye contact with Barbie and her Silicone Squad, none of whom seemed amused.

"A move like this could get you kicked off the dad pool, you know."

"I've seen my competition," he said with a laugh. "I'm not that worried."

We fell right into the expected traps of reminiscing while watching the kids take selfies with their friends. "It's strange, isn't it?" he said. "Them growing up."

I sighed. "At least you still have Max."

"I do," Logan said, "but Maggie is my little girl. Now she's leaving and…I don't know…I can't help but notice that all the girls in my life leave for something better."

Nearly twenty-one years ago, the two of us stood on the boardwalk as he begged me not to leave for college on the West Coast. I wanted to convince myself that I could stay and we could magically grow up overnight and live happily ever after. But the truth was we were eighteen and every bit as immature and irresponsible as that implies. Even though I was terrified to leave, I knew I had to go where life was taking me. And so, I left. It was the right move, but one that he took personally and deeply. He refused my calls and never responded to my letters. We didn't speak again.

Until tonight.

"I have a confession to make," he said.

And here's where he ruins it, I thought.

"I knew you would be here tonight."

"What? But you said…How?"

"Well, I *am* the vice principal," he said with a smile. "I thought I saw you at school night but told myself I was just seeing old ghosts. Then I saw your name on Ben's file. I mean, how many Frances Vanderwoods could there be, right?"

"Why didn't you say anything?"

"I didn't know what to say. I felt like an idiot for never writing you back. And I should have called when I heard about what happened to Ben's dad. I was going through my divorce, I was bitter and, I don't know, I just chickened out. I didn't know how to erase all of that with a hello."

"But Ben and Maggie? Showing up at your house? How did you know—"

"Trust me." He spoke before I could even finish asking. "I couldn't have planned that if I tried. I was just as freaked out as you were."

"I have a purse filled with dirt and pieces of your grandmother's broken vase," I said. "There's no way you were as freaked out as me."

He smiled. "It's good to see you again, Frankie."

The moment broke when the DJ overpowered the speakers and everyone stopped. "If I can get your attention to the dance stage…"

Logan must have been more nervous dancing with me than he let on because he started rolling up his sleeves.

"I highly suggest that everyone get their camera phones ready," the DJ said, "because Vice Principal Green is about to supply you with enough Internet gold to make you more YouTube famous than a dancing panda."

Logan winked and ran onto the stage, putting on a black baseball cap he pulled from his back pocket. He leaned into the microphone and said, "Hey, everybody!"

It was clear from the way they cheered that the students were crazy about him.

"I hope you're all having a great time. There's plenty of night left, but since you all enjoy watching me make a complete fool out of myself…"

They cheered even louder, each fighting for the best camera angle.

"So tonight, I'd like to do a dance that I never got to finish for a special friend many, many years ago, Ms. Frances Vanderwood."

Without hesitation, Marky Mark's voice filled the room as the intro to "Good Vibrations" blared through the speakers.

He approached me with the swagger of an overly confident early-'90s rapper as he lip-synced the lyrics and reenacted the dance moves from the music video.

The students loved it. Even our own kids were laughing and cheering along.

OK, fine. I was, too.

It was corny and hilarious and even a little impressive. He had to have been planning it for weeks, maybe even months. Or maybe there was just a part of him that never really forgot it.

As I stood there, a wave of warm salt air rolled in and I couldn't help but think that no matter what, everything was going to be OK. I might have been terrified of what life had in store for me, but it did bring me back here. And for the first time in years, I felt like I was exactly where I was supposed to be.

In West Philadelphia, Kristin Norton was born and raised. On the playground is where she spent most of her days. Wait, that's the Fresh Prince. Kristin is actually a full-time writer, Muppet enthusiast, and dumpling lover. A native of Philly, she now lives in South Jersey with her husband and kids where she spends her sparse free time reading, road-tripping, and watching the sun set on the river.

Tower Sixteen

By Phil Giunta

Rehoboth Beach, DE — Summer 2006

From atop the fire control towers, you could see forever. At least, that's the way it had seemed to twenty-three-year-old Reggie Prell during the Second World War. Back then, Corporal Prell had been assigned to Fort Miles, where the army had constructed a series of observation towers to protect the Delaware Bay from incursion by German vessels.

"Grandpa, is a battleship the same as a U-boat?"

More than sixty years had passed since those days. Now, Reggie stared out through the horizontal slit in the tower wall alongside his son, Craig, and his eight-year-old granddaughter, Hannah. Outside, densely packed evergreens, awash in August sunlight, eventually gave way to the calm blue waters of the bay in the distance.

"No, a U-boat is a German submarine. The *U* stands for "*Unterseeboot*," which means 'undersea boat.' Now, you see that other tower way over there?" Reggie pointed to the left and Hannah nodded. "These towers were built in pairs so we could triangulate the position of a ship out in the water and radio the coordinates back to base."

"You ever sink any ships, Grandpa?"

Reggie chuckled. "No, they never made it this far. You want a better view? Let's go to the top."

Craig lowered Hannah to the metal landing. "Are you sure you're up to it in this heat, Dad?"

"I'm eighty-four, boy. I'm not dead. Don't need you henpeckin' me. Got enough of that from your mother, God rest her soul. Now, fall in and forward *march*."

* * * * * *

The top level of Observation Tower Seven in Cape Henlopen State Park allowed for a 360-degree view of the park and surrounding water. To their right, the white buildings and massive guns of Fort Miles were visible seventy-five feet below.

Hannah waved down at her mother, Candace, before gripping the chain-link fence with both hands. "I wish Mommy could see this."

"You know Mommy's scared of heights," Craig said.

Hannah pointed to the other tower they had seen earlier. "How many towers are there, Grandpa?"

"There were fifteen along the Delaware coast and four in Jersey," Reggie replied. "They tore down two in the Wildwoods years ago and there are only eleven left here."

"Thirteen," Craig said. "Unlucky number."

"They were built to last, at most, twenty years, and here we are, sixty-one years later. Pretty damn lucky, I'd say."

"How many soldiers were in each tower, Grandpa?"

Reggie shrugged. "About eight, give or take. Back in the day, there were no spiral steps. We had to climb a ladder all the way up and there was a wooden floor at every level. All those little windows near the bottom had glass in them." Reggie sighed. "About the only thing left now is the concrete." *Just a shell of their former selves.*

Reggie looked at Hannah. "You know how long it took to build each tower?"

She shook her head.

Reggie held up a bent, gnarled finger. "One week, start to finish. They'd pour all the concrete in a day and..." Reggie trailed off, staring down at Fort Miles. All of the buildings were gone, and in their places stood olive drab tents. Several men in World War II army uniforms hurried about. Still others were inspecting the guns.

"Dad, are you OK?"

Reggie frowned. "Must be some reenactment."

"What are you talking about?"

Reggie nodded toward the fort. "All those men in uniforms down there, and those tents are like the ones that were there before the buildings."

Craig followed Reggie's gaze. "I only see a bunch of tourists taking pictures. Are you feeling all right? Maybe we should go back down. I think the heat and the walk up here might've been too much for you."

"I'm fine." Reggie removed his sunglasses and rubbed his eyes. When he looked again, the buildings were back and the soldiers were gone, replaced by the usual strolling sightseers. "I know what I saw…"

* * * * * *

Although Reggie would never admit it, life had been lonely since Beverly died. They'd made a lot of friends after retiring to Rehoboth Beach, finally living in the house on Hickman Street that they'd rented out every summer for decades.

Still, everyone else had heard all of Reggie's army stories more than once. Certainly, his son and daughter-in-law were sick of them by now. His granddaughter, on the other hand, was a fresh audience and her enthusiasm helped fill the void left by the loss of his wife— the grandmother that Hannah never met.

Of course, Reggie would never admit that, either. He had a cantankerous image to maintain.

The sight of Hannah and Candace approaching from the shoreline snapped Reggie out of his reverie. With drenched bathing suits and matted hair, each was carrying a bucket filled with water. Hannah dropped to her knees in the sand just beyond the shadow of Reggie's umbrella and emptied her bucket.

Candace set hers down and reached for a towel from one of the empty beach chairs. "Making a castle?"

Hannah shook her head. "A tower like the one we were in today with Grandpa."

With a smile, Craig looked over at his father. "See what you started?"

Reggie grunted a brief acknowledgment but had become distracted by a young man sporting the khaki shirt and matching trousers of a World War II army summer service uniform. The soldier strode purposefully across the beach, and as he drew near, Reggie was able to attach a name to the face. *That's impossible.*

"Zeke?" Reggie struggled to his feet, keeping his gaze fixed on the soldier, noting the rank insignia of technician fifth grade on the upper sleeve of his shirt. "It *is* you."

The soldier didn't weave around the horde of sunbathers and beach chairs in his way—he simply passed *through* them. Yet no one seemed to notice him, except for Reggie. The soldier disappeared behind a group of young people crowded under a canopy. Reggie waited, but the soldier never emerged.

Craig raised an eyebrow. "What are you looking at, Dad? Cute little honey catch your eye?"

Sidestepping Hannah's pile of wet sand, Reggie started off across the beach. Craig shot up out of his chair and caught up with him easily. "Dad, where are you going?"

Reggie didn't reply. There was no time to explain, and doing so would only cause Craig more concern about the state of his old man's mind. Finally, they reached the canopy, but the soldier was nowhere to be found. A petite young blonde in a blue-and-white bikini stepped away from her friends and smiled as she looked from Reggie to Craig.

"Hi! Lose something?"

Possibly my sanity. Reggie looked right and left. "He was just here."

"Who?"

Craig gently took Reggie by the arm. "No one, ma'am. I'm sorry to bother you. My father is just…having a moment."

"Gotcha. No worries. Have a good one, guys!"

"Come on, Dad. Let's head back to the house and get cleaned up for dinner."

This time, Reggie didn't protest. Perhaps Craig had cause to be concerned.

* * * * * *

"Ever since Mom died, I've been worried about him," Craig said. "I knew letting him live here alone was a bad idea. Seems like he's declining fast."

"Maybe it's time to consider a nursing home—one that's closer to us."

"He won't leave Rehoboth without a fight."

"Well, then, I'm sure we can find something for him around here."

In the hallway just outside his spare bedroom, Reggie leaned against the wall, listening to the exchange between his son and daughter-in-law. The door was ajar, allowing him to remain out of sight. It hadn't been his intention to eavesdrop, but damn it, this was his home! No one had a right to conspire behind his back and make decisions about his life. *There's only one way I'm leavin' this house—*

"Grandpa, what are you doing?"

Reggie spun to see Hannah standing behind him. "Don't scare an old man like that," he whispered. "I was just…heading downstairs."

"Can you tell me more stories about the army?"

After a brief pause, Reggie smiled. "I can do better than that. I can *show* you."

Reggie found his old photo album and he and Hannah sat down at the dining room table. Hannah pointed to a picture of one soldier saluting another. "Is that you? You were skinny."

"Yep, that's me as a corporal saluting one of my superior officers, Captain Trusten D. Lee."

Hannah raised her right hand to her forehead in a mock salute.

"No, no. That looks like you're shading your eyes from the sun. Let me show you a proper salute. Stand up and face me."

Reggie and Hannah rose from their seats and stood about four feet apart.

"Straighten up, soldier. Shoulders back. Posture is critical to a proper salute. Start with your right arm straight at your side, hand flat, all fingers together. Now, raise your hand quickly to your brow like this." Reggie snapped his hand up at a slant, index finger gently touching his eyebrow.

Hannah mimicked the movement, albeit clumsily.

"Your upper arm should be parallel to the ground and your forearm at a forty-five-degree angle, just like mine."

Hannah adjusted her arm accordingly.

"Now, turn your hand so that neither the palm nor the back are visible."

Hannah twisted her hand back and forth a few times until she decided it was correct.

"Better. Now drop your arm quickly to your side like this." Reggie lowered his arm in one swift chopping motion.

Hannah did likewise.

"Very good. Might make a soldier out of you yet."

"Not if I have anything to say about it."

Reggie and Hannah turned to see Candace standing in the doorway. "Time for bed, Hannah, if you want to be rested up for Jungle Jim's tomorrow."

"After Jungle Jim's can we go see some more towers, Grandpa?"

Reggie shrugged. "Sure, if your parents are OK with it. We can't go inside the other ones, but we can see 'em. Maybe even walk up to a few of 'em."

* * * * * *

Everyone was fast asleep by the time Reggie crept out of the house for his usual midnight stroll along the boardwalk. There were still plenty of night owls milling about, but as Reggie passed Rehoboth Avenue, their numbers dwindled. By the time he reached Olive Avenue, there was no sign of life at all. Even Obie's outdoor patio was devoid of the usual party crowd.

Reggie glanced over his shoulder and stopped, incredulous at the sight of a boardwalk utterly deserted. *Where the hell did everyone go?*

Shivering against an unseasonably cool ocean breeze, he gazed up at the Edgewater House and over at the Boardwalk Plaza. The balconies were all empty. *Lights are on, but no one's home.*

Further north, from the direction of the Henlopen Hotel, the sound of heavy footfalls gave Reggie hope that he wasn't entirely alone in the night.

Under the boardwalk lights, a group of men jogged toward him. They formed two lines, leaving a gap between them. Even at this distance, it was clear they weren't dressed for summer—but rather for a war that ended sixty years ago.

He recognized the combat uniforms and M1 rifles slung over their shoulders. While Reggie's mind screamed at him to get out of their way, his legs refused to budge.

Four soldiers passed him on either side without so much as a nod.

Reggie recognized the last man on the right as the same one from the beach. "Zeke? Zeke, it's me, Reggie!"

He reached out to grab Zeke's arm, only to grip thin air. Reggie stared as the unit continued on—all but Zeke, who fell out of formation just long enough to give Reggie a casual salute before catching up with the others. Reggie felt another tremor in his chest, but there was no sea breeze this time.

Finally, the men turned and vanished down Rehoboth Avenue. Reggie knew it would be useless to follow.

"Grandpa?"

Reggie's frozen legs nearly buckled at the sight of— "Hannah!"

All around them, life returned to Rehoboth. Obie's came alive with music and laughter. People chatted on balconies.

"Hannah, it's after midnight. What are you doing out here?"

"I followed you."

"Where are your parents?"

"Asleep."

Reggie rubbed his forehead. "I need to sit down a moment."

He led Hannah to one of the white benches and they sat facing the beach. Reggie reached into the pocket of his cargo shorts. After looking around, he pulled out a metal flask and downed a quick snort.

"What's that?"

"Scotch. Don't tell your parents you saw me drinking this. They're looking for any excuse to put me away."

"I won't say a word. Why are you out so late, Grandpa?"

"Oh, I sometimes take walks late at night when the air is cooler and the stars are out. We really should start heading back. If your parents find out you're out here with me, we'll both be in for it. On the way, I'll tell you another story about the towers."

Reggie took her hand as they strolled along the boardwalk. "Do you remember how many were built here in Delaware?"

"You said fifteen."

"Right, and the four in Jersey were numbered twenty-three through twenty-six."

"What happened to the numbers in between?"

"Funny you should ask. Some of us in the battery used to joke that when we died someday, we'd all go to the big tower in the sky. From there, we would look out for the rest of our brothers-in-arms, keep them safe. After a while, we started calling that Tower Sixteen. It became sort of a code.

"Over the past decade or so, many of the guys have…passed away. We ain't getting any younger. The rest of us would see each other at the funerals and we'd say that Ben, or Dwight, or Paul, or…anyway, we'd say they went to Tower Sixteen and we'd all know what that meant.

"I got a letter in the mail last week from a lady whose father served with me at Fort Miles. Zeke Watkins. He and I often worked the same shift in the tower. Anyway, Zeke died a month ago. His daughter even wrote in the letter that he went to Tower Sixteen."

Hannah squeezed his hand as they turned off the boardwalk onto Hickman Street. "I don't want you to go away, Grandpa. Not to a nursing home or Tower Sixteen."

Reggie smiled. "Me neither."

They continued in silence until they neared the house.

Reggie opened the storm door slowly, letting Hannah enter first. "All right, let's be quiet now. Don't want to wake your parents." He took one last glance toward the boardwalk but couldn't see beyond the silhouettes of the eight soldiers standing shoulder-to-shoulder across the intersection.

* * * * * *

The following evening, after returning from dinner at Grotto Pizza, Candace ushered Hannah out to the backyard, leaving the men alone in the living room. Reggie knew immediately that something was amiss. His suspicions were confirmed when Craig motioned toward Reggie's favorite easy chair.

"Dad, do you have a minute to chat?"

Reggie shrugged. "Where else am I going?" He lowered himself into the chair and settled in for what would undoubtedly be an uncomfortable conversation.

"We've been concerned about you lately."

"So I noticed." Reggie leaned forward. "Why don't we get to the point, boy? You want to put me in a home because you think I'm losing my mind, especially after my behavior over the last few days. Well, I don't blame you."

Craig stared at him for a moment. "I'm…glad you're being reasonable about this. I've been worried about you living here by yourself these past nine years."

"And yet I've managed pretty damn well on my own. I have a lot of friends here in Rehoboth and we look after each other."

"But they can't be with you twenty-four seven." Craig waved toward the stairs to the second floor. "What if you fall down these steps, or worse, the basement steps, and crack your head open on the concrete floor?"

Reggie held up his hands. "I'm not arguing, Craig. Every man should know his limits. Tell you what, how about I sleep on it tonight and we'll discuss it again tomorrow—I promise."

* * * * * *

Once again, Hannah waited until Grandpa reached the corner of Hickman and King Charles before setting off after him. This time, she wore sneakers instead of flip-flops and made sure to stay far back so he wouldn't hear her.

By the time she caught up with him, Grandpa was standing at

the top of the closest ramp that led down to the beach. Hannah approached slowly, wondering what he was staring at.

"Grandpa?"

He turned, slowly this time, as if expecting her. That's when she saw the concrete tower at the end of the beach looming above the crashing waves.

Hannah stood beside him. "How did that get there?"

"It's the real reason I've been taking these late-night strolls. I've been waiting for it since I learned about Zeke, and now it's finally come for me."

Hannah's head snapped up to look at him with wide eyes. "Is that—?"

Grandpa nodded. "Maybe from there, I'll find your grandma again."

"No!" Hannah shook her head and threw her arms around his waist. "You can't go! I don't want you to go!"

"It's OK, Hannah."

"No, it isn't!" Tears clouded her eyes, but she didn't care. All that mattered was keeping Grandpa here with her.

He lowered himself to one knee and reached under his collar. He lifted a beaded chain over his head and held up two small metal plates. "These are my dog tags. I won't need them where I'm going." He gently slipped them over Hannah's head. "Now, you tuck these under your shirt and keep me close to your heart and I'll keep you close to mine. Always know that I'm looking out for you no matter where I am."

With that, Grandpa leaned forward and kissed her on the forehead before making his way down the ramp to the beach. Tears welled up in Hannah's eyes as she ran after him, but the sight of the tower, something that once excited her, now filled her with dread. She stopped and watched as he walked toward the tower, then disappeared inside.

* * * * * *

Back at Grandpa's house, Hannah found her mom standing outside. Tears streaked her face. "Hannah Prell, where have you been? We looked all over the place for you!"

Hannah was nearly out of breath from running. "I was with... Grandpa on the beach. The tower...came for him."

Her mother shook her head and took Hannah into her arms. "Tower? No, sweetie, that's impossible. You couldn't have been with Grandpa. Your father went to check on him earlier and...God, I don't know how to tell you this. Grandpa died in his sleep."

Hannah pulled back and shook her head. "No, Grandpa went into the tower with the other soldiers."

Her dad emerged from the house. "Girl, where have you—?"

"I'll show you! The tower's out there on the beach. Come on!" Hannah broke free of her mother's grasp and ran back toward the boardwalk at full tilt.

* * * * * *

Hannah's parents caught up with her at the end of the ramp. They peered in awe at the tower along the shoreline just as a group of soldiers filed out. As they lined up on either side of the door, Hannah counted eight of them. Then, a skinny young man with short brown hair stepped out of the tower. He wore an old-style army uniform, just like in Grandpa's pictures.

Hannah wiped her eyes and looked at his face. He wasn't just one of the men from Grandpa's pictures, he was—

"Grandpa?"

Craig stepped onto the sand. "Dad?" He began running, with Hannah keeping pace beside him. "Dad!"

"Grandpa!" Hannah stumbled as she neared the tower, falling to her knees in the sand.

Grandpa stood over her. "On your feet, soldier. Straighten up.

Shoulders back." He raised his right hand sharply to his eyebrow. Hannah picked herself up and returned the salute, just like Grandpa had taught her. Then, Grandpa turned to his son. "I'm afraid a nursing home just ain't for me, boy."

It was now Craig's turn to cry. "Dad, wait…"

"I'll be sure to give your mother your love." With one last smile, Corporal Reggie Prell turned and stepped into the tower.

The other soldiers followed.

The door closed.

And, as Hannah saluted one final time, Tower 16 faded into the night.

PHIL GIUNTA'S FIRST NOVEL, A PARANORMAL MYSTERY CALLED *TESTING THE PRISONER*, WAS PUBLISHED BY FIREBRINGER PRESS IN 2010. HIS SECOND NOVEL IN THE SAME GENRE, *BY YOUR SIDE*, WAS RELEASED IN 2013. PHIL'S SHORT STORIES APPEAR IN SUCH ANTHOLOGIES AS *REDEUS: DIVINE TALES* AND *REDEUS: BEYOND BORDERS* FROM CRAZY 8 PRESS. IN ADDITION TO CONTRIBUTING SEVERAL STORIES, PHIL SERVED AS EDITOR ON THE SPECULATIVE FICTION ANTHOLOGIES *SOMEWHERE IN THE MIDDLE OF ETERNITY* AND *ELSEWHERE IN THE MIDDLE OF ETERNITY* FOR FIREBRINGER PRESS. A THIRD INSTALLMENT IN THE SERIES IS CURRENTLY UNDER WAY. HIS PARANORMAL MYSTERY NOVELLA, *LIKE MOTHER, LIKE DAUGHTERS*, IS SLATED FOR RELEASE IN LATE 2016. VISIT PHIL'S WEBSITE AT HTTP://WWW.PHILGIUNTA.COM.

The past and the present blend with the beach and war and storm to create a textured tale filled with energy and empathy. A walk down the historic past of Rehoboth and coastal Delaware. Well done and intergenerational. Easy to read and enjoy. This story about the power of love and innocence to see things that others can't see is a touching beach read that makes imaginative use of its Rehoboth setting. A haunting read worth going back to.

Stacy Fischer Can Dance the Tango

By Lonn Braender

It was dark and bitterly cold, and the wind was whipping up the street. It was insane to have gone to the beach, but Stacy had needed to; he had to try. He had needed to see the ocean, to be near its cleansing waves.

Head down, coat pulled tight against him, Stacy hustled away from the boardwalk and the ocean and hurried down Baltimore Avenue. He had had this crazy hope that the power of the waves might wash away his sadness and his pain. Maybe if he had gotten wet it would have worked, but in the middle of January, the ocean was far too cold.

He turned up his collar as a frigid rain began pelting him, the icy droplets burning his face. Halfway down Baltimore Avenue, it started to pour and he began to run. He took cover under the overhang, against the side of a building that housed an art gallery called Anita Peghini-Räber Gallery. The street was deserted, but music and voices from inside the gallery found him. He looked in, and as he did, the door opened. A tall woman in a long, flowing, colorful dress opened the door. She had tangled blond hair pinned in place and a captivating smile.

"Come in, dear. Don't stand in the rain."

Stacy saw people dancing and having fun, but he didn't want to interrupt the party.

"Don't be shy, come in." The woman reached out, taking hold of his sleeve.

"I don't want to intrude." Stacy rubbed at his chin, a nervous habit his wife had tried, and failed, to stop.

"Intrude?" She had a small accent. "We're dancing the tango; you can't intrude."

"I don't dance."

"That's OK, come get warm. You'll freeze out here." Her voice was exotic. *She* was exotic. "I'm Anita."

He stepped up and into a long glass porch. "Stacy, Stacy Fischer."

The main gallery room inside was large and lit by candles. It looked warm and inviting. There were maybe twenty people, some paired off dancing, others standing to the side, talking and watching the dancers. Stacy, unsure, studied the room quickly. There were paintings everywhere, on walls and on easels pushed against the walls. The paintings were whimsical and ethereal, much like Anita.

Couples danced in small circles in the center of the room. It wasn't the fierce straight-line tango that Stacy remembered from old movies. He watched for a second, then caught Anita watching him. He stepped back. He didn't belong there.

"Give me your coat, Stacy. Come dry off." She was still smiling.

"I shouldn't."

Anita coaxed him lightly. Stacy frowned, then stepped into the cozy room. As he entered, some turned and looked, some smiled, and one gentleman nodded, but most kept dancing.

"Earl, Stacy needs a glass of wine," Anita said to an older man standing nearby as she hung Stacy's coat.

She led Stacy in, and when Earl returned she introduced them. "Earl, this is Stacy. He was getting soaked."

"Welcome to tango night," said the slender, gray-haired, sixty-something man.

Rehoboth Beach Reads

"Thank you." Stacy took the glass and watched as Anita moved across the room. She was elegant and graceful.

"Do you like to dance?" Earl asked.

"No, I was just trying to get out of the rain. She dragged me in." Stacy nodded across the room.

"She can be persuasive."

"Insistent."

"In a sweet way."

Stacy looked outside. It was pouring. He sipped the cheap wine and scrutinized the dancers. Most were men and women around his age. One man, who looked younger than most and accompanied an older woman around the floor, was a particularly good dancer. His movements were precise and polished.

Stacy panned the room. He wanted to smile, but his heart wouldn't let him. He sighed, put the glass down, and looked for his coat.

Anita reappeared at his side. "Stacy, you should dance." Her eyes twinkled in the overhead lights. She was a beautiful woman with a perpetual smile.

"I should go."

"Dancing will help you, no matter the sorrow." This she whispered in his ear.

"I can't dance." He rubbed his chin.

"Surely you've danced, at weddings?"

"At weddings." Stacy looked outside. His burden was heavy and squeezing his heart. He wanted to hide.

"Oliver," Anita called to the center of the room. "Can I borrow you?"

The man who had been dancing with the older woman stopped, said something to his dance partner, and then stepped over alongside Anita.

"Oliver, this is Stacy Fischer. Would you be a love? He doesn't know the tango."

Oliver smiled, first at Anita, and then at Stacy. He held his hand out, and his smile broadened. "Well, Stacy Fischer, come, let me show you the tango."

Stacy forgot about all his sadness and stepped back, closer to Anita. He whispered to her. "But he's a man."

"I'm sure he knows that. In Rehoboth, we dance. It doesn't matter, man or woman."

"Stacy, I promise not to bite," Oliver said, this time taking Stacy's hand and gently pulling him to the dance floor. Oliver never lost his smile, nor his gaze into Stacy's eyes. "The tango can be simple and fun or elaborate and seductive. Tonight, we'll do the basics."

Oliver took Stacy's left hand and placed it on his waist. He did the same with his right hand on Stacy. Then he took Stacy's right in his left and held it up. Still smiling, he said, "Just follow my lead." Then he nodded and walked, one, two, three steps. He counted and bobbed as he moved.

Stacy, scared to death, stumbled.

"Relax, let me guide you. Don't be nervous."

Oliver took a step and gently pulled Stacy with him. Stacy, a second behind, stepped on Oliver's left foot, then quickly jumped away. Oliver took hold and pulled Stacy back.

"I'll walk on the bottoms, you can walk on the tops." Oliver laughed at the old joke. He positioned their hands again and smiled. "Ready?"

Oliver took a step, Stacy followed, this time eyes locked on his feet. Oliver took another step and a third, pulling Stacy with him.

When Stacy looked up, Oliver was looking into his eyes, not at his feet. It was odd as hell, dancing with a man. He wondered who was watching. He glanced to both sides; Anita and Earl were, but most of the others were dancing, talking, or sipping wine.

Distracted, he stumbled again. He blushed and looked at Oliver.

Oliver guided him again, stepped to the side, and turned. Stacy followed. "That's it. Not so hard?"

"You're a good leader."

"A good leader needs a good follower." Oliver winked. "Now relax. Dancing can help many ailments."

Stacy tried to relinquish his fear. He looked down again to watch where Oliver's feet were going and missed another step.

"Look up, at me. Your feet will know where to go."

Stacy looked up and frowned as he tripped again.

Oliver took a step and guided Stacy with a slight push and pull at his waist and hand. He nodded as Stacy followed. "There you go. Enjoy the movement."

Stacy looked up and smiled, his first. He relaxed a little and for the first time really looked at Oliver. They were the same height, which made looking into his jet-black eyes natural. He searched Oliver's face, something he hadn't done to another man other than his son. Oliver had fair skin, a slender nose, high cheekbones, and hair that matched his eyes. But what caught Stacy's attention most were Oliver's eyelashes. They were longer than any he'd seen before and perfectly framed his eyes. For an instant, Stacy wanted to touch them.

"You're doing great, Stacy Fischer."

"Umm."

"Ready to pick it up?"

"Uh."

"Feel the music. Let it take you." Oliver pulled Stacy's hand and picked up the pace to better match the beat of the song. He walked Stacy across the floor, keeping his eyes on Stacy's. His smile never faded. He danced Stacy into the rhythm of the song and stepped him gracefully around the room.

Finally, Stacy relaxed into Oliver's lead. Oliver's hand, warm on his waist, expertly nudged him along. His other hand in his, Oliver turned him effortlessly. Soon enough, Stacy felt like he was gliding across the floor, and holding Oliver's hand, firm and strong, not soft like a woman's, no longer felt wrong.

"There you are." Oliver grinned. "The music's got you. You're tangoing."

"I am." Stacy laughed and looked into Oliver's shimmering eyes. "I can tango!"

Oliver glided Stacy around the room a minute more until the song ended. The dancers stopped and clapped. Oliver bowed.

"Thank you," Oliver said as he rose.

"No, thank you. Sorry about your shoes."

"No worries." He laughed.

Stacy looked around and saw the others were milling about. The music started again. Oliver bowed again and turned. "Walter, I think you promised me a dance?"

His voice was clear and bright and made Stacy feel good. He watched Oliver traverse the room, so self-assured. Evidently, Oliver danced with everyone. He watched the two men take up position and start to dance. They flitted about the room, dipping and twirling. Walter, much older than Oliver, seemed focused on his feet. Walter wasn't smiling, as he had, in Oliver's hands.

Stacy stood for a moment and watched Oliver, graceful, fluid; much like the paintings on the walls behind him. As Oliver turned toward him, his smile widened as their eyes met. Embarrassed, Stacy looked away, but when he looked back, Oliver was still smiling at him.

Watching Oliver and Walter dance pushed his sadness further away. Stacy felt better, good even, until he looked outside; the rain had slowed. He felt the tug, his sadness urging him to return to the world he'd known for the last few years. The world of sorrow and sickness that tugged at his heart, wanting him to leave the joy he felt here in this art gallery. He looked back in time to see Oliver spin Walter under his arm with ease and grace, obviously enjoying the motion.

He should go. He took a step, but Anita appeared beside him.

"Stacy, that was good, no?" She clasped his hands.

"It was Oliver." He felt shy.

"It takes two to tango." Her smile, like Oliver's, was a gift.

"Anita, thank you for saving me. I should go." As he spoke, a sadness as heavy as wet snow blanketed his heart. He turned his face, trying to hide.

"Do you have someplace to be?"

"No, but—"

"Stay and dance. It can only help."

He looked back at Anita. Her smile dimmed, turning somewhat sad.

"The tango can help." She held out her hand.

Just then, Oliver stepped over. He was bouncing. "Stacy, dance the next song with me, please. It's my favorite." He held out his hand.

Stacy reached out toward Anita, but Oliver took his hand. He blinked, the second time in his life to hold a man's hand. He followed and smiled when Oliver faced him. The heavy wet snow surrounding his heart started to melt.

Oliver stood for a second as one song ended. His smile widened as the next song started. "This is a great song. You'll see. Just follow me."

The opening bars to "Tango in the Park" burst out of the speakers. Oliver bowed slightly, took Stacy's hand, and turned his head. He nodded once more and walked three steps before stepping left. Stacy followed, letting the firm hand on his waist guide him into the mix of dancing couples.

Stacy double-stepped until he felt the rhythm. After realizing that no one was watching him dance, with a man, he relaxed into the music. It did feel good.

"There you go," Oliver said softly into his ear. "Let the music guide you."

Oliver expertly led Stacy in and out of the other dancers. Stacy followed, moving about the room gracefully, and suddenly he was alive. He was using muscles he forgot he had. Years of sitting at his wife's bedside had taken a toll on his body, and though he'd be sore in the morning, he didn't care. He was *dancing*.

Stacy smiled—not a big smile, but a true one—as Oliver led. At a spin, which caught him off-guard, he laughed, trying to catch up. As he did, they passed Anita and Earl, who applauded. Stacy blushed.

All too soon, the song slowed and stopped. Oliver ended the dance by dipping him, just enough to make a show. Stacy panicked—he had twenty or more pounds on Oliver. He started to resist, but Oliver was skilled and strong. He dipped Stacy with ease and stood him upright before Stacy could stop him.

"Oh my, I didn't think you could hold me," Stacy panted, from dancing, yes, but more from the dip.

"A man never drops his partner." Oliver released Stacy's hand.

"Thank you."

"You tango like Fred Astaire, Stacy Fischer. Thank you." Oliver smiled and bowed again.

Stacy searched his face for insincerity and found none. All he saw was kindness and gentleness.

"Thanks, Oliver, I needed this."

"Anita's not usually so insistent that someone join us. Is everything OK? Are you in trouble? You seem like you have a heavy burden."

"I buried my wife last August." His sadness came into view but didn't overtake him.

"I'm so sorry. I shouldn't have asked." For the first time, Oliver lost his smile.

"Thank you, but it was a blessing of sorts. She'd been ill for a few years."

"I hate that part of life. It's not fair."

"No, it's not. But she's no longer suffering."

"Now you are."

"I'll be OK." Stacy rubbed his chin and looked away.

"Yes, you will. Give it some time. Everyone grieves, but you will be fine." Oliver reached over and hugged him. Stacy froze, then relaxed slightly. "Dancing will help. You should dance every day. You already look better."

Stacy remembered what had brought him to Rehoboth. He'd come hoping to find solace, never thinking he'd find it at an art gallery, dancing the tango, with a man.

"Stacy, you lied to us!" Anita joined them and put a hand on his.

He wondered if this woman did that to everyone, it felt so natural. It felt so reassuring. "Honest, it was Oliver. I did my best not to step on his shoes."

"And you did well." Oliver squeezed his arm. Then he turned to Anita and Earl. "The heart has a way of showing the feet where to go."

"That it does," Anita agreed. "Stacy, have a glass of wine. We're taking a break for a few minutes but we will dance again."

Stacy smiled—his need to run was strong and again he looked outside. The rain had stopped and it wasn't so black. It would be easier now. He'd be OK, he knew. "Anita, thank you. This has helped more than you know."

"Oliver has a way with worry."

"I think you do, too. I don't know how you knew I needed help, but thank you."

"God lets us know when someone needs to dance. That's why it rained on you."

"Stacy," Oliver chimed in, "have a drink with me before you go. I know nothing about you."

Stacy saw that the three of them were smiling at him. "What about dancing? I'm sure others want to dance with you, Oliver."

"They can wait their turn. Besides, we dance every month."

"OK. I'd like that."

"Oh, good! Sit there," Anita exclaimed and pointed at a sofa against the far wall. "Earl, help me with the wine?"

"Come, sit." Oliver gestured to a loveseat, where they sat side by side.

Again, Stacy felt odd, being this close to this man. Oliver was so casual and content being close with men, something Stacy had never been. He wondered, and not for the first time, if Oliver was gay. He'd known a couple of gay men in his life; he worked with a gay man he considered a friend. But he'd never danced with one, nor been this at ease, and had definitely never been as intimate as he felt now. He was thinking these thoughts when he was startled back to the present by Oliver's melodic voice.

"So, Stacy Fischer, what brings you to Rehoboth in the dead of winter?"

The use of his full name was somewhat odd and he shifted in his seat. "I needed a break, to get away."

"Do you have family here? Do you have a place?"

"No, I'm in a hotel on Rehoboth Avenue."

"Why Rehoboth Beach?"

"I was here as a kid and again before getting married. I loved it here. I don't know if it was the ocean, or the people, or something else, but I remember being completely happy here. I came back to find out."

"And?"

"It's Rehoboth. There's some sort of magic here."

"There is—I can attest to that. There's something about this town that draws people like Anita."

"And you."

"Thank you." He bowed his head again.

"Here you are." Anita handed a glass to both. She glanced around to see if she was needed elsewhere, but she wasn't. She took a chair opposite Stacy, and Earl sat beside her. "You tricked us, Stacy. You can tango."

"Honest, I have never tangoed before in my life. Oliver did it all."

"Oliver is a good teacher. He knows just how to hold you."

"That he does." Stacy sipped. The wine burned slightly as he swallowed, which wasn't a bad thing. It reminded him that he could feel again.

"I'm so glad you found us. We need new a new face." Anita raised her glass to him. "And I think you needed to dance. The tango can heal many ailments, especially those of the heart."

"So I've discovered," Stacy agreed, but how did she know? Was it that obvious?

"Stacy, how long will you be here?" Oliver asked.

"I leave Monday."

Oliver frowned. "Too bad. That means I won't see you again. Well, make sure you go dancing before you leave."

"You do like to dance," Stacy said.

"Oliver is an instructor, among other things," Earl added.

"What else do you do?"

"I'm a personal trainer and I teach yoga."

"That explains the dip." Stacy laughed.

"He's excellent," Anita exclaimed. "He's gotten me in the best shape of my life. I can touch my toes again."

"You did the work." Oliver grinned.

"You showed me how." She turned to Stacy. "He's amazing. He can look at you and know what you need."

"It's all in the posture." Oliver leaned in conspiratorially and touched Stacy on the knee.

"You can read a body," she countered.

"And you, my dear, can read the heart." Oliver raised an eyebrow. "You look into a person's soul and know what they feel."

"I'm a painter. That's what we do."

"That's what *you* do," Earl added. He stood, excusing himself. "I'll get the music."

Oliver sipped his wine and looked around the room. The music started and people began pairing off.

"You should go dance. There are people who want their turn," Stacy suggested to Oliver. "Thanks for everything. I really appreciate it."

"You're welcome, but don't leave, or at least promise you'll come back and dance with me."

"I promise." Stacy put his empty glass on the table and stood. He thanked Anita for inviting him in, for saving him. He started to move but didn't get far before she pulled him in for a hug.

"You come back and tango with us again. It's good for the heart," Anita almost whispered in his ear, her small accent flirting with the word *tango*.

He took another step but didn't make it past Oliver, who also pulled him into a hug, big and warm and comforting.

"It was wonderful to meet and dance with you, Stacy Fischer. I hope it's not a once-in-a-lifetime event." Oliver held Stacy's hand. "Please come back."

Stacy promised to return, found his coat, and floated out. Before stepping down the steps, he turned back and looked into the gallery. There, in the window, were both Anita and Oliver, watching and smiling. Stacy gave a quick wave, laughed, and turned toward the hotel.

The street was empty, the air was warmer, and the clouds had passed by, leaving the sky packed with stars. The heavy blanket of sadness that had stifled him was gone. He laughed; his kids would never believe his story. They would never believe that he had danced the tango, in Rehoboth, with a man, with Oliver.

Walking down the deserted street toward his hotel, he didn't care what the kids might think. He felt good, finally. He knew the healing had started; he knew he'd be OK. He now knew there were people who cared, and he loved them for it. And he knew he'd come back, soon. He'd be back to dance the tango in Rehoboth.

LONN BRAENDER IS A JERSEY-BORN ARTIST, PRINTER, BUSINESSMAN, ENTREPRENEUR, AND NOW WRITER. A PAINTER OF LANDSCAPES AND SEASCAPES FOR MORE THAN TWENTY-FIVE YEARS, HE RECENTLY FACED CHANGES THAT FORCED HIM TO FIND AN ALTERNATIVE CREATIVE OUTLET. WRITING HAS FILLED THAT NEED AND HAS BECOME HIS PASSION. LONN HAS WRITTEN A DOZEN OR MORE WORKS, BUT "STACY FISCHER CAN DANCE THE TANGO" IS THE FIRST TO BE PUBLISHED IN A BOOK FORMAT. LONN RESIDES IN BUCKS COUNTY, PENNSYLVANIA, WITH HIS FAVORITE MUSE AND LIFELONG CRITIC, BOTH OF WHOM HAVE A PLAN TO SOMEDAY CALL REHOBOTH THEIR PERMANENT HOME.

JUDGE'S COMMENT

A quiet little story about chance encounters; more importantly, the joys of letting go and seeing, with newly opened eyes, just where your feet and your heart might take you.

I Remember It Was Fun

By Catherine Reed

They are good to us, these assisted-living people. Not all of them are. My cousin says they treat them like children where she stays. We are only two miles from the beach, so I worry it must be costing my kids a fortune, but they tell me Delaware is a good place to be old.

Each day the van takes people somewhere—mostly to doctor's appointments. En route to the medical offices, Alonzo will drop you off at the mall or the library. He drops me off at the beach.

"You got your watch, Ms. McCoy?" he asks, helping me manage the steps to the boardwalk. I know he means my GPS. We wear them just in case we wander off. Later, I will probably only know that it's a watch.

"No swimming," he says with a chuckle. "You know I'll get in all kinds of trouble if you decide to take a dip." He deposits me on a bench where I can watch the people, watch the ocean. "Don't forget your sunscreen," he reminds me, pointing to my canvas tote bag, with its bedazzled peace sign from arts and crafts day.

A dolphin swims by; three more follow. This has always been their routine, for at least every summer since I was seventeen. Can they be the same dolphins? Are they as old as me?

I watched them every day that summer at the beach. I was working over in Ocean City at a big seafood restaurant that hired dozens of high school kids each season. They still do, but now it's Russian kids. We stayed in terrible old apartments owned by the restaurant. The toilets were rusty and the showers only lukewarm. It was noisy and crowded, and they cheated us when they took the rent money out of our paychecks. I worked in the kitchen; it was hot and steamy enough that the crabs barely needed to go into the pot. I was seventeen, away from home, and every day was grand.

One of the dolphins flies up out of the water; she spins and slaps her tail. The folks down on the sand spot it and I hear somebody yell, "Dolphins! Over there—look, look!" Umbrella by umbrella, as the message moves along, people jump from their chairs, point, and cheer. It's sort of like Old Faithful in Yellowstone, or that clock in London—Big Bob, Big Bill, Big—whoever he is. Those dolphins are reliable and come by every day to amuse the tourists. Maybe the Chamber of Commerce has a trainer on salary; maybe he used to work at Sea World.

Technically, I believe they are porpoises.

There was a boy that summer; more than a boy, really. I woke up one morning on the floor of his apartment, with the imprint of shag carpet on the side of my face. It seems I had gotten too comfortable with a bottle of Southern Comfort. Sully lived over a tattoo parlor in an old house on Route 1, with a driveway widened just enough to accommodate a few cars. It had a dark, narrow staircase, and you had to duck your head at the top to get to his apartment. I believe it had been the attic earlier in the life of the house. It was hot up there, so hot; hotter than the restaurant kitchen on Saturday nights in July. Even with open windows and ocean breezes, it seemed you might melt. I stayed with Sully for the rest of the summer. They still took the rent money from my paycheck, though.

Alonzo is pulling the van into the parking lot at Sea Colony. "I'll be just a few minutes. I got to get Mrs. Lewis from her bridge club. You hang tight, OK?" He's wearing a tank top and his tattoos are on display.

I hung out in Sully's tattoo shop whenever I wasn't working. After his last customer had left and his ink was cleaned up, we'd take a blanket down to the beach and be together in the darkness right there at the edge of the ocean. If we got too close to the edge, it would be like the love scene in that old movie, *From Here to Eternity*. I was Deborah Kerr. Sometimes there'd be a noise out in the water—a different sound than lapping waves. I wondered if it was dolphins, if maybe they had a night shift.

I can't find Sully's tattoo shop now, though. We are headed home, driving through Dewey Beach. None of the shops or hotels seems familiar.

"I used to sleep with a tattoo artist in a house along here somewhere," I told Mrs. Lewis. "I was seventeen."

She patted my hand. "No matter, dear, it was the sixties. Those kinds of things happened."

I can still get myself dressed and undressed, although sometimes the buttons are crooked. Does it really matter, though? The night girl is fixing it, getting me a glass of water, making sure I've taken my medicines. She opens the window just a crack; I have to ask her each night to do that.

Sully and I would smoke a joint before we went to sleep. I wouldn't mind doing that now; it made for soft, fuzzy kinds of dreams. We could see the sky through a window from where we lay in his bed. We'd count stars and talk for hours, about what God might be or if there was a God; about blueberries and acid and mountain climbing. We talked about everything and nothing. It was fun.

We were always naked. We had to be—it was so hot and sweaty up there; or maybe that was our excuse. That was also fun.

I'm up bright and early in the morning; it's Tuesday—hairdresser day. Alonzo squeezes seven of us into the van. It's tight even though it's an eight-passenger van. We don't have our bikini bodies anymore. I wear my hair short and although I have no need for a weekly appointment with hot rollers and hairspray, I like to get my nails done and wander around in the shopping center. (Yes, I wear my watch.) There's a CVS, a pizza place, a Candy Kitchen—and a tattoo shop.

Everyone seems to have tattoos now, men *and* women. Once I even thought I saw a child on the boardwalk with one but then realized it was some sort of sticker. Girls didn't get tattoos when I was coming up; they just didn't. Janis Joplin was the only girl I ever saw with a tattoo before I got mine. Sully did a little dolphin on the back of my shoulder. I never wore a tank top or bathing suit around my parents again. A few boys in college dumped me when they saw it. It was a minor embarrassment to both of my husbands—proof of mistakes made before I was "lucky" enough to meet them.

A sign in the window reads, "Walk-Ins Welcome," and so I do. The walls are covered with tattoo art, and I wander around considering the ideas. A young man with a ring in his nose comes from the back of the shop and asks if he can help me.

"How much does a tattoo cost nowadays?"

"A lot more than it cost back in the olden days, lady, I can tell you that." He laughs.

"Oh, mine were always free," I said, winking at him, and turned to leave. *Smart-ass.*

I always wanted another tattoo but never got up the nerve. I like what the marines get, the one that says, "Hell and Back." Sully did a lot of tattoos that summer for guys coming home from Vietnam. I remember one who brought a map; he wanted the outline of the country with the number fourteen in it. That's how many people he killed there, at least how many he was sure of, he said.

Too late now, I guess; it would be hard to draw a straight line on this old lady skin.

No matter how full the moon might be, or how many stars are shining, the beach at night is the blackest of black. Sully builds a little fire and we wrap up in his sleeping bag and spend the whole night out here. He tries to name the constellations. He can always find the easy ones—the dippers and Cassiopeia. His favorite is Microscopium, which he says looks like a microscope, but of course that's just BS. I love his made-up constellations, including the one he calls Nixon's Nose. Sully says the stars are tattoos that God put on the sky. We skinny-dip on the blackest of black nights. No one can see us naked; no one can see my dolphin. The water is so cold.

"Jesus, Jesus, Jesus," I hear Alonzo saying. "Thank God she had her watch on."

On Friday night, a bus takes us to the bandstand. Alonzo's van would have had to make five or six trips to carry everyone who wanted to come. There's always a band here during the summertime; there always has been. Before there was Woodstock, there was the Rehoboth bandstand. It was a party each Friday night in this very same spot where I'm now listening to a country music cover band. There are plenty of seats by the stage, but I find a spot on a bench near Dolle's. I can hear them just fine.

Sully and I and a bunch of other people are dancing in the sand. Is it Creedence Clearwater? No, it has to be a cover band. Sully is singing his head off—it's a song by Bob Dylan—a song about lying in the sand dunes in a big brass bed. So much fun.

On Tuesday, I have my nails painted blue. Pink feels old lady to me today. At the tattoo shop, the same ring-in-nose kid is at the desk.

"How long does it take to get a tattoo?" I ask.

"Depends what you're getting—a little heart, half an hour; a sleeve, all weekend."

My daughter is staying at the Boardwalk Plaza Hotel with some friends; it's her ladies weekend at the beach. She wants to take me to lunch and then do some shopping. She thinks my bedspread is shabby.

"And not shabby in a chic kind of way," she says. "First, we'll go for a manicure."

I look down at my hands. "I just had a manicure on Tuesday."

"But clearly you weren't paying attention, Ma. Look." She reaches for my hand. "They painted your nails blue."

At the outlets, I am guarding her packages and holding her purse while she tries on dresses. I reach in and get her wallet. Folded in quarters are two fifty-dollar bills, hiding behind her license. I take one of them.

A hurricane is coming; I can hear the waves crashing and roaring all around. Sully takes my hand and we fight the wind, sand biting at my face. We find our way to the edge, where it starts to feel wet on our feet. Sully's flashlight is bouncing from the white caps, taller than both of us. I am happy and scared, laughing and screaming with him.

The night girl slams down my window. "Ms. McCoy, it's raining outside. I'm going to close this now."

"Here are our girls!" sings out one of the hairdressers, the one with the spiked hair.

Alonzo has dropped five of us off, each with our money safely tucked into our purses. Mrs. Lewis keeps hers in her bra. I have my daughter's fifty dollars, and another fifty for the hairdresser. Today I'm supposed to have a haircut as well as my manicure. "I'll be back in an hour and a half. Get beautiful, ladies."

When I see the van make the left out of the parking lot, I slip through the door and walk to the end of the shopping center, to the tattoo shop.

"And here she is again," ring-in-nose says. "What would you like to know today?"

I pass him my folded up fifty-dollar bills. "Can you do my tattoo in an hour and a half?" I pull up the sleeve of my T-shirt. "Here on my arm. Put 'I remember it was fun.'"

CATHERINE'S FIRST NOVEL, PUBLISHED IN A SPIRAL NOTEBOOK, WAS WILDLY POPULAR THROUGHOUT THE FIFTH GRADE. SINCE THAT TIME HER WRITING HAS INCLUDED TERRIBLE TEENAGE POETRY, BITS AND PIECES IN HER COMMUNITY NEWSPAPER, AND FORTY YEARS OF MEETING MINUTES AT PRINCE GEORGE'S HOSPITAL CENTER. SHE IS A MEMBER OF THE EASTERN SHORE WRITERS ASSOCIATION. "I REMEMBER IT WAS FUN" IS HER FIRST PUBLISHED PIECE, INSPIRED BY A CHARACTER IN HER (AS OF YET UNPUBLISHED) NOVEL, "JANIS JOPLIN WAS MY BABYSITTER." SHE LIVES IN BOWIE, MARYLAND, WHERE SHE AND HER HUSBAND RAISED TWO SONS. SHE IS A CRUSADER FOR CURSIVE WRITING.

The Triple Mary

By Maria Masington

Rehoboth Beach was back on the radar because I had the unpleasant task of going online to cancel reservations for the wedding my son had just called off. His fiancé, Glenn, had infidelity issues, which my grandmother had referred to as "zipper problems," so she was on my mind as I clicked, called, and lost money. "This is Lou Applebaum calling to cancel the flowers for the wedding. Yes, I realize I'm going to lose my deposit." "Hi, I'm calling to cancel...Yes, I know..."

I looked up the Atlantic Sands Motel on a whim. When my grandmother Nonni died, I'd found an old Atlantic Sands postcard she'd laminated. It now hung on my bulletin board among the wood pulp flotsam and jetsam of my life. The sea-foam green building boasted two huge white seahorses facing each other, and the burnt-orange and turquoise trim of the 1960s. The ad on the back said it all:

ATLANTIC SANDS MOTEL

Open All Year · Private Heated Pool
Restaurant on Premises · Elevator Service
80 Units · Air Conditioning · Phone Service
TV · Individually Heated Rooms

The decision for our grandmother to take my cousins and me to Rehoboth had apparently been a compromise. Our Italian mothers, from the northern part of the Garden State, had always summered at the Jersey shore. Our fathers from "the South," i.e., varying parts of Maryland, had gone to "the ocean" each year, so my grandmother laid down the law and picked neutral territory: Rehoboth Beach,

Delaware. According to Nonni, it was the only week of the year she didn't have to wear a girdle.

Each year, she schlepped her three granddaughters there for a vacation. While our parents struggled with school, bar exams, dissertations, unwanted pregnancies, and marriage counseling, my cousins and I piled into Nonni's powder-blue Cadillac to spend the seven best days and nights of our year.

The first year, 1970, we were seven, eight, and nine, and after buying beach buckets, shovels, and towels from the five-and-dime on the boardwalk, and renting a sky-blue umbrella and thatched metal folding chair for Nonni, we headed for the beach. We were always the first on the beach so we could get the spot closest to the lifeguard stand because "your mothers will never forgive me if you drown!" Everything Nonni said was loud, bold, and written in stone. She said this so often and so emphatically that it was as if our mothers being mad would be worse than one of us being swept off into the Atlantic.

Good Catholic women, every female in our family was named after the Blessed Mother. Nonni was Mary Rose, our mothers were Mary Theresa, Mary Anne, and Mary Grace, and though in the real world my cousins and I went by Lou, Fran, and Kat, our grandmother bellowed out our full names. "MARY LOUISE, MARY FRANCES, MARY KATHERINE, DON'T GO OUT TOO FAR! MARY LOUISE, MARY FRANCES, MARY KATHERINE, STOP RUNNING. MARY LOUISE, MARY FRANCES, MARY KATHERINE, DON'T KICK SAND ON PEOPLE'S BLANKETS!" Always our full names, always in the same order. Between the volume of her voice, with its heavy Italian accent, and three black-haired whirling dervishes who all had the same first name, we got some eye rolls.

Once, a lady in a big hat and huge sunglasses came over to tell Nonni that we had dropped two crackers by her blanket, and then began a diatribe about seagulls and beach etiquette. Nonni looked her straight in the eye and said, "Go peddle your fish elsewhere." I'm sure that woman had no idea that being compared to a fishmonger was the worst insult my grandmother, from the toe of Italy's boot, could think of.

Nonni was owl-like, short and buxom with thick ankles, rhinestoned cat-eye glasses, and a short bluish silver perm, and she never missed a trick. She was only off her game five hours a week. Monday through Friday, rain or shine, no matter the season, and despite the beautiful sand and water, she watched her "story," known to the rest of the world as *All My Children.* She was still sad that *Dark Shadows* had been canceled; Mary Frances said she had a crush on Barnabas Collins.

As our skin grew darker and our hair grew lighter, we spent hours in the ocean.

"Mary Louise, Mary Frances, Mary Katherine, I'm coming down to take a birdbath," Nonni would yell from her beach chair. We'd wave her to the sea, watching her shuffle down in her flowery skirted swimsuit and splash water on her arms and chest. That was a bird bath. She never went in past her calves, yet it never dawned on us that she couldn't swim. Every year she'd make the same announcement the first night at dinner, "One day this week I'm going to go down to the water and go in all the way," but it never happened. As she put it, "I went to Rome, but I didn't see the pope." She got to the water's edge and chickened out.

The year we were nine, ten, and eleven, the war between Nonni and Mary Frances started, because Mary Frances was "boy crazy." As the youngest, I still played with Barbie dolls. Mary Frances said my Barbie needed a more manly man than Ken, so she traded him to another girl on the beach for the girl's brother's G.I. Joe. Mary Frances then proceeded to orchestrate passionate make-out sessions between the two dolls. "If you're not good, I'm not taking you to the crazy clown tonight," Nonni threatened. The "crazy clown" was Funland, but Nonni called it the crazy clown because of the black, white, and red harlequin face painted over the "Freshly Roasted Peanuts" sign on the side of the building.

The best part of the vacation was nights on the boardwalk, where we would have dinner, talk, watch the sun go down, and stay long after dark. Nonni cheated on her diet, crammed herself onto every ride, and waddled behind us among the crowds like a fog horn yelling, "Mary Louise, Mary Frances, Mary Katherine, don't run too far ahead," her muumuued frame clogging the flow of traffic.

We ate dinner at The Avenue, Robin Hood's, or Grotto's, each of us taking a turn sitting next to Nonni. During these meals we talked and talked and talked. She pumped us for dirt on our parents' marriages, careers, and financial situations. "Does your father work too much?" "What does your mother say?" "Does she hear from Uncle Sonny?" And without realizing it, we learned our history—how she'd met my grandfather at a bocce game.

"He said, 'Girl, hold my coat.' Ten days later he asked my father if he could marry me."

"What did you say?" I asked.

"I said, 'Do you even know my name?' He said, 'No.' We got married two weeks later."

"My dad said you'll never remarry because you don't want anyone stealing your money."

Nonni did not confirm or deny, but gave the same answer she would give until she died decades later: "I'll never remarry because I'll never find another man as good as your grandfather."

"My mom says she should have married her high school boyfriend, Luke Dettwyler, because he inherited a lot of money, and now we would be rich," said Mary Katherine, to which Nonni retorted, "You know what happens when you marry for money? You pay for it every day of your life!"

On rainy nights we ate downstairs at the Atlantic Sands and then sat on our balcony, overlooking the water and writing postcards. With No. 2 pencils and six-cent stamps, we wrote to our parents, siblings, friends, and teachers.

One year, Mary Frances bought a postcard of a cartoon nudist beach from The Thunderbird Shop that read, "Well, you wanted a CHEEKY postcard!" Nonni confiscated it, and after that, all correspondence had to be inspected before being mailed from the front desk.

In the light of flashlights and citronella candles, we played cards and strung seashells into necklaces. Then we ended our beach nights by piling into the queen-size bed, listening to the waves hitting the shore, and dreaming of the next day.

The last year we went to Rehoboth was 1975, the year we turned twelve, thirteen, and fourteen. By then, we had one topic of conversation from morning to night: boys. Still the owl, Nonni accompanied us to the beach every day, but she no longer seemed to worry about us drifting out to sea. At dinner, all her questions were about boys and the fact that we were all boy crazy. When Mary Frances was tearful over a breakup, Nonni announced to everyone at the Robin Hood Diner, "Boys are like buses; a new one comes along every ten minutes."

One night, as we prepared for dinner at Grotto's, we came out of the bedroom in a holy trinity of pastel tube tops and cutoff shorts. Nonni rolled her eyes, said, "*Madone a mia*," and proceeded to stomp ahead of us down the boardwalk, as if a shout out to the Blessed Mother was going to give her the strength to make it through the next hour. After dinner, for the first time ever, we were allowed to go to the crazy clown alone, but with strict instructions that we were not to talk to anyone, were to take turns pairing up on the rides, and were to be back in the room at "9:30, not 9:31."

We watched Nonni walk back to the hotel by herself and headed to Funland. But Mary Frances soon ditched us, and with trepidation we returned to the Atlantic Sands at 9:29 p.m. as a duo instead of a trio. At 9:45 Nonni went to the front desk, had them place a long-distance call, and screamed at Mary Frances's mother in Italian. At 10:00, she demanded that the Atlantic Sands staff contact the police, who finally arrived at 11:00 to talk with her. She told us to wait in the lobby "with both feet in one shoe," in other words, not moving.

At 11:10, Mary Frances stumbled into the hotel, smelling of beer. The cop gave all three of us a lecture about safety, but failed to notice what Nonni saw: Mary Frances had come home with her tube top on inside out. When our grandmother demanded an explanation, Mary Frances giggled, flopped into a lobby chair, and said, "Don't worry, Nonni. I went to Rome but I didn't see the pope!"

Nonni said, "We are leaving right now and I am never taking you anywhere again." Within fifteen minutes, everything was packed and the four of us paraded through the lobby. She simultaneously piloted the Cadillac and lectured Mary Frances for the entire two-hour drive, talking about going to confession, wedding nights, disgracing the family, and "never being able to show our faces at the Atlantic Sands again."

While Mary Katherine and I dutifully listened, Mary Frances, still working off the effects of the beer, began to nod off. "Wake her up," Nonni would demand, and then start another diatribe.

As we pulled into Mary Frances's driveway, Nonni delivered her final comment. "You know what they say about girls who give the milk away for free?" To which a tired and cranky Mary Frances replied, "Moo." Nonni dragged her out of the car by her braid and pulled her up the sidewalk like a tired dog on a short leash. We stayed in the car while we watched Nonni swing Mary Frances in past the front door, and listened to her yelling, in English and Italian, until the neighbors' lights went on in the universal language of the sleep disturbed.

Mary Katherine and I were returned to our parents in the wee hours of the morning, and that was the last vacation. The rest of the summer we were not allowed to hang out with Mary Frances because she was a "bad influence," and within the year, life and schedules and different schools pulled us in different directions.

We drifted apart, with the exception of an occasional bridesmaid gig, where we inevitably dug out the tube-top story. Mary Frances was closest to Nonni in adulthood, but none of us stayed close to one another, except through our grandmother. "Have you heard from Mary Frances? She lost another baby," like it was a wayward set of car keys. "You should call Mary Louise. They are taking her right breast." "Think about calling Mary Katherine—she needs to get rid of that lazy loser husband. I bet he has zipper problems, too!"

Sadly, Nonni died in her sleep the year we were thirty, thirty-one, and thirty-two, and subsequently we lost our emotional telephone operator and the clearing-house for our relationships. To be honest, Facebook is now our main connection.

Mary Louise Applebaum posted:

Mary Frances Burke and **Mary Katherine Miller**
remembering Nonni and the Atlantic Sands. We appreciate all your support as we go through the difficulty of canceling Jeff's wedding and hope we can all get together soon.
Love to all!

Mary Katherine Miller posted:

> Weird how all the science and social media does not seem
> to help. We have 4 marriages and 2 divorces between
> the 3 of us. Jeff's betrothed had zipper problems, but our
> grandmother only knew her husband for 3 weeks before
> they got married. They were happily married for 30 years,
> and she spent the next 30 years alone—because no other
> man could ever measure up to our grandfather. She had
> a true love, a good marriage, and a quarter of a century
> broken heart.

Jeffrey Applebaum "liked" and posted:

> What would your grandmother say if she knew she had
> a great-grandson who was broken-hearted over a man
> named Glenn?

And there it came, like a voice front the past:

Mary Frances Burke posted:

> "Boys are like buses; a new one comes along every ten
> minutes."

Maria Masington is a poet, essayist, and short story writer from Wilmington, Delaware. Her poetry has been published in *The News Journal*, *The Red River Review*, *Damozel Literary Journal*, *The Survivor's Review*, *Wanderings*, *The Fox Chase Review*, *Van Gogh's Ear*, and *Currents*, and by the University of Colorado. Her short story "Impresario" appeared in the anthology *Someone Wicked*. Maria is a member of the Written Remains Writers Guild and is active in the Delaware and Philadelphia art scene. She has been a guest on WVUD ArtSounds and invited as a featured reader at the Fox Chase Review Reading and 2ND Saturday Poets. Maria also freelances as an emcee at various artist venues, including the Newark Arts Alliance's monthly open mic.

The Attitude of Gratitude List

By Robin Hill-Page Glanden

June

Hey Juli,

I'm writing this letter to you from Rehoboth Beach in Delaware (which I didn't even know was a state)! LOL!! It's been 3 days and I already miss you and New York City and all my friends. My dad is working on his next book and he and Mom rented a condo here that overlooks the ocean. That's way cool, but the condo is tiny. I do have my own bedroom, but I miss our big penthouse and there is no doorman here. Well, my Parental Units say I need a change of scenery and an attitude adjustment. WTF??!! So—get this, they took my iPhone away for the whole summer! OMG—can you believe it?! And—I have to write letters to send by snail mail. So you will be hearing from me this summer—in writing—by hand—with a pen—on paper. And I have to walk to the post office today and buy stamps. How lame is that? Mom says I need to learn how to <u>really</u> write instead of just texting, tweeting, and emailing. And I only get 2 hours a day on my laptop, plus limited TV time and NO video games—at all!! How bad does that suck?!

I'll try to email you and catch you on Facebook when I can, but I still have to write these letters. And—I've got to spend time outside every day! They rented me a bike to ride and I have to go for a walk with Mom EVERY day. I have to get up off the sofa, they say, and MOVE. This is gonna be one long freakin' summer. Oh, and the other thing I have to do is write a list of 10 things I'm grateful for EVERY NIGHT before I go to bed. Mom calls it my "Attitude of Gratitude List." I mean, really?? Is that a corny idea or what? So my first list was this: "I am grateful that this summer is only going to last for 3 months." I wrote that 10 times. My Mom looked at my list and shook her head and said that we have a lot of work to do. I'm gonna have to celebrate my 16th birthday in July here in Smalltown USA. Great. Real great.

Your pissed off BFF,
Madison (just call me Sad and Mad Maddie!) ☹

Hey Maddie,

Wow, bummer about your deal there. Please don't be sad. I miss you, too. But you were lucky you squeaked thru and passed all your classes. I flunked English and math and have to go to summer school. It's totally the worst. So here's the thing—I made the mistake of telling my parents about your summer plans, and they saw the letter you wrote when it came in the mail, so now they think it's a good idea for <u>me</u> to write letters, too. My Mom talked with your Mom on the phone and now I have to write back to you all summer. AND they are taking <u>my</u> phone away during meals AND making me sit down at the dinner table with them every night with no phone, tablet, iPod, or TV. They're also limiting my time on the internet and playing video games. I had to take a walk in Central Park with my Mom today. She likes to go for a long walk every day that the weather is good. So now since YOU have to walk with YOUR mom, I have to walk with MY mom. It was hot and we walked for almost an hour. Yuck! But I'm glad I'm still in the city.

I'm going out with Lindsey, Teresa, Marco, Brent, and Tyler tonight. Wish you were here to go with us. Oh yeah, thank your parents for getting me in on their stupid summer plan. Like it's not bad enough that I gotta go to summer school. Thanks a helluva lot! We'll survive this summer. Somehow.

Later girl,
Juli

Hi Juli,

Got your letter and I was so happy to hear from you, but this is such a drag. I'm being tortured. Mom makes me pile on the sunscreen and go outside at least once a day. The beach is really nice, but we have to walk together and we have to walk fast—she calls it "power walking." There is one awesome thing about Delaware—tax free shopping! Yeah baby!! No tax on anything!!!! They have these huge outlet shopping centers up the road and Mom and I are going there later this week.

We had to rent a car. There are no subways here! There's not much public trans in general—not like in New York. I don't know how people stand it. You pretty much have to drive to get anywhere. They have lots of designer stores, so when we go to the outlets I'll look for one of those leather bags you like. Oh—and the pizza here is good. Not exactly New York pizza, but pretty decent. And there's snow cones, caramel popcorn, fudge, beach fries and salt water taffy. Yum!! But Mom has put me on a healthy eating diet thing with her and Dad, so treats are limited and I'm eating a lot of fresh fruits and veggies from local farms. Yes, there are farms close to here. Oh, man, I am so out in the boonies!

I am really jealous that you guys are going out. Where did you go and what did you do? BTW, how's Brent doing? He is soooo good looking. He plays guitar really well. He told me he wants to be a rock star. I bet he will be. I can hardly wait to get back home to see him. And you, of course. I am not feeling particularly grateful these days, but I am looking forward to the outlet shopping. Miss you so much.

Stranded like a beached whale,
Madison

July

Hey M,
So did you say NO sales tax—on ANYTHING? Wow—I mean, WOW! Can you look for one of those cross-body bags for me (red is my first color choice) and see if you can get the new iPod? I have enough saved up from my allowance to pay your mom back.

I'm doing OK, I guess. We went to a street fair in the village on Saturday and then out for ice cream. Brent asked about you. I think he likes you, but he's kind of a jerk. We went to this cool vintage shop after the street fair and he stole a couple of things when the owner wasn't looking. He thinks shoplifting is fun and cool.

The Attitude of Gratitude List

And he teases me sometimes because I'm a little bit chubby. Yeah, he is pretty hot, but I don't like him very much. If you're thinking of dating him when you get back, you might wanna think twice about that. But whatever. We had time off school for the 4th of July. You missed the Macy's fireworks. Awesome as always!

Miss you,
J

Hey J!

They had a band playing at this big gazebo by the boardwalk on July 4th and they had good fireworks. That's gross about Brent. Shoplifting is so <u>not</u> cool. He is gorgeous, but I always thought he was kind of rude. I met this really nice guy here. He's born and raised in Rehoboth. I met him on the boardwalk on the 4th of July. His Dad was playing drums in the band at the gazebo and he was there with his whole family. His name is Ben and he's 16 and has his driver's license. He's kinda cute. We're going out for pizza tomorrow night with his older sister, Beth, and her boyfriend. I don't think Ben would ever steal anything. Mom and I went to the outlets. I got some cool stuff and I found a red leather bag I think you'll like. Mom said no to the iPod for you—and for me. She said we're addicted to tech and we need to ease up a little on that. There was a cool breeze blowing in off the ocean today. The weather has been nice here.

Later Gal Pal,
M

Dear Maddie,

Well, it is so flippin' hot here I can't believe it. The sidewalks in NYC are steaming. The humidity is so gross. I haven't had a good hair day in over a week. I just stay in the air conditioning. I told Mom I felt sick today so I could get out of walking with her. Brent's dad found the stuff he stole and he had to return it to the store and now he's grounded for the rest of the summer. What a dumb creep. I'm bored.

Blah,
J

Hello!!

Hey Juli, you'll never guess what I did! I went into the Atlantic Ocean!! When Mom and I went to the outlets, she bought us swim suits. She got a cute navy-blue one-piece and she got me a bright-red tankini. We went into the ocean and it felt great! I don't know how to swim, but it felt good just being in the water. We sat on the boardwalk afterward and had some really delish fat-free frozen yogurt. I'm getting a little bit of a tan and losing some weight. How are you doing? You sound kinda depressed. I hope you feel better soon. Serves Brent right for stealing stuff. Maybe that'll teach him a lesson and he'll straighten up and get his act together. I've been doing my list of gratitude for Mom every night. She won't let me go to bed until it's done. It's getting a little easier to think of stuff I feel grateful for.

Hugs,
Maddie

Hey Birthday Girl!
Just wanted to wish you a Happy Birthday! I'll give you your card and gift when you get home. I think you'll like what I got you. So how does it feel being Sweet 16?! I won't be 16 til November. What did you do to celebrate your birthday? Wish I coulda been with you. We'll have lunch at the Hard Rock Café to celebrate when you get home.

Miss you,
Juli

Dear Juli,

Thanks for the birthday wishes. I look forward to celebrating with you at Hard Rock. I had an awesome birthday. My parents and friends threw me a surprise party! I wish you had been here. Dad and Mom gave me a birthday card, some distressed skinny jeans, and a beautiful beaded bracelet, and then we went out for breakfast. In the afternoon, I thought I was just going over to Ben's house to hang out, but my parents and his family and a lot of the people I've met here were hiding in the dining room and they jumped out and yelled "SURPRISE!" when I walked in! I got lots of really great gifts, a big decorated cake (chocolate of course!) that Ben's mom made, and balloons. Wow, was I surprised! Ben gave me 16 red roses. How sweet is that?! I'll send you pictures of my party and post them on Facebook. I had a lot of things on my gratitude list tonight, especially:

1. My super fun surprise birthday party
2. Homemade chocolate cake (with vanilla frosting)
3. My birthday presents

Your officially 16-year-old BBFF (Beach-lovin' Best Friend Forever),
Madison Leigh Burnett

August

Hey Maddie,

Your party sounds like it was fun. Glad you had a really happy birthday. Wish I coulda been there. Sounds like you're having a pretty good time. Summer school sucks. The good news is that I'm passing both English and math. It's still hotter than Hell here in the city. Wish I could come down to the beach and hang out with you. I can't wait til it cools off. Lindsey and me went to Bloomingdale's yesterday and this girl was texting on her phone as she crossed the street and she walked right into the side of a cab! She fell down and hit her head. I don't think she was hurt bad, but they took her away in an ambulance. I always walk around texting. I guess that's not a real good idea, huh? Lindsey took her mom's Bloomie's credit card without asking and charged up a whole bunch of stuff. Now she's in trouble with her parents. She bought all these killer outfits and shoes and some jewelry, but her mom is making her take a lot of it back. She charged a pair of jeans, earrings, and a jacket for me—she said it was OK, but obviously it wasn't because I have to return that stuff, too. Bummer.

Still missing you,
Juli

Hi Juli,

Wow, that must have been crazy seeing that girl walk into the cab. I used to text while I was walking around, too. You know, I don't miss my phone as much as I thought I would. I mean, when I go out now I look around since I don't have my phone. I go for walks and see interesting people and look at the scenery.

Last night Ben and I took a walk on the boardwalk after dinner. As the sun set, the ocean turned a kind of greenish-blue color that was so awesome and when it got dark, there was a big, bright full moon and it shimmered like gold glitter on the water. It was just so beautiful! When I go walking up the Avenue, I see lots of cool clothes in the store windows that I want Mom to buy for me. I like smiling at people and saying hello and most times, people smile back! And at dinner it's actually kinda nice talking with my parents at the table. They are really interested in what I have to say and what I think and feel. I also like going out with friends and talking with them. Ben and his sister and their friends don't text a lot. They have phones, but they aren't on them all the time. They don't even have video games. We go out and play miniature golf and beach volleyball. Beth took me to a yoga class with her and I really liked it a lot. I am definitely losing weight and I feel great.

My mom and I talk a lot when we walk. I never talked with her much before. I always knew she was an English teacher, but I never knew that she double-majored in English and theater in college. She and my dad met when they were both cast in a play at NYU. She decided to go into teaching instead of acting. My dad did some plays just for fun. He was always into history, teaching, and writing, but Mom said he was a pretty good actor. And my Grandma Jenny—she was at Woodstock! Mom said she was a wild flower child in her day. And my Grandpa Joe was a singer and played guitar in a rock band back in the 1970's! My family is pretty cool.

Peace and Love,
Maddie

The Attitude of Gratitude List

Hey there Madison!

Well, I'm getting through summer school OK. Looks like I'll get B's in both classes. Mom says I did better because of more exercise and less phone, TV, and video games. I don't know about that—maybe. I'm just glad it's almost over and I got pretty good grades. So when are you coming home? School starts the first week in September, you know.

See you soon,
Juli

Dear Juli,

I'll be home next week. Mom and I went shopping for school clothes at the outlets yesterday and we got lots of great buys. My new clothes are 2 whole sizes smaller! You know, I've had a really great time here in Rehoboth. I can't believe it. The town is beautiful and the people are so nice.

Last night I went for a drive in the country with Dad, Mom, and Ben. We visited a couple my parents met at the gym and got to be friends with. They have 3 really nice daughters and they live in a neat old farm house. We sat on their patio out back and had dinner. Mrs. Mason made chicken and what they call "slippery dumplings" and they were so good! After dinner some of their neighbors came over for dessert and we had fresh-baked peach pie made with peaches picked from trees on their farm. Nick, one of Ben's friends, played guitar and we all sang and danced. Juli, I have never seen so many stars in the sky! You can't see them that well with all the city lights in Manhattan, but out in the country they sparkle like diamonds and there are zillions of them. And we saw 2 deer in the field behind their house—real live deer!

I've made some really good friends in Rehoboth. And here's the best thing ever—the condo we rented is up for sale and Dad is going to buy it! So we'll be back here next summer and you're invited to come with us! Now, the deal is that we have to do really well in all our classes this year so nobody has to go to summer school. I agreed to lighten up on the video games and the internet/phone stuff. I hope you'll go along with me on that. And I think maybe we'll have to rethink our choice of friends. Kids like Brent are not so good to be around. Just wait until you meet Ben—he's a really great guy! He's going to come up and spend Thanksgiving with us so you'll get to meet him then. I know you'll really like him.

Well I guess this is our last letter of the summer and then I'll be seeing you live and in person. I hate to say it, but my parents might have been right about my attitude. Writing the nightly Attitude of Gratitude List has become pretty easy and kinda fun. Mom gave me a journal that I can draw and write in so I'm going to keep up with writing the gratitude lists when I get home. Here's tonight's list of things I'm grateful for:

1. Being able to visit a beautiful beach town for the whole summer
2. Beating my dad at miniature golf yesterday
3. Losing weight so I look hot in my new school clothes
4. Root beer snow cones and caramel popcorn (with peanuts)
5. Yoga classes
6. The Atlantic Ocean
7. Ben and all the new friends I've made in Rehoboth
8. The silver heart ring Ben gave me last night
9. Having Juli for my best friend
10. Having 2 parents who love me enough to teach me how to live a better, happier and healthier life

I'm a very lucky girl, Juli, and you are, too. I'm looking forward to starting school. We're gonna have a great year—I just know it! See you real soon.

Love you,
Madison ☺

ROBIN HILL-PAGE GLANDEN WAS BORN AND RAISED IN DELAWARE. AFTER COLLEGE, SHE WORKED IN THE ENTERTAINMENT INDUSTRY AND AS A FREELANCE WRITER IN PHILADELPHIA, NEW YORK CITY, AND LOS ANGELES. SHE ENJOYED THE CALIFORNIA BEACHES, BUT REHOBOTH BEACH HAS ALWAYS HELD A SPECIAL PLACE IN HER HEART. SHE WAS THRILLED TO HAVE HER SHORT STORY "ELAYNEA AND THE WALK OF BOARDS" PUBLISHED IN THE 2014 REHOBOTH BEACH READS ANTHOLOGY *THE BOARDWALK*. ROBIN SUMMONED HER ALIEN ALTER EGO TO WRITE THAT STORY, AND NOW SHE HAS CONSULTED HER INNER TEENAGE GIRL IN ORDER TO WRITE "THE ATTITUDE OF GRATITUDE LIST" FOR *BEACH NIGHTS*. ROBIN IS CELEBRATING HER TWELFTH YEAR AS A BREAST CANCER SURVIVOR AND KEEPS HER OWN PERSONAL ATTITUDE OF GRATITUDE LIST. ROBIN LIVES IN NEWARK, DELAWARE, WITH HER HUSBAND, KENNY, AND THEIR TWO FINE FELINES, TEDDY AND LUCY.

Fifty-Five

By Mark Polo

Marty steadied himself as his son Joe rushed around the back of the car to open the door for him. Joe grabbed Marty's arm as he exited the car, but Marty pulled it sharply from Joe's grasp.

"I know, I know, but we've done this for fifty-four years and I will not disappoint on the fifty-fifth—period."

"Can't I talk you two out of this?"

"No." Marty was abrupt. "Look, I let you help with the groceries, get the sunfish out from under the deck, and turn on the water and the power. I think you've helped enough."

"It's getting too hard for you."

"I told you this weekend is important to us. I don't want another word about it. Mom is going to be annoyed that it took so long. Let's just get on with this, OK?"

Marty grudgingly let Joe guide his uneasy steps and carry the provisions for the weekend. It was a small consolation, Marty thought, to stop this incessant conversation about not opening his beach house for another season.

"Well, I'll check up on you later. Tell Mom I'll call her tomorrow."

"Whatever." Marty waved his son off without turning around.

"Love you, Dad," Joe said to Marty's back as he climbed the stairs.

"Back at ya."

Years past, getting to his house on New Castle Street presented little difficulty. He would unpack the trunk of his car and bring the groceries up to the side porch, with copies of the *Cape Gazette* and *Coast Press* rolled up and tucked under his arm. Gina would meet him, holding the screen door and complaining that he did not buy enough of something. He could never be sure what it would be—

but it was always *something*. Secretly, though, he lived for that moment, that opening of the door, not only of the house but of another Rehoboth Beach memory.

He and Gina had opened up the Rehoboth house every year since before they were married. It was originally Gina's parents' place, bought with the saving and scrimping of dimes and nickels that her father earned as a factory supervisor. This was the only house they had ever owned. Her parents could only afford one and they chose to own this one, relegating their months up north to being tenants.

After their engagement, Gina and Marty would help her parents each season, pulling the curtains open, removing the sheets covering the furniture, and opening the windows to let in the wet, salty air. The walls and the furniture seemed to gasp as if revived. The blues and greens and whites, faded from the sealed incarceration brought on by winter, intensified once again. The soft yellows of the walls glistened with the newest layer of salted air hitting their surface, adding a place for the morning sun to bounce and shine.

For their wedding three years later, Gina insisted on being married at the beginning of summer, on the sand between the house and the rolling blue. This always made coming to the beach a double celebration.

"Another year under our belts," Marty would say.

"Wonderful weekends filled with children and grandchildren. I'm going to be exhausted," Gina would say. Words that were all part of the tradition.

But each year, the first weekend was theirs. They shunned family, friends, and opening-season invitations to be together, alone.

"Sorry, can't. It's our anniversary," they would tell people. Now, more recently, one of their pockets would vibrate and the same words would be repeated into their awkward choice of a less-than-smart phone. The house was now theirs. It had been theirs for more than thirty years, since Gina's parents passed suddenly, one from disease and the other, soon after, from the void.

But beyond the shift of season and events, both Gina and Marty enjoyed the sand and the rhythmic waves just outside their door. The steady motion and sound calmed them and erased the winter months that grew more difficult as the years passed. It would be just them for two days and one glorious night, allowing space between the stress and the tensions automatically built into life and the daily negotiations of family. Magically, the elixir of the salted westerly breezes softened callouses brought on by life, healed cuts of disinterest, and relaxed their touch so they could connect again. The newness would be revived and last through the year, each year, from the beginning of the spiral of copper leaves piercing the front lawn of their northern house to the budding of the magnolia tree in the back signaling the new warmth of yet another summer. The cycle of healing would last each year through children, financial tensions, and marital squabbles. Rehoboth patched the wounds and allowed them to heal just enough to get to the next season at the beach.

Marty stood for a moment before he opened the screen door. "I'm back."

"Did you get enough milk? You never get enough milk." Gina's impatience was at the ready.

"I think so," he said, secretly happy that all the traditions would continue, including the complaints.

"Joe sends his love and says he'll call tomorrow."

Gina registered what Marty said but was on her summer mission of righting her ship as quickly as possible.

They put things away in silence, as always, each dividing the tasks that years of repetition assigned.

"I'm almost done. I just need help with the beds," she said, on automatic.

"Aye, aye, my captain." Marty saluted Gina to acknowledge her territory. Tucking and folding, they made them all, for the beds would be used and reused all summer long.

The sun kissed the chimney of their house as their tasks were completed. White billowy clouds swelled with steam, giving dimension to the intensity of the electric blue sky.

Gina readied lunch. Gingerly balancing cloth and dishes, she walked, as she had always done, to the screened porch. But this time, it was with an increasingly uneasy gait. Marty watched her from behind, noticing the frailty that was attacking their lives. It was sweet for the years of memories but bitter for the inevitable result. She spread the striped cloth on the table. Its blue matched the sky and brought it to them close and warm. She set the table and patiently waited for Marty to finish bringing their food.

They sat together and toasted, "We've done it. Another year."

Gina tapped his glass with hers. "I'm glad we're here." Her eyes filled. They always did. Each year it was as if they crossed a finish line together.

"Happy anniversary, my love."

"Back at ya," he said.

Their midday meal lasted well into the afternoon as they absorbed the warmth of the day and inhaled the smell of the sea through the open porch windows. They lifted their faces and automatically closed their eyes to feel the new season on their skin.

"Do you feel it?" Gina whispered.

"Yes." He touched her hand as he spoke. The healing would begin.

After lunch, they walked on the beach arm in arm through the late afternoon sun. Walking arm in arm was more of a necessity now, as it allowed them to become stronger, as one.

They inspected the sameness and the change of the dunes and the grasses, remarking on the differences a year brings. The result was that no matter how it changed, how the houses along the edge grew and dwarfed their own, they knew that the beach was about canvas and billowy white, sand and weathered wood, and them as a couple and as a family. They turned to go back, a shorter distance with each passing year.

The first evening together began in the living room. This was most important time to Marty. The night of the first day represented everything for which they worked. Sitting in the rocker that his father-in-law made, he felt the velvet stillness of the night air brushing against his skin, catching the rhythm of the ocean as he rocked. He looked around the room and drank in the photos of years past on the walls: family dinners at local restaurants, parties on the fishing boats they rented, and nights at Funland with the children, where every stuffed animal tucked in every closet came into their lives. He looked over the fireplace to see a succession of photos, all with his family sitting around the dining table. Photo after photo of the same people aging, changing, maturing, gave him a comfort and security that he fit somewhere. He was part of and responsible for the cycle of their lives. The proof was on the walls of the living room. He would remember each year, as he sat there the first night. This was what it was all about—the struggle, the laughter, the tears, and the joy. He had proof that it was real, that it was true, that it was his.

As he rocked, he would lay his head back on the rail of the chair and slowly look at each wall, inspecting its age and its history. He chuckled at the patches and repairs quickly done so the day would not be wasted on anything but the beach. This was the only place where quick and done could replace proper and well executed. His eyes fixed on the ghostly outlines left on the darkened wood walls of this room from paintings moved, replaced, and taken away. It was a scrapbook in itself.

After ensuring that everything was right with his memory of this place, Marty continued his night, reading his "locals." He broke for a moment as he turned the page, and peered at Gina's silhouette as she sat on the sofa facing the ocean, crocheting a blanket for the newest grandchild. This was as much a tradition as coming here. Marty followed the outer edges of her face from forehead to nose to chin, seeing it as he always did, like it was the first day. He did this every first night so he would never forget her softness, her grace. He saw the gentle folds that gathered under Gina's chin and thought how beautiful they were. Marty drank in the peace of this and shook his head as if dismissing his silliness.

As the years passed, bedtime became increasingly earlier. They found their spots carved into the mattress as they lay there year after year and waited to drift off to the sounds of the water hitting the shifting sands. Its rhythm lulled them like a cradle. This time, as he lay in bed, he turned just to look at his wife. He watched as her eyes slowly relaxed and the purse of her lips flattened.

Feeling his stare, she opened her eyes, "Why are you looking at me?" She giggled lightly as if half admonishing him and half embarrassed by him.

"No reason. Can't I look at my girl?" He grabbed her hand. "Let's go to the beach."

"Now?" She had not forgotten, but wanted the invitation. He needed to ask and she needed to say yes.

"Yeah, now. I need you and the blankets and the sand. Right now."

This was familiar territory for them. Over the years this had become their time. Whether alone as it was in the beginning or when there were children. They made this time their time. Every year, once a year, in the night.

"I thought you might have forgotten." She grasped his hand more tightly now and pulled him in her direction.

"How could I forget?" They stood and he followed her from the room.

With slightly unsure steps, they helped each other shake off their fog. He grabbed the quilts from the chest by the door as he followed her and then caught up. They stumbled together, holding each other, making it to the dry side of the water's edge.

Marty smoothed out the sand and created a platform for their nest. He gently helped Gina sit. He sat down beside her and wrapped them both in the blankets. They sat huddled, cloaked in the speckled blackness that joined the sea and sky. He put his arm over her shoulders and pulled her close. Together they looked at the lace of the stars that formed the canopy above them. He was at peace again with his girl. Time melted away and there was no past and no future. Each year, this time of the night became all that there was. They exhaled deeply in unison. There was nothing to say.

Intermittently, they explored places that were familiar to each of them after all these years. There was no excitement for entering the newness of uncharted territory, but there was passion for the ownership of all those places that were theirs to touch, by right of fidelity and God.

Kissing Gina, it brought all the memories back: the first time he held her hand, the first time he embraced her in the boat, the first time she yielded to him, her skin, her smell. Gina wondered how Marty could be so clumsy when making a bed but could explore her body with such care and completeness. Clinging to him erased all the years. It was today, it was yesterday, it was fifty years ago. This moment's passion grew but with new insight that only time could enhance. No longer the heat of just the physical, it became the passion of happiness that they could claim, protect, and enjoy. Long-standing respect made different sounds than other passions. It became less about the "where" of the touch, as each place of physical joy subtly changed over the years. The places within were the places that needed to be touched now. And they did. Again. Sounds free and random overtook the crash of the waves.

The sun cracked the seam between sea and sky that the night joined so tightly. As horizontal light grew in intensity, the glow from Marty and Gina's renewal waned. They sat, huddled and entwined.

They were together again and through it all: children and illness, building and falling down. Their passion for each other was not made on perfection but on failure and forgiveness, stumbling and getting up. It was the house they built together on a weathered foundation.

"I've always been glad it was you...."

Marty absorbed the words and could only nod his head as he closed his eyes.

He touched her forehead with his. Gina understood for the fifty-fifth time.

MARK ALAN POLO, AN INTERIOR DESIGNER FOR MORE THAN THIRTY YEARS IN NORTHERN NEW JERSEY, RECENTLY MOVED TO REHOBOTH BEACH WITH HIS HUSBAND, NORMAN COHEN, AND OPENED A NEW BRANCH. ALONG WITH HIS INTERIOR DESIGN BUSINESS, HE BROUGHT HIS AVOCATION, FICTION WRITING. ALTHOUGH HE IS AN ARTIST BY EDUCATION, HE FINDS WRITING EXPRESSIVE, EQUALLY SATISFYING, AND PORTABLE. POLO HAS WRITTEN ARTICLES FOR TRADE AND ASSOCIATION MAGAZINES AND AUTHORED PIECES FOR HIS OWN WEBSITE AND NEWSLETTERS THAT HAVE BEEN PICKED UP AND REPRINTED BY PUBLICATIONS SUCH AS *ASPIRE MAGAZINE*, THE BERGEN *RECORD*, AND THE *STAR-LEDGER*. MARK'S WRITINGS ARE FILLED WITH AN INTENSE SENSE OF PLACE, INFUSING VISUAL DETAILS THAT MARRY HIS TWO LOVES: DESIGN AND WRITING. MARK IS FINISHING HIS FIRST NOVEL, *MOSQUITOES AND MEN*, A SOUTHERN TALE OF FAMILY, HISTORY, AND A BLACK SHEEP RETURNING AFTER TWENTY-FIVE YEARS. IT WILL SOON BE PUBLISHED BY DEVIL'S PARTY PRESS.

Benny

By Joey Masiello

I celebrated my twelfth birthday during the summer of 1969. Yes, this was the summer I sold myself for a roll of nickels, although technically, I sold myself for an entire evening of Skee-Ball. I looked at it as a win-win situation. Hell, I got an evening of free Skee-Ball, and all I had to do was spend a little time with my benefactor, or so I thought.

I can still remember the heat of that late afternoon. The air had a thickness to it—my grandmother would have described it as close. I just remember the stillness of the day. It was as if everyone was in slow motion. On any other day the ocean would have served as a refreshing diversion from the sweltering heat, but the jellyfish had made their annual pilgrimage to Rehoboth Beach, and no one was taking any chances.

My boardwalk scenario could be described as the perfect storm. Perhaps if just one of the variables had been missing I wouldn't have found myself wandering off the beach and into Funland just before sunset, into the world of Skee-Ball, cotton candy, and an enigmatic fortune-teller who resided inside a glass enclosure. However, as fate would have it, all the elements were aligned perfectly, and the summer of 1969 was being set in stone.

On the pivotal day, I meandered through Funland, oblivious to my surroundings. My thoughts were on high finance; I had some major decisions to make. Tucked into the back pocket of my Birdwell Beach Britches were four brand-new quarters. Preoccupied with the complex decision of how to divide my fortune between the Skee-Ball machine and the sticky pink confection known as cotton candy, I strolled through Funland unaware of the imminent danger.

Things might have been different had I checked in with the fortune-teller first, although he was probably programmed only for fortunes of happiness and unrequited love.

Gorging myself with as much sugar as possible proved to be far too great a temptation for the likes of a twelve-year-old boy. Deciding to forgo a game or two of Skee-Ball, I found myself standing in line among other emancipated preteens. As I ordered my pink cotton candy and large Mountain Dew, I felt free, grown, and almost euphoric. Although both hands were now occupied, I managed to attack the cotton candy by diving headfirst into the pink cloud of sweetness, simultaneously jabbing my tongue into its center as the pink cloud teetered precariously on the end of a long white paper cone. Not only did I receive a mouthful of sweet cotton goo, but also my entire face emerged hostage to the sticky confection. I now looked more like a pink angora sweater than a member of the human race. Looking back on this snapshot in my mind's eye, I can only imagine what the other people of Funland thought when they saw me.

Why is it that I cannot remember the date of my best friend's birthday or the title of a movie I watched last week, but I can recall every detail of that summer evening as if it happened yesterday? I felt special that night, and I believed that everyone was admiring my summer look: bright yellow T-shirt, candy-apple red beach trunks, kelly green Chuck Taylors tied with brand-new white laces, and most important, white puka shell necklace contrasting against the tanned skin of my neck. Yes, I had every prop imaginable, and I was sporting all of them simultaneously.

It wasn't until I had finished throwing my last ball into the rounded hoops of the Skee-Ball machine that I noticed Benny. He wasn't tall, he wasn't handsome, and he wasn't unattractive. He was just Benny. But the first time you met him you couldn't help but notice his large birthmark, or as he referred to it, his raspberry snow cone stain. It sat at the top of his forehead, cascading gently to the space between his eyes, forming a shape much like the state of Texas. Dallas was perched on his forehead, while the Rio Grande rested peacefully between his bushy eyebrows.

Perhaps I didn't take notice of Benny initially because he was as much a part of Funland as the pinball machines. Benny was a local, one of the characters at the beach that everyone talked about—someone you always expected to see but never gave much thought to until he was standing right in front of you. He jokingly said his colorful marking was from eating too many raspberry snow cones and claimed it appeared suddenly one morning as he tilted the remains of the cone-shaped cup into his mouth to savor the last drops of melted ice. After hearing the tale, I quickly took raspberry off my favorite flavor list.

Had it not been for the rounded object Benny balanced in the palm of his hand, I probably would have been on my way seconds after my normal polite hello; but that's not what happened. The object that occupied Benny's hand looked like a faded piece of brown construction paper, rolled perfectly into the shape of a tube. Without a word, Benny handed it to me. I was surprised to find it was much heavier than I had anticipated. I was suddenly a millionaire—the proud owner of a roll of brand-new, shiny nickels. There must have been at least one hundred nickels tucked neatly into the tightly rolled package.

Every evening Benny paraded the boards, wearing his long-sleeved shirt and khaki trousers, bellowing with the vibrato of a rock star: "Take your tongue on a sleigh ride with the best snow cones in Rehoboth Beach." He spent hours drumming up business for his tiny snow cone shack on the second block of Wilmington Avenue. Benny was as much a part of Rehoboth Beach as Thrasher's French fries or old Mrs. Pickens, the cat lady. We saw him every day, either behind the counter of the snow cone shack or walking up and down the boardwalk crooning his jingles. Benny seemed to have one purpose and one purpose only: snow cones.

For June, July, and August, riding the waves, collecting Funland tickets, and spending my evenings crunching down a batch of warm caramel popcorn from Dolle's were everyday occurrences in my world. My parents gave me freedoms unheard of today, and I could explore any and all territories three blocks north and south of Rehoboth Avenue. Each day served up a new adventure, and every evening ended with the cool taste of a Benny's blueberry snow cone. I didn't realize then that my summers were about to change.

My friends and I would brag about our beach houses, touting their proximity to either Funland or the ocean. Although I lived several blocks from the ocean and just as far from Funland, in my heart I knew I had the best cottage because I lived right next door to Benny's snow cone shack. Peering out my bedroom window, I was able to gaze upon the shack, with its smiling penguins wearing ski hats. It was almost as if they too knew how lucky they were to be able to live so close to the coolest place at the beach.

Benny opened the shack on Memorial Day weekend and shut it down the Tuesday after Labor Day. I took comfort in knowing that my penguin friends would diligently stand guard over the snow cone shack until my parents and I returned once again for another summer.

I took great pride in being Benny's first customer each season. Greeting me as if he had just seen me yesterday, he would jokingly ask, "Hey, champ, you gonna go with the blueberry, or are you gonna give one of the other flavors a try?" Already scooping into the huge metal vat of ice, he knew the answer before he asked the question. With each lick of the frozen treat came the richest blueberry flavor imaginable, and within minutes my mouth developed a deep blue hue, a shade even Papa Smurf would envy. I would proudly enter

Funland with the trademark smile that proclaimed Benny was once again open for business.

I wasn't sure how many Skee-Ball games the roll of nickels would buy, but I was willing to accept Benny's gift without trepidation. Within a split second I had forgotten Mrs. Babson's entire "stranger danger" lesson. I can still recall the filmstrip with the strange animated man lurking around the local park, waiting in the shadows with a disturbing smile, eyeing the unsuspecting children playing on the swings as dramatic music droned in the background. None of this seemed to matter now that I was being offered free Skee-Ball games. And besides, Benny wasn't really a stranger, he was the snow cone man. He was just one of those characters everyone knew in Rehoboth Beach.

This should be the part of the story where Benny drags me off to some dark place, the dreaded second location, the place where no one survives, especially twelve-year-old boys with Chuck Taylors and puka shell necklaces. In any other story, Benny would wrap a chloroformed bandanna around my nose as I beg for my freedom. Well, as you've probably surmised, this is not one of those stories. There was no chloroform and the only bandannas were being worn by the teenage boys who were stalking an altogether different type of prey.

Absorbed in the cacophony of carousel music and the clanging bells of the pinball machines, I had forgotten all about Benny and the fact that he had given me enough money to play Skee-Ball for the entire evening. Suddenly, I was pulled from my haze by a tug on the end of my T-shirt. Benny was no longer there. He had been replaced by my sister, standing beside me, arms akimbo, foot tapping as she impatiently waited for me to respond. She told me that I needed to return immediately to our beach house. My night of fun and freedom had come to a screeching halt.

Although I was not expecting a warm reception, I certainly was not expecting to be catapulted into the scenario that awaited me once I entered the tiny kitchen. There, in front of the refrigerator and behind my father, stood Benny. Before I could speak a word, my father started congratulating me on my decision to help Benny in his snow cone shack the following evening. He went on to tell me how proud he was that I had promised Benny to help him on one of the busiest nights of the summer season. He also asked me if I wanted him to hold the roll of nickels I had been paid in advance, or was I just going to put it in my bank.

Throughout this entire conversation Benny remained silent. I guess he was hoping I would go along with his deception. And go along I did. After all, my choices were limited. I could admit to accepting money from someone I hardly knew for no apparent reason and worse yet, have nothing to show for it, or I could try to explain the entire situation, which appeared to be hopeless. I had now become Benny's indentured servant, a fact that he seemed to relish, as he delivered a wink in my direction, telling me he would see me tomorrow night at dusk.

* * * * * *

I regretted my promise even before we began. More than once an awkward silence hung in the air as if it were a storm cloud bursting through the humidity of the early evening hours. Benny didn't seem to notice the silence. I, on the other hand, tried unsuccessfully to think of topics that might break the uncomfortable quiet. Then something happened that diverted my attention: As Benny raised his arms above his head to place a bottle of cherry syrup on a high shelf, his T-shirt pulled away from his belt, exposing his lower back. Much to my astonishment, I could see what looked like another raspberry stain. If the one on Benny's forehead could be described as Texas, this mark surely included all fifty states, as well as Mexico and at least part of Canada. From what I could see, Benny's back was covered with this mysterious raspberry-colored mark. Before I was able to decipher the markings, Benny tugged his shirttail back into his trousers and continued waiting on customers.

At that moment I had come to another realization about Benny. Not once in all the summers I had known him had I seen him wear anything other than a long-sleeved T-shirt and khaki trousers. He didn't wear sandals or flip-flops and he never went without socks. His head was the only skin exposed to the elements—and the only piece of him exposed to the human eye. In this moment of clarity, my attention turned toward Benny's hands. For years I had mistaken the discoloration of his palms as some type of stain having to do with the mixture of syrups they were often immersed in. Benny was always trying to come up with the flavor of the summer, the one that would surely take your tongue on a sleigh ride. Now I saw them in a whole new light. Benny's hands carried the same trademark color as his forehead and lower back. I couldn't help wondering if he was covered from head to toe in his raspberry birthmark.

After spending several hours with Benny in the snow cone shack, my perspective changed. Not being able to erase that image from my mind, much like a crossword puzzle after I had filled in a few blanks, several other pieces of information became clear. I couldn't help believing that perhaps Benny wasn't the snow cone king by choice; maybe he had other desires, other wishes. My mind's eye began to place him on the beach, riding a wave, or taking part in the Fourth of July fireworks on the boardwalk. It pained me to think of Benny standing behind the window of the shack, night after night, selling frozen ice treats as the entire town carried on without him. Perhaps he longed for a walk on the beach or a chance to lose himself in the excitement of the boardwalk.

On the last day of summer, just before leaving for my first day of school, I headed toward the snow cone shack to bid farewell to Benny. As always, he was elbow-deep in a metal vat of colored ice, adding to the rainbow stains of his apron. As I said good-bye to Benny, I assured him I would be back next summer, and perhaps I could help him out again, just in case he needed a break. With that proclamation he just smiled and continued with his work. Waving good-bye, I surreptitiously left a gift for him on the shelf of the snow cone shack, something I hoped he would someday enjoy.

Throughout that year, thoughts of Benny were often on my mind. I found myself wondering if he was celebrating Christmas with his family or visiting friends in another town. I made a promise to get to know more about him; perhaps we could become friends. I looked forward to talking with him. I was no longer afraid of the awkward silences, and I felt confident I would be able to fill those gaps with questions about Benny and his mysterious life.

The following summer was unlike any summer I had experienced. I sensed something was different as we turned into the drive of our cottage. The snow cone shack was dark. Any other summer evening in May would have found Benny preparing for his first day of business. I found it ironic to see the smiling penguins still keeping a watchful eye, as if they too were expecting Benny's return at any moment. Hoping that Benny would be up bright and early with his newest flavors displayed upon the wall of the shack, I went back to my cottage. Much to my disappointment, Benny didn't open the snow cone shack the next day or the next. Benny's snow cone shack remained closed for the entire season. I couldn't bear to look at the empty little white building. It was much like finding a discarded Christmas tree in February—some of its tinsel clinging on for dear life, but the beauty and glory of its original purpose long since expired. Each time I passed the shack I couldn't bring myself to look at the closed door, nor could I meet the ever-peering eyes of the penguins that had stood guard for so many years.

Although many rumors circulated, no one knew what became of Benny. Some people said he moved to Hawaii to sell ice all year long, while others had him living in Fiji. As the summer continued, the rumors became more and more outlandish. The bottom line was, Benny had vanished.

Had I known Benny was not going to return to his snow cone shack, perhaps I would have let him know that I knew his secret, or perhaps Benny would have told me that he knew what I had seen that day in the shack. Maybe I would have told him how special he made my summers, and perhaps I would have made good on my promise to work the shack for him while he took a well-deserved break. I often think of him and wonder where he is today. I like to imagine him wearing the royal blue surf trunks I left on the shelf of his shack that final day of summer, embracing his colorful skin, and smiling as he walks down the beach knowing they are the exact same color as the blueberry snow cones that made so many people so very happy.

DURING HIS THIRTY-YEAR CAREER AS A TEACHER, JOEY MASIELLO WAS HONORED TO HAVE BEEN AWARDED TWO FULBRIGHT SCHOLARSHIPS. THE FIRST SCHOLARSHIP TOOK HIM TO BRIGHTON, ENGLAND, WHERE HE TAUGHT SIXTH-GRADE ENGLISH AND DRAMA. THE SECOND FULBRIGHT SCHOLARSHIP LANDED HIM IN TOKYO, JAPAN, WHERE HE WAS ABLE TO PARTICIPATE IN AN IN-DEPTH CULTURAL EXCHANGE. IN ADDITION TO HIS ADVENTURES IN JAPAN AND ENGLAND, JOEY WAS HONORED TO REPRESENT DELAWARE AS THE 2011 STATE TEACHER OF THE YEAR. HE IS NOW RETIRED AND LIVING IN LEWES, DELAWARE, WITH HIS PARTNER, JOHN. JOEY SPENDS MOST OF HIS FREE TIME WORKING ON A BOOK HE HOPES TO COMPLETE SOMETIME IN THE FUTURE.

Flight of the Songbird

By Kathleen Martens

Cora Jean Johnson had experienced plenty of *firsts* throughout her childhood. Not many of them good.

Cramped with her mother in their one-room, second-floor walk-up on Columbia Avenue in North Philly, Cora remembered the first time she looked into dead eyes, the first time the gangs ripped the antennas from the cars and whooped her cousin, the first time she felt the ache of her empty stomach, before her mother got her maid's job at the Nelsons.

There was at least one great *first* in Cora's young life. At twelve years old, stretched out on the gleaming hardwood floor doing homework in her mother's small maid's room, when she first heard a recording of Billie Holiday crooning through Mrs. Nelson's parlor door. Her mother's employer loved jazz, all the greats.

Cora's momma only liked her singing hymns for the Lord with the Zion Baptist Church choir. But something different happened inside Cora when she heard that jazz. Jazz made her woozy, tingly; it swirled inside and sent chills down her arms. More moving, more stirring than the feeling she had when singing anything else. Except, maybe, "Amazing Grace," she thought.

By eighteen, Cora had memorized every line, captured every vocal nuance, for every song that was delivered to her through that crack in those double mahogany doors. Sarah Vaughan, Ella Fitzgerald,

Dinah Washington, and her favorite, born right in Philly, too—Billie Holiday. Cora loved the spirited church choir harmonies, but when she heard her own smoky, velvet, lone voice, she felt freedom living right inside those jazzy notes. Most beautiful thing she ever felt, with just a little edge of wrong.

She had different kinds of *firsts* in the summer of 1959, as the first high school graduate in her family—the first time on a long-distance bus, first time out of Philly, first time to the ocean.

Her momma wanted her out of the steaming sweat of the city. Wanted her breathing soft air. Somewhere clean and happy. Like where she was headed by bus for the summer, Rehoboth Beach, Delaware. Funny name.

With a coy smile and her chin tucked into one raised shoulder, Cora sang the Billie Holiday hit "I'll Be Seeing You" to her mother at the bus stop in North Philly. It would be Cora's first time away from her, and Cora imagined seeing her mother's sweet moon face in every lovely summer day while she was away at her Aunt Edna's. She sang the lyrics about all the light and new things she would see that would lift her up from her life in the swelter and relentless threat of the city. Cora swayed with one arm around her mother, the other holding her small satchel of clothes. "Thank you. Thank you. I love you, Momma."

The most surprising graduation gift she could imagine, a bus ticket to a summer with her mother's favorite sister, Edna, who owned a café in Rehoboth Beach. Cost her mother nearly all her savings. Cora would clean rooms at the Henlopen Hotel to earn her keep. The hotel sat right on the boardwalk next to the beach. The thought of seeing the Atlantic Ocean…that *first* alone made Cora smile. She'd go home with a fist full of dollars, too, Aunt Edna had said.

"Cora, don't you be singing that around Sister Edna. That jazz music, it's got sin in it. Not the way to use your God-given gift. You ever look at where those women like Billie Holiday end up?" her mother said, after Cora let the soothing farewell notes float from her mouth.

She felt the weight of her mother's words on her heart. At her Aunt Edna's house, Cora was hoping for another *first*. Cora's older cousin had told her there was a jazz club at the Henlopen Hotel where Cora would be working, and she had heard them rehearsing through the walls. Hearing those songs *live*, well, that would be beyond any *first*.

And Cora was grateful for some *lasts,* too: the last time she would see fear in her mother's eyes as Cora left for school; and the last time she would climb the brick steps to do her homework at the Nelsons' house, to hear her mother's aching sighs, and smell the scent of bleach and that new Lemon Pledge. A job at the Nelsons' was waiting for Cora, too. Third-generation maid. They were good people. It was honest work, but honestly, Cora wanted more. She knew that's why Momma helped her go away.

Cora had no idea where her life would take her—possibilities had always felt impossible—but she was moving. That was a good feeling; just moving somewhere felt like possibilities coming her way. But *what* to dream? She was beyond dreaming.

"Make me proud." Her mother's face ran tears, as she waved her handkerchief.

Cora knew where to go. She stepped up onto the bus, and with her head lowered, she walked down the long narrow aisle, passing the rows of white people. Cora glanced sideways at her mother, memorizing her face through scratched window after window until she reached her proper seat in the last row. Fingering the yellow foam through a long slash in the seat, Cora watched the reflection of her own face floating in the window.

The sun kept winking at her from between crumbling buildings, then came out full, as the towns gave way to highways and on to endless farm fields with scarred red wood barns. She knew she must be getting close to Rehoboth. Aunt Edna said she would see lots of cornfields. But they weren't growing too high on that June day. More like fields of green tufts.

How wonderful it would be to sing right out there in the open air in those fields. Just to let her voice go as loud as she could with those soulful lyrics, carried by the wind to somewhere far off. Not like holding back in her little bathroom, with the water running in the tub to cover up the sinful tunes, or in the back hallway of her school.

Cora kept her eyes cast down as she rode and found herself singing, "God Bless the Child That's Got His Own." Another favorite by Lady Day, Billie's nickname. She sang about the haves and have-nots. Cora wanted to have, but what? The space out the window let her breathe, let her thoughts go out a long distance away, about a handsome young man, maybe. A job where she could use her mind, not her hands.

She felt eyes on her, sky eyes, green eyes, some brown, staring from white faces. A child gripping the back of the seat, frozen, with his blue eyes peeping at her. Keeping her chin down, she glanced up again for just a flash. Their looks seemed mostly curious, but a few were unkind. Cora stopped singing. She didn't want trouble.

Cora was the last one to descend the ridged metal stairs. Uncrumpling the walking map her auntie had sent, she put her back to the scribbled, wavy lines that represented the ocean, and headed toward the sunset that was dropping fast at the west end of the small beach town. Aunt Edna said, where the paved main road turned to crushed clam and oyster shells heading west, Cora would find the Negro section.

Cora stopped. Feeling a pull behind her, she turned around and walked east toward the water. She just *had* to see the ocean for the first time. The Atlantic Ocean. Aunt Edna wouldn't worry if it was a short time; Cora would walk fast.

She got a few strange looks from white people, so she hugged the outside of the sidewalk tight-rope-walking the curb. Jim Crow flew far, she thought. Still the town seemed more gentle than Philly, for sure. Reflected in Snyder's candy store window, tall as she was, and stylish in her one Sunday blue dress, she thought she looked fine. Older than your years, Momma had said, and *so* pretty. Well, that was her momma talking, she thought. The sweet aroma was coming from the shop door, and Cora took a deep breath of the alluring, sugary scent.

A group of four women who looked a lot like her momma, dressed in bright white maid's uniforms, walked by toward the boardwalk. Cora folded in with them just to be safe. Something was changing. Maybe her hopes. Hopes that seemed to rise with the salty breeze that lifted the hem of her dress, just as the sidewalk turned into rough wood boards. At the end corner was Dolle's salt water taffy that Aunt Edna said she loved. Cora wanted to buy her aunt's favorite, maple walnut, but she didn't know the rules for Negroes in the town.

Peeling off from the group, Cora made her way to the edge of the boardwalk and leaned over to touch the hot sand. She remembered the smell of her mother's ironing on her day off, watching the TV that Mrs. Nelson had given them.

A round-faced, white-uniformed lady called out, "Chile, you alone? Lookin' for the colored's beach? Crow's Nest, they call it." She pointed. "By the big drainage pipe. 'Tween those two rotten ole jetties. See? Just by the big, white Henlopen Hotel up there, where we work. Never mind, you best walk with us."

"Thank you, ma'am." Cora walked along listening to the women talking about how easy it was to get a summer job with all the tourists around. "There you go, missy. Just stay in that small beach section and you'll be fine. You be careful going home, you hear?"

"Yes, ma'am." Cora walked beside the big storm drainage pipe in between the jetties to the water's edge, put down her satchel, and took off her shoes. There were just a few people on the beach and the sun was low, scattering diamonds of light on the ink-blue water. The milky meringue sizzled over her feet. It was so hard to leave the rolling sound, the waves arching, then collapsing in a sigh, the calling gulls drifting and dipping overhead. Heaven. She breathed in the balmy salt air, leaned back, put her face to the sky, and whispered, "Thank you, Jesus."

Strolling, shoes and satchel in hand, she walked the boardwalk barefoot, to see the Henlopen Hotel where she would work with her cousins. It looked fine. And then the beautiful sounds, faint but familiar, caught up in the summer air and passed on as a gift to her ears. Jazz.

She followed the tempting lilt to the side door of the hotel. That familiar feeling filled her, sizzling like the foam from the rhythmic waves. She knew the song, every word, every note. Leaning her back against the wall around the corner from the door that was leaking the melodic sounds into the evening air, she swayed her head. A warm male voice delivered Sarah Vaughan's melody from inside the hotel. He sang "Misty." Funny to hear a man singing about being a helpless kitten up a tree. Cora looked up at the darkening sky streaked with white fluff. She too was clinging to a cloud, as the lyrics went.

She didn't know how long she stood there enraptured, but the dark descended around her and the lights of the hotel blinked on above. Her voice rang out in the alley and echoed back to her. The music stopped, and she heard a door open and close around the corner from her. Then, no sounds. She resumed her medley, serenading the night sky. No stopping, eyes closed, Cora freed the dozens of songs that were stored in her heart, freed them like a fluttering of birds from an opened cage.

"You've got *pipes*, miss." The liquid tenor voice of a man startled her. She turned to leave.

"Wait, slow down. Excuse me. Hello? I'm just a songbird like you. No harm here. Sammy Farrow, from DC."

"Cora Jean Johnson, Philly."

He shook her cautious hand.

"That's my band in there, Sammy Farrow Quartet. Where'd you learn to let go like that?"

She sized up the gentleman. Kind eyes. Looked like Reverend James in her first church. "Choir at church, I suppose," she said.

He smiled at Cora. "Ha, I meant, your *style*? Dead ringer for Sarah Vaughan, *and* Billie *and* Ella…Where do you sing now?"

"Here. Just started here, Mr. Farrow. Oh, and in school hallways and our small bathroom."

"So we had the same start, huh?" His laugh had a relaxed tone. No sass. He lit a cigarette, drew in, leaving a long raging red ash, and blew out slowly from the side of his mouth with one eye half-closed. Pushing his white tails back, he slipped his left hand in his pocket and leaned against the wall. "So, you play the Henlopen? I've never heard of a Cora…oh, I get it. You must use a stage name, huh?"

She smiled and looked out to the ocean, trying to seem older, confident, mature.

"Listen, Miss Cora, I'm missing my lead female singer tonight. Getting by with my inferior male vocals, as you heard."

She said nothing.

"Miss Sarah Vaughan sings 'Misty' better than me, don't you think?" He smiled and tilted his head, and his warm laugh escaped again. "Am I being too bold to ask, do you want to sit in? Pay's good."

"*Pays?*"

"Well, maybe not what you're used to in Philly."

Cora nodded. It wasn't in her control, that nod. A kind of lie, she knew. Another *first*. She would let herself have this dream. A dream she hadn't known enough to want. Then her mother's words made her stomach twist. "There's sin in that jazz." Cora promised herself she could be good. Would avoid the sin in it. I'll let the end justify the means. Money and a dream beyond dreams. Momma would be happy in the end, she thought.

Cora looked at Sammy's formal tails and swiped her hands down her Sunday best dress. Was it nice enough for this fancy place? She stepped back and wrapped her arms around herself.

She just knew the joke would end. He'd see her for the girl she was. She'd be a fool to think... And singing in front of all those fancy people?

"By the way, meant to say, you look fine in that blue dress, Miss Cora, just fine for the stage." He seemed sincere.

Another moment of hesitation. This chance would never happen again, she thought. Not in a million years. Cora saw her momma climbing the brick steps to her cleaning job, aching back, and Cora doing the same. "I happen to be free. When shall we start?"

How did it get dark? Aunt Edna. The time. The walking map was melting in her sweaty hand. She was about to turn.

A lean young man, cocoa-skinned like her, but midtwenties, with the same kind eyes as Mr. Farrow, came out of the heavy metal door. "Hey, man, we're on."

"Jackson, meet Miss Cora." Then his words that made it all real. "She's fronting our band for the next set. Why don't you two make a song list that suits her. I'll be right in." He took another long drag.

"Sure, Sammy. Please, this way, miss." She saw Jackson glance back at Sammy and lift his shoulders.

* * * * * *

"Ladies and gentlemen, please welcome to Jazz Night at the Henlopen, all the way from Philly, Miss Cora," Sammy announced, and he gestured for her to move to the big silver microphone. Her name rang out and was swallowed by the applause. She stared through the nearly blinding spotlight into the ballroom, filled with tables, set with silver, white tablecloths, white faces. Men in jackets and ties, ladies in dresses. A fancy and curious audience smiling at her, politely clapping their hands together. For *her*.

Being on the stage chased the Crow away, she thought. Amazing Grace.

The room went silent. A few stray voices were hushed by the attentive audience, some leaning forward, setting chins on fists, elbows on the table.

She heard the lead-in, closed her eyes, put her moist hand around the silver mic stand, and whispered the opening notes. Then, her tight throat opened. It freed. She held onto notes an impossibly long time, letting the words *breeeeze* and *treeees* wrap like loving arms around each listener as she sang the soulful tune "Tenderly." She kept her mind on the soft, salty evening breeze that had sent its quivering breath through the trees that lined the main street of the town.

Then she was in the open fields. Her voice was going out far into the air, as she warbled through a dozen songs. Again the roar of appreciation, and Cora hung her head in gratitude and tried to breathe.

"Miss Cora, there are no words for you." Jackson was beaming, and she felt a shiver from his warm smile from across the stage. Such sweet, kind eyes.

Indeed, she had no words for the vibration of the thundering applause, the whistles, the hoots and woo-hoos, and the standing ovation at the end of the set that drove into her soul. The possibility that had seemed an impossibility. The most beautiful thing she ever felt with no edge of wrong.

"They want an encore. You up for it, Miss Songbird of the Sea?" Sammy stepped beside her.

She whispered her selection into his ear amid the throng of applause.

A man in a fine suit came to the edge of the stage, shook Sammy's hand, and handed Cora a business card. He cupped his hand and yelled into her ear. "Phil Miller. Pleasure. Call me when you're home. I've got a band who needs you in Philly, Miss Cora."

Sammy nodded his approval and pointed his chin at the departing man. "He's *the* man in Philadelphia. Hard to get." He winked and tilted the mic. "Ladies and gentlemen, one more time, the one and only Songbird of the Sea, Miss Cora, with a Billie Holiday favorite."

Cora stepped up to the mic, again. "Thank you...so much." Her voice trembled. Her head lowered. Talking was different from singing.

The crowd settled. "Shh! Shh!" A few customers chastised the talkers.

The band started poppin' the beat, and Jackson called out, "*Yes, Miss Sister Sea!*" He lifted his horn to his lips.

Cora had a new feeling inside. A knowing. Singing was her gift; she'd give it. "This is dedicated to Sammy and his trio..." She looked at Jackson, and then the audience. "And every one of you fine ladies and gentlemen." And for you, Momma, she thought.

Applause encircled her. Then a call came from the audience. "Miss Songbird of the Sea, let's hear it."

She moved the mood from mellow to upbeat, and let it out, singing Billie's "T'Aint Nobody's Business If I Do."

The perfect lyrics almost made her laugh out loud. Cora closed her eyes, rocked her shoulders left and right, rolling her happy head side to side.

Yes, if she went to church on Sunday, and then sang jazz all Monday...

"T'Aint Nobody's Business If I Do."

KATHLEEN L. MARTENS IS AN ACTIVE MEMBER OF THE REHOBOTH BEACH WRITERS GUILD. WITH A B.A. IN ENGLISH LITERATURE AND AN M.A. IN EDUCATIONAL PSYCHOLOGY FROM THE UNIVERSITY OF CONNECTICUT, SHE PURSUED A CAREER IN INTERCULTURAL COMMUNICATIONS WHILE LIVING AND WORKING IN THAILAND AND INDONESIA. HER TRAVELS THROUGHOUT ASIA RESULTED IN HER WRITING THE AWARD-WINNING MEMOIR OF MARGARET ZHAO, A SURVIVOR OF THE CULTURAL REVOLUTION UNDER CHAIRMAN MAO, *REALLY ENOUGH, A TRUE STORY OF TYRANNY, COURAGE AND COMEDY*. SHE IS CURRENTLY WORKING ON HER OWN MEMOIR, A COLLECTION OF SHORT STORIES, AND A NOVEL SET IN A MODERN STONE AGE SOCIETY IN THE REMOTE MOUNTAINS OF IRIAN JAYA, INDONESIA, BASED ON HER OWN CONSULTING EXPERIENCE IN HER TWENTIES. HER RECENT SHORT STORY, "MOLTING," WON A JUDGE'S AWARD AND WAS PUBLISHED BY CAT & MOUSE PRESS IN *BEACH DAYS*, 2015.

JUDGES' COMMENTS

This is a lovely rhythmic tale with delicate emotional resonance. It's perfect for a cloudless night. Excellent writing and details. The story fit the theme and was sensitive without tugging at heartstrings. Characters were rounded and readers were engaged from beginning to end. No soft spots in this selection. A heartwarming, evocative tale about a talented teenage jazz vocalist who visits Rehoboth from Philadelphia that skillfully imagines the 1950s era and creates a multilayered, real world—despite the space limitations of the short story form. Could easily envision its expansion into a full novel; the main character is that resonant and strong, while the supporting characters are plot-perfect and well drawn.

The Vampire Surf Club

By David Strauss

"The Vampire's on," is all he says. "The Vampire's on." He punches Empty in the shoulder and walks out the door.

I'm standing next to Empty at the bar, refilling the ice bin, the never-ending job of the summer bar-back. "What's the Vampire?" I ask.

Empty looks over, a huge grin spreading across his face. "I don't know what you're talking about. Vampire? What Vampire?" He laughs and strolls the length of the bar to wait on a pair of pretty blondes.

Empty—or MT, Michael Topper—as the bar's owner will only call him, is a year-round worker here in Rehoboth, one of those college kids who—not unlike myself—came down to work and party and surf during summer breaks from classes. Ten years ago, he once told me, he made the decision to stay. "Why go to work in the *real* world for thirty or more years hoping to one day retire down here and enjoy the beach life? I'm skipping the boring part and going right to the beach life."

It is my first summer working for Empty as a bar-back, and my last before graduating college, which will happen next spring. I've been weighing his words for most of the summer now, trying to decide myself about staying or going. Going to the corporate world, the suits and schedules, the right house and the right car, and the money: the boring part?

* * * * * *

The world is a vampire…

Tonight is turning out to be one of those nights: the tourists were trapped inside for two days while a hurricane churned offshore, sending whipping winds and stinging rain along the streets of Rehoboth. Families packed tiny hotel rooms, eating delivery pizza and watching television, and getting on each other's nerves. Tonight is one of those nights: clearing skies and gentle breezes, clouds drifting lazily overhead, rimmed with the soft golden light of sunset as every trapped tourist and local alike emerges and descends on tiny downtown Rehoboth determined to celebrate the return to normalcy.

The bar is bustling with hungry diners, fathers needing that extra drink, young adults extending happy hour long past seven, and me running buckets of ice and restocking beer coolers, grabbing new bottles of liquor, emptying trash, and losing track of time amidst the chaos of summer until I hear Empty ring the bell and yell out, "Last call."

Another hour or so of scrubbing down stainless steel and washing dishes, emptying more trash, and sweeping and mopping, and then just before three thirty, as I'm being tipped out, I notice him standing outside, beneath a dome of yellow light, backpack strung over bony shoulder.

"The Vampire's on."

I turn to Empty, looking for a sign, but he's busy finishing up, moving in that fast-motion mechanical way that bartenders and servers do at the end of their shift, the same wiping and stocking and counting they do every night, months and years at a time, so that it's become second nature, almost involuntary, like the blink of an eye.

Empty grabs his backpack and exits out the front door without a word, greeting his vampire friend with a handshake, and they hurry off together. I'm outside trying to follow them when I see the figures emerge from the murkiness of night, from side streets and alleyways, walking barefoot toward the soft sands of this Atlantic beach. I've got this image of them all waking at midnight and shuffling like the risen dead from cramped apartments and old beach houses scattered across town as they descend on unsuspecting Rehoboth at almost four in the morning. The scene is surreal and eerily silent except for one sound: the sonic boom of large waves breaking and crashing somewhere out there in the black.

And then I notice it, the common denominator in this confusing equation playing out in front of my eyes: the figures, each and every one of them, has a surfboard tucked under his arm.

Touched by madness…

They converge on the beach, still wrapped in their blankets of night, a loose circle of surfers, barefoot on the cool sand, passing clouds partially hiding a full moon, its Cyclops eye watching silently over the proceedings.

Empty is front and center, and these surfers—bartenders and businessmen, drunks and stoners, family men and thirty-something man-children—all of them somehow vampires, watch and listen with respect. I am surprised by this; I've always thought of him as kind of a loser. But here, on this beach in the middle of the night, Empty is *the man*. And although I can't hear them, it's obvious they hang on his every word; Empty, the master of ceremonies.

They huddle together and chant something I can't quite understand, and then silently, one by one, the vampires walk to the water and disappear into the chilly void that is the Atlantic Ocean, big waves breaking and booming somewhere out there in the night. It could have been the tug of the moon or the pull of the tides, but I'd like to think it was the bite of the vampire that drew me toward the ocean's edge. In any case, I soon find myself knee-deep in those dark waters gazing intently at—*what?* I don't know what I expected to find, but I can see nothing, save for the occasional lifting of the clouds, and then, like a ghost emerging from the haze, I spy the image of a man gliding across the ocean, a white board sliding across the face of a black wave breaking, and then the clouds drift across that unblinking eye and the specter vanishes. I stand for a bit, like some lunatic in a trance, transfixed, feet sucking deep into cool, wet sand.

Surfing vampire apparitions appear from nowhere, and then just as quickly fade from sight. But the sounds, the sounds, never disappear.

The crash and boom, the cut of a board across this open ocean face—like paper being torn, the suck of water back toward its primordial deep, ebb and flow, ebb and flow. The joy of laughter, hoots of pure ecstasy, the noises of unbridled happiness in the unknown of night; these are sounds I haven't heard since childhood.

The veil of darkness is lifting.

One by one they emerge from the midnight blue Atlantic like spirits gliding from the mist, white surfboards like tombstones, the first shafts of sunrise glowing across the chop of ocean water, a million sparkles of brilliant light glittering against the disappearing dark.

Empty is the last to wander from the sanctuary of the sea, his body glowing ghostly white—a clear sign he spends no time in the sun. He is smiling and shaking his head, brushing wet strands of long hair from his face, when he sees me sitting alone in the sand, watching. Empty drops his board and ambles over.

"Now you know what the Vampire is," he says, matter-of-factly.

I look toward the horizon, the bright curvature of this new sun beginning to rise, and then at the surfers scattered along the beach, finally settling my gaze back on Empty. "No, I… "

He sits beside me in the sand. "The Vampire Surf Club is a group of guys who live down here year-round. Most of us work in the restaurants and bars around Rehoboth, so we don't get a chance to get out much during the day. A few years back we came up with the idea of night surfing, and, like the vampire, we always find our way back home by sunrise."

"The Vampire," I whisper. "Cool." I squish my feet in the grainy sand. "But why do you do *this*—I mean, it doesn't make any sense. You can't see anything, and it's dangerous."

Empty smiles. "Exactly. That's why."

"What?"

A hundred yards out a pod of dolphins glide by, chasing schools of fish, their slate gray dorsal fins rising and sinking, rising and sinking.

"Do you know what they give to people who have ADHD?" he asks. "Stimulants. They give stimulants to people who are hyperactive. Crazy, right?"

I have no idea what he's talking about.

"Stimulant medications boost concentration and focus while reducing hyperactive and impulsive behaviors. You'd think just the opposite—give a hyperactive kid a depressant, something to calm him down. But in reality, it works the other way 'round."

"OK."

"Listen. This life, the beach life, can be a bit crazy..." Empty stares into space, clearly seeing something I know nothing about. "Sometimes the only way to balance out the insanity of beach life is to do something even more insane. A lone surfer slides across a perfect wave in the emptiness of a black ocean and feels liberated— and yet no one else is present to witness this experience—no one except fellow vampires. I always feel reenergized after a Vampire session. It helps to rebalance, to recalibrate things."

Wisdom is a gift...

Empty continues, "I'm going to tell you a story I've never shared with anyone before. When I was in college at Towson University, there was this old building, Stephens Hall—one of the original three college buildings on campus, all brick and stone and mortar, a beautiful shell with a majestic-looking bell tower looming over the town, but woefully inadequate in terms of modern conveniences. So anyway, halfway through my junior year, they boarded the place up and set about scheduling renovations. There was this gap in time between the boarding up and the new construction, and so this building, this history, just sat empty for months. One night, two of my friends and I snuck in, worked our way up to the attic, and from there, climbed rung ladders and went through trap doors, 'til we found ourselves up high in that bell tower, perched on the edge of the world, three kings on our stone throne, a couple of beers in hand, watching the landscape unfold around us—every single person on earth unaware of where we were and what we were doing. We just sat there in silence and watched. These little pieces of a lifetime that belong to you, and you alone. A life lived between sunset and sunrise."

He traces a spiral in the sand with his finger.

"Sometimes, it's amazing how the same piece of real estate can look different from a new perspective. We watched that sunrise from our secret throne, the quiet spread across the land, fuzzy purple campus lights shining across empty parking lots, those many commuter students slumbering away at home, totally unaware that this other world even existed."

Empty rubs his thumb in slow circles across the fingerprint of his index finger, sand sprinkling back to the beach.

"The Vampire Surf Club is my bell tower. And though I'll never be wealthy—I'm a bartender—and I'll never be respectable, I will, at least, make an attempt to understand this gift. This gift of life, of time."

And for the first time, maybe ever, Empty looks me straight in the eye, his cold hand on my summer-tanned shoulder. "This life— *your* life—is about time. And what you do with it, how you spend it, is up to you."

A shaft of sunrise sunbeam smacks us both in the face, harsh and warm all at once. I shiver and he rises, brushing sand from his shorts. "We can always use another vampire." And with that Empty grabs his board, wraps the leash, and walks away, sunlight illuminating his form as he disappears up the walkway and down a side street—the vampire retreating back to the darkness of his lair, tourists blissfully unaware.

I face the horizon and watch the waves break as they've done for a billion years now, big and empty, hollow swells of green saltwater pounding against this Rehoboth shoreline, slate gray dolphin fins rising and sinking, rising and sinking silently into the harsh wedge of reflected starlight shining off this immense ocean surface—and the light, the light hurts my eyes.

DAVID STRAUSS GREW UP VISITING OCEAN CITY AND CLEARWATER BEACH EVERY SUMMER. HE SPENT HIS COLLEGE SUMMERS LIVING AND WORKING IN OCEAN CITY, MARYLAND, AND HAS HAD POETRY AND/OR SHORT STORIES PUBLISHED IN *THE SCARAB*, *THE DAMOZEL*, *SELF X-PRESS*, *DIRT RAG MAGAZINE*, AND *THE BOARDWALK*. HE HAS ALSO PUBLISHED TWO NOVELS, *DANGEROUS SHOREBREAK* AND *STRUCTURALLY DEFICIENT*, THROUGH CREATESPACE. HE LIVES IN BEL AIR, MARYLAND, WITH HIS WIFE, MIRELLA, AND HIS SON, LIAM, WHERE HE TEACHES U.S. HISTORY.

A fun twist on the "carpe diem" tale that engages the need for locals to carve out a space in a tourist area. This story really sticks the ending. Nice job of the backstory of who and what keep Rehoboth visitors satisfied. Excellent use of the night theme, and the favorites: surfing and vampires, only missing the garlic for effect. Engaging and well written. While Rehoboth famously proffers its sunlit beaches and booming surf, this story looks at the flip side—revealing the hidden depth of meaning that those who surf the Atlantic at night find most evident when the summertime sun is nowhere in sight.

The Portrait

By Robin Hill-Page Glanden

Eva was deep in thought as she drove from her Manhattan apartment to the rental cottage in Delaware. Her recent divorce and the death soon after of her best friend, Amy, had left her sad and emotionally exhausted. Now, the final chapter of her second novel was due in ten days and her mind was paralyzed with a bad case of writer's block. After the great success of her first novel, Eva was terrified at the thought of disappointing with her second book. How could she top or even equal her first novel if she couldn't find a strong ending for the sequel?

She had been working on the book for months in the apartment she once shared with her ex-husband. Every corner held a memory. Lonely, depressed, and unable to concentrate that morning, she logged onto Facebook to take a quick break. That's when she saw the ad:

> *Quaint Victorian cottage in a private setting,*
> *minutes from Rehoboth Beach. All amenities, but*
> *with Old World charm. Two bedrooms, one bath,*
> *well-appointed kitchen and lovely front porch.*
> *Cozy, quiet retreat. Low off-season rates.*

Before she had a chance to change her mind, she dialed the number listed.

A man with a sexy British accent answered. "Daniel Wedgeworth here."

"Hello, my name is Eva Markwell. I'm a writer in New York who's working on a novel and I desperately need a change of scenery. I saw the ad for your cottage. I'd like to rent it this week if it's available."

"Well, hello, Eva Markwell. I'm the owner, and it is indeed available. When would you like to check in?"

"Well, how much is it for the week?"

"How much would you like to pay?"

How strange, Eva thought. "Uh, I don't know. How about $500 for the week?"

"That will be fine," Daniel replied. "You may check in this evening, if you like. I'm occupied during the day every day, but I'm always available in the evenings after seven."

"Perfect," Eva said. "I'll arrive around seven, then."

"When you turn into the driveway, the cottage will be on the right. Continue up the drive to my home and I'll give you the key."

Eva packed quickly, put the address into her GPS, then followed the driving instructions to the property in Rehoboth. The cottage was surrounded by trees, hydrangea, and rose bushes. Golden lights shone in the windows, and two lanterns on either side of the front door illuminated the porch. A flagstone walkway with a rose-covered arbor led to the door. It reminded Eva of a scene in a Thomas Kinkade painting. She continued down the driveway and there, partially obscured by stately trees, was a huge Victorian mansion. Although the exterior was a bit shabby and the yard needed some TLC, the building was magnificent.

As Eva parked in the circular driveway, the door opened and a man stepped out onto the wrap-around porch. He was tall, slender, and handsome, but his attire seemed oddly formal for someone who lived at the beach. As she approached, she noticed he was wearing black trousers, a starched white shirt, gray pin-striped vest, and a wide tie that looked more like a silk scarf.

He smiled and greeted her with that dreamy British accent.

"Welcome, Miss Markwell. Please excuse the shabby appearance of the property. My gardener has taken leave and I need to have some work done on the exterior of the house, but I just haven't had the time nor the inclination lately to address those issues."

"Hello. Please, call me Eva."

"I certainly will, if you agree to call me Daniel," he said, opening the door and stepping back to invite her inside.

"It's a deal."

The opulent foyer featured a sparkling crystal chandelier and led to a spacious parlor with high ceilings, arched windows, and a marble-mantled fireplace with its blazing fire taking the chill off the late-September evening. Oil paintings adorned the walls of the room, which was furnished with elegant Victorian furniture.

"Please sit and have a cup of tea. You must be tired after your long drive."

Eva settled on a tapestry loveseat and Daniel brought in a silver tea service with china cups and saucers. He poured two cups of fragrant tea. "A teaspoon of sugar, no milk?"

Eva was surprised. "How did you know?"

"Lucky guess," he replied with a grin.

He sat down across from her in a leather wingback chair.

"Oh, let me pay you for the rental," Eva said, rummaging through her purse. She handed him her $500 check in an envelope.

"Thank you," Daniel said, accepting the envelope and placing it, unopened, on the end table beside him. He looked at her so intently that Eva felt uneasy.

"So, tell me about these paintings," she said.

"Well, I'm an artist, and these are paintings I've done since I've lived in Rehoboth," Daniel explained. "My wife and I were born and raised in London and we fell in love with this town and this house when we visited on holiday. We moved here and I started to paint seascapes. I'm a bit of a local celebrity, so please don't mention that I'm here or that you're staying at the cottage. I'm trying to get a special painting completed. Since my wife died, I like to be left alone to work."

"Oh, I'm so sorry about your wife," Eva said.

Tears welled up in his eyes. "She went back to visit her family in London one summer and was killed in an accident. She was so beautiful; I loved her dearly and miss her so." He paused, then cleared his throat. "Well now, enough of that. Let me show you my work."

He led her around the room, pointing out details in each painting. With a wave of his hand, Daniel indicated a painting bearing his likeness. "I always thought that every artist should paint a self-portrait. I was going to paint my wife's portrait after I finished mine, but she passed away before I could. After her death, I just couldn't bring myself to do it."

He led her back to the loveseat and sat down again in his chair, then stared at her as if he were trying to see into her soul. "I would very much like to paint you, Eva."

"No, I don't think so," Eva said, flustered. She felt panicked, realizing that this might be a dangerous situation. *Here she was alone with a strange man in his home at night. Now, after a brief conversation, he wanted to paint her? With or without clothes?* "I think maybe this was a mistake. I'll stay at a hotel in town."

"You misunderstand, Eva. I would just like to paint your portrait." He went to a closet and took out an exquisite, dark-purple velvet cape. "I can see you wearing this—with your blond hair and blue eyes, it would make a lovely portrait. I have no sinister motives, I assure you, and I don't paint nudes, if that's what you're thinking. If you feel uncomfortable about sitting for the portrait, I understand, but please stay."

Their eyes met and she suddenly knew he was sincere and that she had nothing to fear. "OK, I'll stay. And I'll think about the portrait."

"Think about it overnight, and if you decide yes, just come by at seven tomorrow evening."

He took a key out of the end table drawer. "Here's the key to the cottage. Make yourself at home and if there's anything you need, please call. I'm always up late."

Eva smiled. "I'm a night owl, too."

She drove back to the cottage. It was immaculately clean and tastefully decorated in soft blues, seafoam greens, and buttery yellows. There were china vases full of her favorite flower—pale pink roses—in every room. What a lovely coincidence, she thought.

Eva brought her suitcases in and set her laptop up on the dining room table. The kitchen cupboards were well stocked. Again, another curious coincidence: on the table were a china tea cup with a pink rose pattern and a small matching plate with her favorite cookies—shortbreads. She made a cup of tea and took her snack to the dining room as she powered up her laptop. Suddenly, an idea popped into her head and she started typing. Words flowed out of her mind and into her fingers as they flew across the keyboard. Finally, at 4:00 a.m. she stopped, exhausted. But she nearly had the ending for her book.

The brass bed in the master bedroom was soft and comfortable. For the past few months, Eva had been plagued by insomnia, but she fell asleep immediately and slept soundly. When she woke, bright sun streamed through the window. Eva made a pot of coffee and went back to work, feeling refreshed and inspired. Her writer's block had vanished.

At five o'clock Eva drove into town. She chose a restaurant on the boardwalk with Victorian décor and an ocean view. The combination of the mansion, the cottage, and the restaurant made Eva feel as if she had been transported back in time to the Victorian era.

After dinner, she sat on a bench on the boardwalk and looked out over the water as the daylight faded. A warm breeze stirred and Eva felt a peace she had not known in a long time. She returned to the cottage having made a decision.

When she knocked on the front door of the mansion, Daniel appeared immediately.

"You're going to let me paint you?" She nodded her consent. "That's wonderful!" he exclaimed.

Daniel set a blank canvas on an easel in his studio. He posed Eva on an emerald-green velvet chaise in the center of the room next to a small table with a vase of pink roses. He draped the purple cape around her shoulders and tied her hair back with a satin ribbon. Each time he touched her, a shiver ran through her body. He meticulously adjusted the lighting, then stepped back. "Perfect!" he proclaimed, and began to paint.

That week was one of the best of Eva's life. Her writing flowed effortlessly as she worked during the day. The final chapter seemed to almost write itself. Then, each evening, as day turned to night, she walked to Daniel's house. First they worked in the studio, then they retired to the parlor and talked over a glass of wine or a cup of tea. She told him of her distress after the disintegration of her marriage and the death of her friend. Daniel spoke briefly about his wife. They had been together nearly twenty-five years but had no children. Eva asked to see pictures of his wife. He said they were all put away because looking at pictures of her made him too sad. Eva told him about her life in New York and about her passion for writing. Daniel told her stories of growing up with his wealthy family in London and about his painting career.

All too soon it was Eva's last day in Rehoboth. She had completed her novel and emailed the manuscript to her editor. She didn't want to leave, but she had to get back for a meeting. She loved the cottage and Rehoboth and she had grown very fond of Daniel. She was sure he felt the same way about her. They had formed a special bond, and she felt their connection might lead to something deeper. She pushed that thought to the back of her mind, not wanting to get her hopes up.

That night, Eva strolled down the driveway at the usual time. Daniel was seated in one of the wicker chairs on the porch and greeted her with a warm embrace. Her heart skipped a beat.

"Come in and see your portrait," he said with excitement. "It's finished."

Daniel escorted her to the parlor where he had arranged the painting on an easel by the fireplace. Eva gasped with delight. The colors were rich and vibrant and her likeness had been captured perfectly. Her skin appeared luminous and Daniel had painted her eyes with such depth that they seemed to peer out from the canvas and look around the room. The pose on the chaise, the way Daniel had styled her hair, and the velvet cape with its black lace collar made her look as if she had just stepped out of a Victorian romance novel. Once again, as in the boardwalk restaurant, Eva had a strange yet familiar feeling that she was living in a bygone era. "Oh, Daniel, it's beautiful. I love it!"

"Well, thank you," Daniel said modestly. "You're a beautiful subject, so it was easy to create a good piece of work."

They sat together on the loveseat, had tea and shortbread cookies, and talked late into the night.

Finally, Eva looked at her watch. "I hate to go, but I'd better get some sleep. I have a long drive back to the city tomorrow. What time should I check out?"

"Whenever you like," Daniel replied. "No hurry."

Eva decided to open the door for an invitation to return. "I have to be back in New York for a meeting, but after that I'm free. I'm relieved to have the novel finished. It was so easy to write once I got here. I love Rehoboth and your cottage. I feel right at home."

"I'm glad it worked out so well," Daniel said, smiling. "And I am so pleased I was able to create this painting of you. I believe I'll put it in my next exhibit."

"How exciting!" Eva exclaimed. "Please let me know the details and I'll be there."

"It will be somewhere local," Daniel said. "I'll be sure to let you know."

There was an awkward silence. Eva stood up. "Would you like your key now?"

Daniel nodded. "Yes, I won't be available tomorrow during the day when you leave. Just lock the door from the inside and pull it shut behind you."

He took the key from her and their fingers touched. He kissed her lightly on the cheek. "I have enjoyed our time together this past week, Eva. You don't know how much it's meant to me."

"I've enjoyed it, too," Eva said breathlessly.

After another awkward silence, Eva walked to the front door and Daniel followed her onto the porch. As she walked away, she paused to take one more look at the mansion. He was standing there watching her. She waved, hoping he might call her to come back, but he just returned her wave, then went into the house.

Eva wondered why he hadn't seized the opportunity to suggest a plan for them to meet again in Rehoboth. She thought there was a strong, mutual attraction. Perhaps when her portrait was on exhibit, he would call and ask her to come back for a visit. She went to bed and fell into a deep sleep. She dreamed that she and Daniel were dancing in a grand ballroom. He was dressed in a tuxedo and she was wearing a lavender satin gown and the purple velvet cape. An orchestra played a waltz as they glided along the dance floor.

Suddenly, a loud noise jarred Eva awake. It was morning. She dressed quickly and went outside. Engine sounds were coming from the direction of the mansion. She ran down the driveway and saw construction vehicles. Workmen were fencing in the area around the house.

"Excuse me, what are you doing?" Eva called out to one of the workmen.

A tall, heavy-set man sauntered over. "Hi, I'm John, the foreman. You'll need to stay out of the way. We're tearing this house down."

"What? There must be a mistake. Daniel Wedgeworth lives here. I saw him just last night and he said nothing about this. Are you sure you have the right property?"

"Yes, ma'am. This old mansion is structurally unsound. The property was bought by a developer and he ordered the demolition. He's gonna build townhouses here."

"No, that can't be. Daniel lives here—this is his home."

"You mean the artist?" John asked. "Yeah, this *was* his home a long time ago, but it's been abandoned for years. I heard his wife died and he passed away soon after. Story is he died of a broken heart."

"But I rented his cottage this week. I've spent every evening here with him. He painted my portrait."

John took off his hardhat and scratched his head. "Miss, I don't know what you're talking about. This place was really something back in the day, but it's a mess now, as you can see. You couldn't have been inside it recently."

"But I was," Eva insisted. "Go inside; it's beautiful. You'll see."

John sighed and took the key out of his pocket. He opened the front door and stepped aside so Eva could enter. The interior was in shambles and a musty odor hung thick in the air. In the foyer, strips of paint and chunks of plaster had fallen from the walls and ceiling.

Eva ran to the parlor and steadied herself against the doorway as she gazed at the bare walls and the empty easel next to the fireplace.

All the paintings were gone. Every piece of furniture was draped in sheets and covered with dust and cobwebs.

"You all right?" John asked.

"I don't know," Eva replied. "He finished my portrait yesterday. It was on that easel last night and his paintings were all over the walls. What happened?"

John shrugged. "I don't know what to tell you. Why don't you go to the Rehoboth Museum? Martha Williams knows local history and might be able to help you."

Eva ran back to the cottage, her head spinning. She loaded her suitcases in the car, then with one last look, she locked the door and pulled it shut behind her.

An elderly woman sitting behind a desk in the museum looked up as Eva entered.

"Martha Williams?"

"Yes. May I help you?"

"I hope so," Eva replied, and proceeded to tell her story.

Martha listened politely, yet looked increasingly perplexed. She shook her head, "Daniel Wedgeworth's wife died in 1902 and Daniel passed away the following year. His sister came from London to clear out his personal belongings. She donated all his paintings to the museum. The property has been tied up in red tape for years, but a developer finally purchased it. A shame that charming home is being razed. But come, we have a room devoted to his paintings."

Martha led Eva to a room in the back of the museum. The paintings were ones she remembered seeing at the mansion. But in an alcove were two paintings that took her breath away—Daniel's self-portrait and the portrait he had painted of her.

Eva took the woman's arm and pulled her over. "That one of Daniel was in the parlor and this is the portrait he painted of me this past week!"

The woman looked at Eva with obvious confusion. "I'm sorry, dear, that's a portrait of Mr. Wedgeworth's wife, Evangeline. But my goodness, you do bear a strong resemblance to Evangeline Wedgeworth."

Eva trembled and tried to speak, but the words wouldn't come.

"See the pink roses in the painting?" Martha said. "They were her favorite."

* * * * * *

Eva drove back to New York, turning the events of the past week over in her mind. Nothing made sense.

Back in her apartment that evening, Eva did some research on Daniel Wedgeworth. The information from Martha Williams was accurate.

Eva moved through the week in a daze, running errands and catching up with friends. She didn't mention her week in Rehoboth to anyone. She asked her bank about the $500 check she had given Daniel and they said it had never been cashed. She attended the meeting with her editor and was happy to find that he was pleased with her manuscript. He was also intrigued to hear that her next book would be set in Victorian-era Rehoboth Beach, Delaware.

Robin Hill-Page Glanden grew up in Harrington, Delaware. After college, she spent twenty years in Philadelphia, New York City, and Los Angeles working in the entertainment industry and as a freelance writer. Robin continued writing after moving back to the East Coast. Her short story, "Elaynea and the Walk of Boards," was published in the 2014 anthology, *The Boardwalk*. This year Robin had two nonfiction stories published by Guideposts—one on their website and another in *Mysterious Ways* magazine. Her haiku recently appeared in *The Cicada's Cry*. Robin enjoys reading her poetry and prose at various local venues. She and her husband, Kenny, teamed up as a poetry/percussion duo and have performed on the World Café Live stage at The Queen Theater in Wilmington, in the Arden Gild Hall, at Newark Arts Alliance, and at the Jackson Inn. Robin is a University of Delaware alumna and lives near the campus in Newark, Delaware.

Cooking Lard and Candle Wax

By Rich Barnett

Billy was sitting at the kitchen table poring over the latest edition of *Photoplay* when Linda Katie came barging through the back door wearing a faded yellow towel wrapped around her head.

"Damn it! I've really done it this time. I can't compete in the pageant looking like this." She removed the towel to reveal a head of fiery red hair.

"Wow!"

Linda Katie was a shoo-in, everyone said, to win the title of Miss Strawberry Queen 1959. But that was yesterday, when she was the prettiest girl at Rehoboth High; today, she looked like a cross between Lucille Ball and an Atomic Fire Ball.

"All I wanted was a little red. Then I found mother's cigarettes and Carol phoned and—damn it!—I left the dye in way too long."

Billy giggled and she threw the towel at him.

"You've got to help me!"

Billy wasn't good at hitting a baseball or throwing a football. Nor was he interested in cars like most teenage boys. His dad often said Billy's engine just ran with a little sugar in the tank. That, however, didn't stop him from employing his youngest son in the family barbershop after school and on weekends, because Billy had a way with hair. His scissors could transform an average Joe into an Ivy Leaguer or a Hollywood heartthrob. The young men lined up for Billy's haircuts on Saturday mornings. Then, after lunch, he skedaddled across town to his Aunt Lottie's beauty salon to do hair for the blue rinse brigade.

Billy grabbed a can of Comet Bleach Powder from under the kitchen sink and mixed it with some shampoo to make a gooey paste that he worked all through Linda Katie's hair. "Let it sit half an hour," he instructed.

While they waited, he read to Linda Katie from *Photoplay*. It took an additional thirty minutes, but Billy was able to tone her hair down almost to the strawberry blonde shade she'd been aiming for.

"You're the most, Billy, the most. How can I ever pay you back?"

"How 'bout we go for ice cream?" Besides movie magazines, Billy loved ice cream. Given the chance, he'd eat it every day. He liked pistachio best because he'd read it was Tab Hunter's favorite.

That night, Billy was in line for a cone—Linda Katie was outside flirting with one of the Apostolakas brothers—when he overheard someone asking for pistachio ice cream. He craned his neck to see who it was, but he didn't recognize the handsome sullen boy with the perfect DA haircut. His family must be renting a house for the summer. Billy wormed his way to the counter.

"I'll take one too!"

The teenagers looked at each other, both holding cones of pale green ice cream. "My name is Billy." He stuck out a hand.

"Cooper," the boy replied, shaking Billy's hand.

Cooper was different from Billy's friends in Rehoboth, who were loud and always showing off for girls on the beach. Not only was he from Washington, but also he stayed mostly inside and out of the sun. Cooper had a portable phonograph and a huge stack of rhythm and blues records that he played nonstop, all the while pretending to be a radio disc jockey. He knew as much about Chess Records and the Apollo Theater as Billy did about Universal Studios and the

Brown Derby Restaurant.

"Where's Rosedale Beach?" Cooper asked Billy one afternoon as they sat in Cooper's bedroom, listening to the Isley Brothers' new song "Shout." He handed Billy an advertisement cut from the *Coast Press*—one night only, James Brown and the Fabulous Flames, nine o'clock, at the Rosedale Beach dance hall.

"It's the colored beach, over on the other side of the bay."

"Boy, wouldn't it be a blast to see James Brown in person? They say he does the splits on stage."

The advertisement got Billy thinking. Summer was coming to an end and Cooper would be leaving soon. Billy might not ever see him again. "Let's go," he blurted out. "My dad has a motorboat he keeps down on the bay. I hate to fish, but he lets me drive it."

Cooper looked directly into Billy's eyes, with an expression that was both excited and questioning, yet he said nothing.

"Tell your folks you're sleeping over at my house. I'll tell mine I'm spending the night at yours. Linda Katie and me do it all the time. Works like a charm."

* * * * * *

It was almost twilight when Billy pushed off from the pier in his dad's aluminum bass boat. He and Cooper paddled quietly out into open water, then Billy cranked the engine to life and they sped off, past Thompson's Island with its spooky Indian burial mounds and south across shallow Rehoboth Bay. It was a smooth ride, even after they hit the cross currents of the Indian River.

Though Billy had never been to Rosedale, he had heard about its hotel, boardwalk, and dance hall. Some white people from Rehoboth went to hear the colored music on Friday and Saturday nights. They wouldn't actually go in the dance hall; they anchored their boats offshore and listened.

Rosedale attracted the best black talent traveling from Philadelphia south to Norfolk, Virginia Beach, and the Carolinas. It was one of the few hotels catering exclusively to black folk on the entire Delmarva Peninsula.

Billy and Cooper, however, weren't content only to listen. They could do that with records. No, the boys came to see James Brown, whom Cooper believed was a legend in the making. Just beyond the dance hall and the other boats, they kicked off their penny loafers, jumped out, and pulled the boat through the cool, shallow water to shore, where Billy tied it up to a large pine tree.

Barefoot, and using the cover of trees and bushes, they carefully crept over to the dance hall, a single-story, wooden, white, frame building with aluminum awnings over its windows. A loud crowd had gathered on the front steps to greet James Brown, who had just arrived. From their hiding spot they heard how Brown and his band had been stopped for speeding and then detained at the county jail for a couple of hours.

The boys took advantage of the commotion and made their way to the back of the dance hall and darted inside. Cooper seemed to know what he was doing, so Billy followed. "There's got to be somewhere in the dressing room we can hide."

Sure enough, Cooper found a supply closet. There was no door, merely a thin, green cloth nailed up. They ducked in just as James Brown and his band burst into the dressing room, carrying suitcases and band equipment.

"Gimme a drink," Brown ordered, and sat down heavily in one of the few chairs in the sparsely furnished room. A well-dressed man they called Bird handed him a bottle of Canadian whiskey. Brown took a couple of very long swigs. "Goddamn crackers," he yelled. "Thought they was keeping us locked up all night." Members of the band were unpacking their instruments and changing clothes.

"Where's the girl gonna conk my hair?" Brown hollered, feeling more relaxed from the effects of the brown liquor on an empty stomach. Bird explained that she'd gone off with her boyfriend when it looked like the band might be stuck in jail all night.

"Hellfire. Who gonna do my hair? James Brown can't go on stage looking like this." He kicked a suitcase. "People pay to see a show, they expect a show." The noise from the crowd in the dance hall was getting louder.

"Wear a hat," one of the band members yelled.

"Wear a hat? When you ever see James Brown wear a goddamn hat?" He took another swig of whiskey.

At that moment, Billy stepped out of the closet. "I can style your hair, Mr. Brown."

"Whoa, Nelly!" James Brown leaned back in his chair, almost falling over backward from surprise. "Who this skinny white boy?"

Bird pulled a gun. Cooper screamed as Bird grabbed a struggling Billy by the arm and pushed him up against a wall. "What you doin' here, boy?"

"We came to hear music."

Bird seized Cooper and shoved him up beside Billy. Both boys were trembling like wet puppies. He continued to point the gun at Billy and Cooper.

Alarmed, Brown spoke up. "Now hold on, Bird. Be cool. We just got *out* of jail and I ain't going *back*. Let me have a word with the little cracker."

Bird led Billy over to James Brown, holding the boy's arms behind his back to keep him from running. Brown eyed the barefoot blond teenager in his pressed chino pants and plaid button-up shirt with the carefully rolled up sleeves.

"You got one minute before I throw yo white ass outta here." Bird released him.

Billy quickly explained how he styled hair and his dream was to go to Hollywood and find a job doing hair for the stars when he finished high school next spring. Overly excited, he began to lisp, which caused the band members to snicker.

"You know how to do *black* hair?"

"Can't be any harder than Mrs. Dantonio's hair. I barely get a comb through it."

"Don't listen to the little sissy!" Bird, who had been part of James Brown's band from day one, was protective and cautious around new people, especially white people.

"You got a better idea, Bird? You want to do my hair?" Bird went silent. "Humph. I didn't think so." Brown turned back to Billy. "Got any supplies?"

"No."

"Then *how* you gonna style James Brown's hair?"

Billy reached out to feel Brown's hair, running it through his fingers. "Doesn't need to be conked. I can make pomade with cooking lard and candle wax. They'll have both in the hotel kitchen." For rollers, he had to think fast. Remembering the supplies in the closet, Billy grabbed a roll of toilet paper and pulled out the brown cardboard tube. "I'll cut and use these."

"You ain't puttin' toilet paper on James Brown," Bird yelled at Billy. "Ain't right."

Brown, however, was amused and impressed by the boy's nerve. He took the cardboard tube from Billy's hand and examined it up close. After a long silence, he finally spoke: "I'm gonna give the sissy a chance. What's your name, boy?"

"Billy."

"All right, Billy." Brown held out his hand to shake. "You got yourself a gig. Bird, take Billy to the kitchen. And tell the crowd we'll go on in an hour. Ain't no damn speeding ticket gonna stop James Brown."

* * * * * *

After successfully procuring the needed supplies, Billy set a chair in front of a small mirror hanging on a wall. He put newspaper on the floor and draped a tablecloth over Mr. Brown to prevent the homemade pomade from dripping onto the singer. Billy carefully coated the singer's hair with the lard and wax mixture, then swept it up and wrapped it around the toilet paper tubes to create Brown's signature curls. He used tin foil to create a cap, which he put over the hair to keep it all in place.

Cooper, meanwhile, was peeking out of the door leading from the dressing room to the stage and beyond. The dance hall was full. The audience was sitting and drinking at small mismatched tables and chairs or standing by a makeshift plywood bar painted all different colors. Most of the men were wearing suits and the women were in dresses. The room was loud and smoky. Red-and-white gingham curtains fluttered from the slight breeze.

Bird came up behind Cooper and looked out. He was more relaxed now that his boss was happy. "How many you think we got tonight?"

"I'd say about two hundred. When 'Slippin' and Slidin'' played on the phonograph, everybody was dancing."

Bird looked down at Cooper. "How a white boy like you knows Little Richard?"

"I listen to WOL radio in Washington. He and Mr. Brown are my favorites."

Bird nodded. "Your daddy know you here?"

"No, sir! Billy took a boat and we sneaked over."

"That so." Bird finally cracked a smile. "Well, you boys all right."

Billy's homemade pomade and cardboard tubes worked even better than he'd expected. High on whiskey and wearing a new electric blue suit, James Brown dazzled the crowd at Rosedale nonstop for ninety minutes, putting on one of his most energetic performances. At least that's what Bird told the boys in the dressing room after the show. Brown's shiny hair never moved an inch, and it looked just as good after the show as before.

Bird handed Cooper a bottle of whiskey. "Drink?"

Without hesitation, Cooper took a sip. Then another. "Thank you, Mr. Bird." He passed the bottle to Billy, who took a big swig. It burned going down and he coughed.

"Not too much," Bird counseled. "You ever drink before?"

"No, sir."

"Well, what you wanna do is take little sips. Enough to fly, but not get sick."

Billy nodded. "That why they call you Bird?" The musician grinned as Billy took another drink, more cautiously this time, feeling the whiskey's warm embrace.

A short time later, Brown called Billy over to where he was changing clothes and handed him an engraved white business card. Billy had never seen anything so glamorous and he said so. Brown chuckled. "You got talent, boy. When you get to Hollywood, you look up this cat named Mr. Ray. Show him this here card and tell him James Brown said give you a job. Mr. Ray styles everybody who plays the coast—Ella, Duke, Fats. He'll help you out." James was looking at his hair in the mirror. "Damn fine job."

"It's getting late." Bird interrupted James's preening. "I've lined us up some barbecue like you asked. Finest chopped barbecue in all of Rosedale."

"Sure am hungry. What's her name?" At that, the band started hollering at Bird to fetch them some barbecue too.

Brown looked over at Billy and Cooper. "You boys want some chopped barbecue?" When they didn't reply, he continued on. "No? I didn't think so. I'm guessing you like the T-bone." Billy and

Cooper blushed, but Brown was amused. "It's OK by me if you got a taste for the bone. Means more barbecue for me. Plenty of fellas like a T-bone.

"Listen here, I'm gonna give some advice and I want you to pay attention to what James Brown got to say. Don't be ashamed cuz you like the T-bone. One thing I've learned in this business is you got to be yourself. Can't try to be somebody else. Ain't nobody in music today like James Brown." The band members nodded. "But you got to be real careful, you know what I mean?" Brown continued, his tone turning serious. "Not everybody is cool like James Brown and the Flames. Lots of mean folks out there won't think twice 'bout hurting boys like you."

Motoring back down the bay toward Rehoboth, Billy kept thinking about James Brown's words. Finally, he cut the engine and the boat slowed. Soon, only the currents gently pulled them eastward. Billy opened the bottle of whiskey James Brown had given them as a token of thanks and took a swig before passing the bottle to Cooper. He watched his friend drink. Heart pounding, Billy leaned over and kissed Cooper, whose lips were wet and tasted sweet. Thankfully, he didn't pull away. Billy might have been a sissy, but nobody ever accused him of being shy.

RICH BARNETT IS THE AUTHOR OF *FUN WITH DICK AND JAMES* (2016) AND *THE DISCREET CHARMS OF A BOURGEOIS BEACH TOWN* (2012). HIS "CAMP STORIES" COLUMN FOR *LETTERS FROM CAMP REHOBOTH* JUST CELEBRATED TEN YEARS. RICH'S FICTION AND NONFICTION WORK HAS APPEARED IN *REVEALING REHOBOTH: AN INSIDER'S GUIDE, SAINTS AND SINNERS: NEW FICTION FROM THE FESTIVAL* (2014 AND 2016), *THE BEACH HOUSE,* AND OTHER PUBLICATIONS. RICH EARNS A LIVING IN WASHINGTON, DC, BUT MAKES A LIFE IN REHOBOTH BEACH, DE.

JUDGE'S COMMENT

A tale of identity, rebellion, and coming of age with all the necessary ingredients: James Brown, booze, hairstyling, a borrowed boat, and a well-earned kiss. This piece is deeply satisfying on many levels, with economic language, rich imagery, and characters that will stay with you.

Mermaid's Moon

By Jeanie P. Blair

Shear panic. Addison Finley empathized with the kids who were being strapped into Funland's Freefall ride for their very first time. She felt their pain. Why had she ever agreed to a blind date? With the faint rumble of thunder in the distance, Addison made her way inside to the kiddie boats, where she had agreed to meet her friend Micki. She rolled her eyes. She had sworn off blind dates—especially with anyone Micki's boyfriend recommended. Brad Davis and his friends were nothing more than a bunch of over-aged frat boys. But Micki assured her that Brad's cousin Gage was different. First, she emphasized that he wasn't Brad's friend, but his cousin. *Some defense. Brad's personality traits could be genetic.* Micki also touted that Gage had money. Wow. Their opinions of the perfect man were polar opposites. *It's going to be a long night.*

* * * * * *

The only child of a struggling, single mother, Addison had no idea how to relate to the affluent. Her mother had once worked for a very wealthy family, but Addison knew nothing about them. They had lived in one of the houses on the family's estate, but Marian Bennett made it a point to keep young Addy far removed from her employers. Addy only caught a rare glimpse of them when they'd call their young son back to the mansion. Trip snuck down to see Addy on a few occasions, but they never played together for long.

The last time she saw him, they were no more than about five or six. He gave her a tiny wooden bear on a red string. He said it was his favorite Christmas ornament, and he wanted her to have it. That was the day her mother came home from work upset. Addison cried as her mother packed up all their belongings—with no explanation—and said it was time for them to leave.

The next several years were a struggle. They lived with her grandparents in Lewes, but Addison's mom still worked two jobs. It wasn't until she married Ray Finley that things changed for them. Ray adopted Addison and raised her as his own. Her mother never discussed what had happened that day. Addison still thought about Trip and kept his gift tied to her rearview mirror.

* * * * * *

"Addison!" Micki Pierce trotted over to her friend and gave her a big hug. She grabbed Addison's hand and pulled her toward the boardwalk exit. "C'mon, the guys are waiting."

"Where are we going?" Addison asked.

"To Grotto's."

Addison halted. "Wait. I thought we were all meeting here." Funland meant games, snacks, and *minimal* conversation. Dinner was a much bigger commitment, with very few options for a fast escape.

"I know, but Brad's really hungry."

Addison smirked. "That's *his* problem."

"Pleeeease. It'll be fine. You'll love Gage. He's so hot. Like—*Channing Tatum* hot."

Addison frowned. "You owe me."

"You're the best!" Micki screeched, embracing her friend.

They hastened their pace down the boardwalk as the claps of thunder grew louder. Grotto Pizza was packed with patrons anxiously awaiting a table and shelter from the looming storm. The two weaved through the mob and found Brad, who lip-locked Micki as she threw her arms around his neck. *Gag.*

Brad turned to Addison. "Hey, Addison. Nice to see you."

She forced a smile. "Hi, Brad. You, too." *Not.*

Micki scanned the crowd. "Where's Gage?"

Maybe he bailed, Addison hoped.

"He's checking on our table," Brad answered.

Damn. No such luck.

"Here he comes," Brad said, motioning beyond Addison.

Addison spun around and almost lost her balance at the sight of the broad chest nearly touching her nose. She lifted her gaze to a pair of piercing hazel eyes.

"You must be Addison." He smiled. "Gage Riley. Nice to meet you."

The two exchanged handshakes. "Um...nice to meet you," she said.

Brad interrupted. "Dude, what about our table?"

Gage shrugged. "They said we're next."

At that, the hostess tapped Gage's arm. "Mr. Riley, your table's ready." She winked and motioned for him to follow, seemingly offering more than just an available table. Addison found herself strangely annoyed.

A server took their order and returned with a Coke and a trio of beers.

"Not a drinker?" Gage asked, motioning to Addison's Coke.

"Sometimes," she said. "On special occasions, mostly."

"I thought this *was* a special occasion."

Seriously? Get over yourself, pal.

She shrugged off his comment. "So what do you do, Gage?" Addison acted as if she knew nothing about him.

"I'm in real estate," he replied.

"Oh, you're an agent?"

"Actually, I'm more of an investor," he answered.

"Fascinating." She continued the ruse. "Tell me more."

He started to fidget. "I'd much rather talk about you. I hear you're a photographer?"

"Only part-time. I'm a full-time tutor, but I'd like to do photography full-time someday," she said.

"Cool," Gage said. "I'd love to see your work sometime."

They both glanced at the other couple, who were off in a snuggly little world of their own. Fortunately, the pizza arrived just in time to quell the awkwardness.

The group's dinner conversation was much less intimate. Addison was pleased to find that Gage was not the immature narcissist she had expected. The foursome finished their meal and proceeded out to the boardwalk, surprised to find that the storm had missed them.

"Anyone for a stroll on the beach?" Micki asked.

With no objections, they kicked off their shoes and hit the sand. Micki and Brad trekked ahead, then stopped for some huggy-kissy time.

"Care to cop some sand?" Gage asked Addison, clearly not interested in a close-up of the smoochfest.

"Works for me."

Gage pointed at the sky. "Wow. Check out that ring around the moon."

"It's beautiful," Addison said. "My grandpa used to call that a mermaid's moon. I know there's a scientific explanation, but he used to say a halo around the moon meant that a mermaid made a wish, and something or someone you lost would come back to you."

Gage grinned. "I like his version much better."

"Me, too." She smiled.

As they spent the next hour talking, Addison felt her guard start to slip.

"It's getting late," Addison said. "I think we'd better corral those lovebirds."

"Yeah, I suppose so. This was really nice, Addison. Listen— knowing my cousin's track record, I'm sure you weren't eager to do this. But I'm very glad you did."

"Me, too, Gage. And I'm sorry, I have to admit I *was* afraid that

Brad's personality might be genetic." She chuckled.

Gage let out a burst of laughter. "God, no!"

As they stood up, Gage offered his hand and Addison took hold, but she lost her footing and fell backward, pulling him down with her. They both rolled onto their backs, laughing hysterically. Gage managed to get up first and again took Addison's hand. "Let's try that again." He chuckled.

She stood up easily this time, and they both brushed off their clothes. Gage turned to her as she shook the last of the sand from her long, auburn hair.

"There," she said. "I think I got it all."

"Wait." Gage swept his finger down her cheek. "You missed some."

Before she could thank him, she locked onto his gaze. He palmed her cheek and leaned in. Her heart nearly jumped out of her chest, and she felt his warm breath on her lips as he pulled her closer.

"Hey, you two!"

Startled by the sound of Micki's voice, Addison jerked backward.

Micki waved at them. "We have to get going."

Brad turned to Gage. "Dude, Micki'll take me home."

"Oh, OK." Gage looked to Addison. "I'll walk you to your car."

"Nah, that's OK. I'm not far away."

"Me neither," Gage said. "C'mon, we'll walk together."

Gage wrapped his hand around hers. She didn't pull away, though she knew she should. They continued to talk and laugh—mostly about Brad—until they reached her car. Addison slid her hand from Gage's and fished her keys from her purse.

"Thanks again for dinner," she said.

"My pleasure." He paused. "Hey, my family's hosting a party tomorrow night. Would you like to come?"

Panic. "Oh…uh…," she stammered.

"It's nothing formal, just a big beach party, really."

Those eyes. Dammit. "Um—OK."

His big, brilliant smile sent a spark through her.

"Great," he said. "It starts at seven. I'll text you the address."

The street was still abuzz with people, so they traded cell phone numbers and exchanged a quick hug. Addison slid into her car, closed the door, and rolled down her window. Gage leaned down and eyed the wooden bear hanging from her mirror. "Hey, where did you get that?"

"Oh, a friend of mine gave it to me a long time ago," she said. "Why?"

"Just curious. It looks familiar, that's all."

"I think it was a Christmas ornament. I'm sure there are millions like it."

"Yeah, probably. Well, goodnight, Addison. Drive safely."

"Goodnight, Gage. And thanks again."

* * * * * *

Addison awoke to the shriek of her alarm clock. She was surprised she had even slept, with the angst of the Rileys' party on her mind. She decided on a trip to the salon and was happy to score an afternoon appointment. While she sipped coffee, she searched her closet for something to wear. The only designer thing she owned was a Coach purse her mother had given her for Christmas. Not thrilled with her options, she finally settled on a print halter sundress and a pair of beaded sandals. They weren't designer, but Micki always said the dress highlighted her best assets. Addison showered, threw on shorts and a tee, and cinched her hair with an elastic band. With her appointment still two hours away, she decided to run some errands on the way.

When she returned to her Lewes condo, Addison looked in the mirror, pleased she had gone to the salon. Her hair was twisted up in curls, a few loose wisps framing her face, and her makeup was model flawless. She changed her clothes, took a final spin in front of the mirror, then touched up her lipstick and left for Rehoboth.

*　*　*　*　*　*

The Rileys' beach home was magnificent. Addison couldn't imagine how much it was worth. It was the largest home on East Lake Drive, with a private stretch of beach just outside the back door. She inhaled deeply as she killed the ignition. *Relax, Addison. These people are no better than you, just richer.* She jumped when the door opened before she grabbed the handle.

"Hey, Addison." Gage stood before her, barefoot and wearing a pair of khaki shorts and a black Polo shirt. His sandy hair was perfectly spiked, his eyes as bright as his smile.

"Hi, Gage."

He helped her out of the car and pulled her in for a hug. *Damn, he smelled magnificent.* When they parted, she grabbed her purse and a pink box from her front seat.

"I brought some goodies," she said, handing him the box.

"Oh, thanks." He stepped back, eyeing her up and down. "Wow. Addison. You look beautiful."

"Um, thank you." Heat crept into her cheeks.

As they reached the top of the stone steps, Gage stopped. "Addison, before we go in, there's—"

"There you are!" A petite, older blonde flung open the front door, a crystal champagne glass clenched in her perfectly manicured hand, her diamonds glistening in the porch light.

Gage looked flustered. "Uh, Addison, this is my mother, Kay."

Addison extended her hand. "Hello, Mrs. Riley. It's very nice to meet you."

Kay pulled Addison in for an unexpected hug. "It's so nice to meet you, too. Please, call me Kay." She grabbed Addison by the elbow and led her through the double doors.

Gage rolled his eyes. "Mom!"

Ignoring her son's beckoning, Kay led Addison out to the patio, where a large crowd was assembled. "Come, dear. I want you to meet Gage's father."

As they weaved through the clusters of guests, Gage disappeared behind her. A wave of unease overcame her. They finally stopped in front of a tall, burly man with salt-and-pepper hair—basically an older version of Gage.

"Ben," Kay said. "This is Addison."

"Well, hello, Addison. So nice to finally meet you," he said.

Finally? "Nice to meet you, too, Mr. Riley."

Gage reappeared. "Mom, Dad, would you excuse us, please?" Without waiting for an answer, he grabbed Addison's hand and bolted toward the house.

Addison jerked his hand and stopped. "Gage, what's going on?"

"Well, I'll be!" A portly, bald man stumbled out of the crowd.

"Oh, shit. Uncle Carl." Gage was clearly unhappy to see the approaching man, and continued on toward the house. "C'mon, Addison."

Despite Gage's efforts, their pursuer caught up to them. The drink in his hand was clearly not his first; he smelled like a walking bottle of Dewar's.

He placed his chubby hand on Addison's shoulder. "So, this is little Addison, is it?"

Hesitant to respond, she said, "I'm sorry, have we met?"

Gage interjected. "No, you haven't."

Gage tried to pull Addison away, but Carl clutched her shoulder. "Wow. You certainly are a beauty—just like your mother."

Addison's mind reeled. "You know my mother?"

"Sure. Didn't ol' Trip tell you?"

Addison looked at Gage, who was clearly mortified. *Trip?* "Gage, what is he talking about?"

"Your mother used to work for us," Carl slurred.

With that, Gage pulled Addison from his uncle's grip and led her inside to a large, wood-paneled office and closed the door.

"Addison—" Gage began.

"Gage, what the...Who is Trip?"

"*I'm* Trip. As in, *triple*. The *third*. My name is Benjamin Gage Riley, *the third*," he said. "Carl is the only one who still calls me Trip."

Addison felt a sudden wave of nausea. It all started to make sense. The Rileys were that horrible family her mother used to work for. And Gage was the little boy who used to sneak away to see her.

"Oh. My. God." She fell backward onto an overstuffed couch. "You knew about this? Why didn't you—" Tears filled her eyes.

Gage combed his fingers through his hair. "Addison, I'm so sorry. I tried to tell you when you got here, but—"

"When I *got* here? Why did you wait until tonight?"

Gage sat down next to her and grabbed her hands. "I didn't even find out myself until just before you arrived. Your name is different, you obviously look different...but then I mentioned you to my mother and she put it together. That's why I tried to tell you outside—"

The two jumped when the door opened and Gage's parents entered, both wearing anguished expressions. Ben spoke first. "Addison, my apologies for my drunken brother-in-law. Please, let us explain. When you were little, your mother worked for us. One day, Carl made a pass at her. When she refused him, he was so angry he told everyone that she was the one who pursued *him*. Your mother was humiliated and resigned instantly. We begged her to stay, but the damage was done. Please know that we never turned our backs on you and your mom. At the very least, we wanted to help financially, but she refused us."

"Addison," Kay chimed in. "Gage told us he had invited someone, but never told us who until tonight. We were thrilled. Your mom kept a tight rein on you back then. We never had the chance to know you."

Addison sensed their sincerity, but, at that moment, all she wanted to do was get as far away from them as possible.

"I'm sorry, but I have to go." She darted out of the room and out the front door.

Gage followed. "Addison, wait!"

She couldn't answer. As she reached her car, Gage caught up to her. He grabbed her shoulders and turned her to face him.

"Addison," he breathed. "I'm so sorry. Please don't go." He tried to wrap his arms around her, but she pushed him away.

"Don't," she sobbed.

"I can't let you leave like this. Please believe me. I had no idea—about *any* of this."

Addison fought back tears. "I just want to go home." She turned and quickly got into her car. She sped off, with Gage in her rearview mirror, watching her drive out of sight.

* * * * * *

During the next several days, Gage left numerous messages, but Addison didn't answer any of them. She hoped at some point he would come to realize, as she did, that it just wouldn't work with them. Micki had left messages, too, but Addison just couldn't rehash the nightmare. She finally connected with her mother, who confirmed the Rileys' story. She even suggested Addison give Gage another chance. Marian also said that, Carl aside, the Rileys really were a good family. No matter. Addison resolved to steer clear.

* * * * * *

Addison decided that some time behind her camera might help her forget about the Rileys. After hearing there'd be a full moon, she planned an evening trip into Rehoboth. To her, nothing was more exhilarating than the beach at night. The briny scent of the misty air, the intensity of the boardwalk lights, and the exuberance emanating from Funland. Then, just yards beyond, the pitch-black serenity of the beach and the surf that could be heard, but not seen, from the boardwalk.

Addison began with a few shots of the bustling boardwalk. Next, she headed several blocks south, far from the lights, so she could capture the brilliance of the full moon. As she set her camera bag on the wooden bench, her cell phone chimed. Another text from Gage.

I really need to see you. PLEASE call me.

Her heart skipped. She wanted to see him, too, but knew it was a bad idea. She sat on the bench, closed her eyes, and took some long, slow breaths of the crisp night air. She jumped when her phone rang, but sighed with relief when she looked down, then tapped the screen.

"Hi, Micki."

"Where the heck are you, Adds?"

"In Rehoboth. I needed some time to clear my head, so I came down to shoot some pictures."

"Are you OK?"

"Yes. I'm fine," she lied. "I'm on the boardwalk at Rodney Street. Don't worry, there are plenty of people around."

"OK, but please call me when you get home."

"I will." Addison ended the call and followed the sandy trail toward the surf.

Addison chose a spot and spread out the blanket she had packed, then sat to adjust her camera for the next series of pictures. The moon was magnificent, casting a bright path from the horizon to the surf. It was clear and sharp and looked close enough to touch.

She removed her lens cap, then raised her camera for the first shot. She gasped at the large figure blocking the moon. "Gage!"

"Hi, Addison."

"What are you doing here?"

"I had to see you. I couldn't leave things the way they were with us."

"How did you know I was here?" *Of course.* "Micki."

"Yes. But don't be mad at her. I begged her to help me find you."

Dammit. She had forgotten that East Lake Drive was just beyond this end of the boardwalk. "I'm sorry I didn't return your calls. It's just best if we don't see each other."

Gage sat down next to her. "Addison, what happened was eons ago. It has nothing to do with us now."

"It doesn't matter. We're from two different worlds."

"Exactly," he said. "That's what I love most about you. I can tell you have no interest in my money. We just enjoy being together. I've never had that. With anyone."

She fought back tears. "I do enjoy being with you. But it's just not meant to be."

"Listen. I'm not superstitious," he said, "but I can't help but believe there's a reason we reconnected after all these years." He wiped a tear from her cheek with his thumb. Gage smiled as he looked to the sky. "Look." He pointed at the moon, which was suddenly surrounded by a big, bright ring.

Addison gasped. "A mermaid's moon."

Gage nodded. "Just like the night of our date. Now—can you honestly still tell me we aren't meant to be together?"

"No, I suppose I can't. Guess my grandpa was right about the mermaid's moon. Something lost is being returned to me."

"He sure was right." With that, Gage took her face in his hands and planted a long, soft kiss on her lips. When they parted, he wrapped his arms around her.

Addison held onto him tightly and whispered as she winked up at the moon, "Thanks, Grandpa."

A NATIVE DELAWAREAN, JEANIE PITRIZZI BLAIR RESIDES IN NEWARK WITH HER HUSBAND, SAM, AND THEIR MINIATURE SCHNAUZERS, SCHATZIE AND BELLA. SHE HAS POSSESSED A LOVE FOR READING, WRITING, AND THE ENGLISH LANGUAGE SINCE SHE WAS A CHILD, WHICH SHE LARGELY ATTRIBUTES TO HER GRADE SCHOOL ENGLISH TEACHERS. JEANIE'S FIRST PUBLISHED PIECE WAS A POEM THAT SHE ENTERED IN A NATIONAL POETRY CONTEST. HER STORY, "SOMEWHERE BETWEEN CRAB CAKES AND COCKTAILS," PUBLISHED IN *BEACH DAYS,* WAS HER FIRST PUBLISHED SHORT STORY. THOUGH SHE WORKS FULL-TIME AS AN OFFICE ADMINISTRATOR, JEANIE CONTINUES TO PURSUE HER DREAM OF BECOMING A SUCCESSFUL ROMANCE NOVELIST AND HOPES TO HAVE HER FIRST NOVEL PUBLISHED IN THE NEAR FUTURE. JEANIE WOULD LIKE TO THANK HER DEAR FAMILY AND FRIENDS FOR THEIR CONTINUED SUPPORT AND ENCOURAGEMENT. SHE HAS SPENT HER WHOLE LIFE VACATIONING AT THE BEACH—HER FAVORITE PLACE AND THE INSPIRATION FOR MANY OF HER STORIES. SHE GREATLY ENJOYS SPENDING TIME WITH HER FAMILY IN LONG NECK, DELAWARE.

Jazzed

By Connie L. McDowell

2 weeks, 3 days, 8 hours, 17 minutes.

He'd purchased the funny little clock on the Internet. Its purpose, to count down the time before a special event. Milestone birthday. Anniversary. Retirement. His momentous occasion—more sinister—but for him, far more pleasurable. A night to remember. He studied the clock again.

2 weeks, 3 days, 8 hours, 13 minutes.

That's how long he had to wait, until his date with death.
Murder, to be precise.
He'd spent months plotting Audrey's demise. His blood pressure rose in anticipation. The rat-tat-tatting of his heart reverberated like machine-gun fire. Fast, loud, staccato beats echoed in his brain. He could barely think. How he'd dreamed of the day he could rid himself of that shrew. The taste of freedom seared his throat as he reviewed his foolproof plan once more.

Every night, he ran on the hard-packed sand near the ocean. His strategy unfolded, crystallizing in his mind with every step. Tonight, the moon lit the sky like a gigantic torch. The sand turned golden, illuminating his path. Soon, he'd escape his dark prison, unfettered from his wife's incessant nagging.

Then she'll have no one to carp at, except the devil himself.

Winded, he flopped on the sand and stared out to sea, fantasizing about his future. *I can hardly wait to start anew.* Kyrra and Audrey—polar opposites. Kyrra is day to Audrey's night; compassionate rather than malicious, good-humored instead of ill-tempered. *Kyrra loves me. Audrey loathes me. My world will be perfect, once I build a new life with the woman I adore and eliminate the one I detest.*

He listened to the pounding surf. Waves thumped in, sliding upon the sand, like pale suds in the moonlight. An ocean breeze, pregnant with the scent of salt, feathered his skin with a briny mist. Its tangy smell consumed him. Minutes passed. The wind gusted. Cresting higher, breakers crashed with a tumultuous roar. They pummeled the shoreline, leaving behind frothy trails. He leapt up to avoid getting soaked, then trudged homeward.

He'd never loved Audrey. Early on, he'd liked her. Smart. Witty. Decent in the sack. Discovering she was heiress to a shipping dynasty added to her allure. Boatloads of dough to fund a carefree existence. But over time she'd begun grating on his nerves, nitpicking his every move. She held up her friends' mates as constant reminders of his shortcomings.

"Why can't you be like Gloria's husband, Darrin? His company grossed over ten million last year," Audrey shrilled. "Look at Millie's boy toy, Mel. He won $50K at that poker tournament in Brussels. Even Angela's Bob, not the brightest bulb, outshone you in the dance competition at the country club last week. Blah-blah-blah…"

Relentless, Audrey poked and prodded every chance she got. Now she'd run out of chances. Soon he wouldn't be forced to endure her put-downs. He'd not only break free; he'd inherit a bundle. Three gorgeous homes. A half dozen fancy cars. The sleek, new yacht. Sweetest of all—enough lovely green stuff to keep everything humming along, the remainder of his days. The daily target of Audrey's sniping and snide jabs, he felt zero guilt. He'd earned this inheritance.

After a respectable mourning period, I'll bring Kyrra here. No, we should winter at the villa in Bermuda and return to the DC penthouse in early spring. Then I'll bring her here to Rehoboth next summer.

Cool heads prevail, he reminded himself. First, he must commit the perfect crime. No room for error. The husband's always the primary suspect.

Audrey suffered from a heart condition. During two previous hospitalizations, her status was critical. Unfortunately for him, she'd rallied and survived. Too mean to die. Even the devil doesn't want her.

Dr. Westphal urged Audrey to stop smoking and adopt a healthier lifestyle. The cardiologist prescribed digoxin, unwittingly providing the perfect weapon.

He pilfered two pills every three months, squirreling them away until he had enough. Then he smashed them to the appropriate consistency. Painstakingly, he opened two packets of artificial sweetener and poured out the contents. He measured the quantity in each, replacing a portion with digoxin. Then, he meticulously filled and resealed the packets. It was impossible to detect signs of tampering.

A few hours after Audrey ingested tea sweetened with the substitute, she'd lapse into unconsciousness. Given her age, weight, and compromised health, he estimated he'd added enough digoxin to trigger a massive heart attack—then death.

1 week, 2 days, 9 hours, 27 minutes.

If the need arose, he'd concocted a plan substantiating his innocence. The Rehoboth Jazz Festival opened next weekend. Following the afternoon show, Audrey and he would dine at the Rudder. While seated beside him, she'd request sweetener. He'd conceal the special ones in his palm and pull two others from the holder. Using sleight-of-hand trickery perfected in front of a mirror, he'd slip the regular packets into his pocket and pass Audrey the altered ones. She'd empty them into her tea, and...

The game of murder will commence.

Audrey had invited guests to the house afterward, for dessert and cocktails. He and Audrey would be among friends when death called her name.

1 day, 6 hours, 32 minutes.

Friday dawned with a chill in the air and a melancholy presence. Low-hanging clouds, laden with moisture, huddled overhead. A murky, pewter sky appeared ready to weep. Clouds descended, shrouding the landscape in a foggy mist.

Lost in thought, he finished his morning brew. Streetlamps cast eerie swaths of light and shadow amid the haze. The filmy vapor distorted ordinary objects, evoking ghostly images.

Sirens wailing in the distance punctured the silence, giving him the "goosies."

It hadn't always been like this. Audrey and he'd met when he became the festival producer's assistant. A huge jazz aficionado, Audrey was a major benefactor. Bonding over their love of syncopated rhythms, they discovered other shared interests. Audrey fell hard. Smitten, and accustomed to getting whatever she wanted with a wave of green, she tossed temptation in his direction. He dashed to collect.

Following a six-week, whirlwind courtship, they wed in a low-key ceremony and flew to Bermuda for a brief period of matrimonial bliss. Upon their return, the honeymoon ended. Although marriage included numerous benefits, certain accessories Audrey insisted he wear he found unpalatable. The oppressively tight collar, attached to a painfully short leash, cramped his style.

Her refusal to take his name also irked him. Audrey claimed she couldn't bear being last in an alphabetical listing. He believed she simply didn't wish to relinquish the Babcock name. Eventually, she conceded to hyphenation. *My name tacked on—like an afterthought.*

On occasion, his jazz festival duties required out-of-town trips. He obtained contract signatures for big-name performers and sought new talent. While on a scouting junket, he met Kyrra, an exquisite songbird with a smooth-as-satin voice, singing in a Milwaukee jazz club.

Zing went their heartstrings—instant infatuation. Meeting Kyrra was serendipitous, the impetus driving his deadly obsession. Otherwise, he would've remained tethered to Audrey forever.

He stole away often to the OC condo where he'd stashed Kyrra. Their relationship was finely tuned; there was never a discordant note. Their harmonious rhythm frequently struck a passionate pitch. Jazzed about their future, they made beautiful music together. Maybe someday, they'd make beautiful babies.

Whenever he traveled, Audrey demanded daily updates, requiring that he account for every moment. It amused him she appeared clueless about Kyrra. Yet Audrey's controlling nature gnawed at him until his insides resembled a dog's three-day-old bone, jagged and mangled, the marrow sucked out.

10 hours, 28 minutes.

Mentally reviewing his plan, he showered and dressed. His hand trembled as he unlocked the desk drawer. Stowing the sweetener in his pocket, he went in search of Audrey.

Despite the gloomy day, Audrey seemed in high spirits. Smiling, she clasped her hands beneath her chin. "Prayer works wonders! The weatherman's predicted clearing skies. And everything's ready for my soiree."

Too bad you won't be around to see it end, he mused. *Then my prayers will have been answered.*

At Convention Hall, they located their seats—front row, center.

He scurried backstage to check whether Dexter needed assistance, while Audrey performed her social butterfly act.

The show, a sell-out for months, was spectacular. Its star performer, Grammy award winner Al Jarreau, sang his hits, including "We're in This Love Together" and "Lean on Me."

Audrey grasped his hand while they watched Al croon "Let's Stay Together" to the rest of the room. She leaned in, softly mouthing the lyrics into his ear. Her unexpected attentions, and those words, heightened his anxiety. A knot the size of Texas filled his throat.

His breathing hitched. *What the—Stay calm. Smile.* Struggling to regain his composure, he reassured himself. *There's no way she could suspect. I've been so careful.* He squeezed Audrey's hand and pecked her cheek.

Celebrated Parisian artist Marc Antoine opened his set with "Cabrillo." He and his guitar conjured acoustic alchemy, melding funk, jazz, rock, and R&B. Contemporary jazzman Steve Cole followed Marc. He slowed the tempo, allowing the audience an opportunity to catch its collective breath. For the finale, Steve performed a haunting version of "Angel." Standing ovations and thunderous applause ensued.

Turning to embrace him, Audrey whispered, "Bravo, darling. Best show ever."

"You're congratulating the wrong person. I'm merely the assistant."

"You're the power behind the scenes. Dexter receives the credit, but you're the detail-oriented one."

A scrap of guilt tugged at his thoughts as Audrey praised him. *This is so unlike her. Although, she was full of bonhomie at the beginning. Perhaps she senses my unhappiness.*

"Th-thanks, Audrey," he stammered.

7 hours, 4 minutes.

They were last in their party to arrive for dinner and couldn't find seats together. Instead, their chairs were across from each other.

Hmmm—conditions not ideal, but workable. Immediately, he located the sweetener. "Please pass the Splenda," he said to the person on his left.

"Why do you want that, dear? You always order sweet tea."

He smiled at Audrey. "Since you've given up sugar, I've decided to join you. And, I knew you'd want it."

He caught the waiter's attention. "Two unsweetened teas, please."

His neighbor passed the basket. Deftly, he palmed two packets, then placed the doctored pair beside Audrey's silverware. The waiter set down their teas. Stirring a packet into his drink, he watched Audrey put one in hers. She stirred and tasted.

"You won't be content without another one."

Emptying the second packet, Audrey smiled. "You know me so well."

His mission complete, he excused himself. *All's going according to plan.* Smiling, he hummed a jazzy tune all the way to the men's room.

When he returned, everyone proceeded through the buffet line. He eyed Audrey during dinner. She appeared fine. The pills required five, perhaps six hours to take effect. It wasn't an exact science.

Audrey remained quiet during the drive home. The moment they arrived, she darted into the powder room. When she emerged, he asked, "Everything OK?"

"Why so nosy? You watched me like a hawk throughout dinner. FYI, I had to pee so bad, my eyeballs were floating." She rubbed her stomach. "Too much tea, I suppose. Now, get a move on. Show our guests inside while I check the arrangements."

He stood rooted in place. Audrey studied his face, then frowned.

"You're the one who doesn't look so hot. You're pale as a ghost." Impatiently, she said, "Have you gone deaf? The doorbell's ringing."

Despite his pounding heart, he was relieved to hear her harangue. *The tyrant's returned, ordering me around like the hired help. After tonight, I'll be calling the shots. She'll be stretched out on a slab in the morgue, freezing her buns off, along with the rest of her anatomy.* The mental picture elicited a loopy grin. *I know it's wrong, but I can't help myself.*

He greeted everyone, ushering them into the music room, and hung their coats, while his queasy stomach lurched and roiled. *Get a grip. It's almost over.*

Suddenly he felt dizzy—nauseated. He dashed into the bathroom, narrowly averting disaster with Audrey's expensive, new, Chinese rug. *She would have chewed me a new one in front of everybody if I'd upchucked on her prized Aubusson.*

As he flicked off the light, the scent of food forced his stomach to stage another revolt. Three more trips to the bathroom persuaded him to refrain from food or drink. *I must've picked up a bug. Life's unfair. Audrey's supposed to be the sick one.*

The guests had departed. All that remained of the party was the jazz playlist, one song relentlessly following another. Totally sapped, he winced, collapsing onto the sofa. Dagger-sharp pains knifed through his gut. *Why's it taking so long? Did I screw up—give her the wrong packets?* He glanced at his Rolex—almost eleven fifteen. *Something's wrong. Enough time's elapsed. Audrey should be unconscious.*

"What's with you?" Audrey's voice slashed through his thoughts. "You spent more time in the john than with our guests, and I had to invent excuses for your rudeness. Now, I see you're actually in pain."

Vehemently, he denied her observations. Yet his tautly stretched face revealed a man under considerable duress.

Then Audrey said, "Perhaps it was something you ate—or drank."

His head snapped upright. Audrey's emerald-green eyes bored into his, glinting cold and hard, like the stone itself. *She possesses all the charisma of a barracuda.*

"After you excused yourself at dinner, I swapped our teas. Mine was too sweet, once you insisted I add another sweetener."

Audrey heard his gasp, as she paced before him. Her arms flailed, seeking a target to punch. Zeroing in, she landed a jab to his chest. Her voice dripped acid. "I know you adore sweet stuff."

An icy finger of fear inched down his neck and wormed its way toward his back. His body convulsed with a violent shudder. He stared at her, wild-eyed, and ran his hands through his hair.

His teeth chattering, he whispered, "How'd you figure it out?"

"I didn't—until now. I was positive you wouldn't divorce me for 'Miss Bubble Brain.' Our prenup doesn't provide for the lifestyle to which you're accustomed. I'd steeled myself to overlook your little fling. Foolishly, I believed you'd soon tire of her. Instead, you hatched a plot to...m-murder me? Do you hate me that much?"

"How'd y-you f-ind out about Kyr-ra?"

"She called here one day. You were out." Audrey's strong, jutting chin trembled. Her voice quavered. "You should've chosen brains over beauty. She proved to be the flaw in your otherwise perfect scheme. Your little 'cutie-pie' fabricated an innocent-sounding excuse for contacting you. But I'm nobody's fool. I engaged a PI. He soon discovered your cozy love nest. For weeks, I've stared at pictures of you cavorting with that blond hussy—young enough to be your daughter."

He stared at Audrey. Her ashen face and pinched expression added ten years.

"*You* want to discuss *age?* Technically, I could call you 'Mother.'"

Audrey's face contorted with fury. "You ungrateful gigolo!" She leveled him with a withering stare. A vein throbbed visibly in her forehead. Spittle struck his face as she shrieked. "I'd drop-kick you right into Satan's fire pit, if possible." Like a petulant toddler, she stamped both feet. "At the very least, I'll tap dance on your grave!"

"You don't get it, do you? I was your possession—your lapdog— never your partner. You became a female version of your father. That overbearing, pompous SOB required everyone to obey his every command. When he died, you snatched the reins and latched on to me. Unfortunately, I permitted myself to be bought."

"Worst purchase of my life! Besides, you've never complained about the rewards you've reaped these past four years."

"I've paid dearly. Few men would've accepted the vitriol you've dished out."

Audrey's shoulders drooped; her body sagged. She sank to the floor, curling in on herself, like a burst balloon.

Empty and deflated.

He felt a brief rush of sympathy before doubling over in agony. A retching moan tore from his throat. Once the spasm subsided, he hauled himself upright and stumbled toward his office, disoriented, drenched with perspiration, struggling to breathe.

"You can't do anything right, can you?"

He spun slowly to discover she'd followed him. He'd believed Audrey was down for the count. Yet, like a champion prizefighter, she'd bounced back.

Ready for round two.

Her shadow projecting onto the wall behind her, Audrey dominated the doorway. Standing there, taunting him. A Cheshire-cat grin plastered on her face, seemingly amused by the turn of events. For once, he agreed. *I can't do anything right.*

The sight of Audrey hardened his expression; his body stiffened.

I could wring her wretched little neck! But strength had deserted him. Frustrated, he turned and staggered toward his desk. He clutched the stupid little timepiece. Even through clouded vision, he saw every number flashed red: **0 weeks, 0 days, 0 hours, 0 minutes.**

Good-bye, my dear sweet Kyrra. Knees buckling, his legs folded. Charlie Parker's sax squealed a mournful, strangled wail; the last sound he heard before merciful darkness swooped down and swallowed him. His body crashed to the floor.

His date with death had arrived.

"You loved money, power, prestige—but never me. If only you'd wanted children." Viciously, Audrey toed her husband's still form. "*They* would've loved me!" Crumpling to the floor, she wrapped him in her arms and wept.

Eventually, Audrey rose. She spoke, her voice harsh as winter's wind. "There's no rush, I suppose. You'll be just as dead tomorrow. Elena will discover your body. Portraying the distraught widow, I'll deliver an Oscar-worthy performance for her and the police. Magnanimous soul that I am, I'll even provide you an elaborate departure. The devil will anxiously await your arrival."

Audrey closed the door. With the threat of tears muddling her sight, she dragged her spent body upstairs.

* * * * * *

The housekeeper arrived at six. Elena was surprised neither employer, both early risers, was up. An hour later, she heard no signs of anyone stirring. Deciding to check, she knocked on Audrey's door. No one answered. She turned the knob.

Elena's screams echoed throughout the house.

Audrey was dead. Two shots to the heart. Numerous bullet wounds marred her once-lovely face.

Her husband, also deceased, slumped by the bed. In repose, he appeared to smile, his expression frozen in time. One hand gripped a revolver; the other clenched a scrawled note:

> *Audrey,*
> *I, Joseph Allen Zimmerman,*
> *finally got something right.*
> *Jaz*

* * * * * *

Eight months later.

Sunlight bounced off headstones on a balmy day in May. A young woman walked along the path, carrying flowers and another small bundle.

"Hey, love, I brought someone to meet you—our beautiful baby boy, Jaz. My heart melts whenever I gaze into his chocolate-brown eyes, indistinguishable from yours. I'm heartbroken, but forever grateful to have part of you with me. Jaz will learn about his wonderful daddy, I promise."

She laid the flowers on a grave.

"Honey, I have strange, but amazing, news! Jaz is Audrey's heir. She drafted a new will the week before you…before she died. It stated that in the event of her death, her estate would pass to any child she or you conceived.

"*Or*—not *and*. Weird, huh? Like, maybe she knew I was pregnant with your baby.

"Distant relatives of Audrey's contested the will, but the judge ruled in our favor. We move into the mansion tomorrow. I guess I'll never understand what happened that night. Only you and Audrey know the true story." Sighing, Kyrra rose. "Funny how life works out. Like the words from our favorite old jazz tune, 'The Lush Life,' Jaz and I'll live the dream life—a life here at the beach."

CONNIE L. MCDOWELL, A NATIVE SUSSEX COUNTIAN, LIVES IN GREENWOOD, DELAWARE. AFTER THIRTY-TWO YEARS AS AN EDUCATOR FOR THE WOODBRIDGE SCHOOL DISTRICT, SHE RETIRED IN 2010. SHE HAS ALWAYS LOVED TO WRITE, BUT RETIREMENT HAS PROVIDED HER THE FREEDOM TO PURSUE THIS INTEREST. HER WORK HAS APPEARED IN BEACH DAYS AND REMINISCE MAGAZINE. IN ADDITION TO WRITING, SHE LOVES READING, ANTIQUING, AND LISTENING TO MUSIC. SHE OFTEN INCORPORATES HER OTHER INTERESTS INTO HER STORIES.

CONNIE WOULD LIKE TO THANK BROWSEABOUT BOOKS AND CAT & MOUSE PRESS FOR SPONSORING THE CONTEST. SHE IS MOST APPRECIATIVE OF THE EFFORT NANCY SAKADUSKI DEVOTES TO HER AUTHORS. SHE IS ALSO GRATEFUL TO THE JUDGES FOR THEIR EXPERTISE AND TIME. SPECIAL THANKS TO THE JUDGE WHO GAVE "JAZZED" AN AWARD!

JUDGE'S COMMENT

I am always happy when I read a good mystery and this one didn't disappoint. I felt there was good characterization from the beginning. The author did a good job of moving it along until the twisted ending!

Burning for Rehoboth

By Tom Minder

"Hey, the Mariner in Rehoboth has a two-night special. How about some sun, sand, and waffle fries?" He examined the fine print. "Sunday check-in. We can do that."

Lana walked to the table and peered over Sam's shoulder.

"Two-fifty a night, Sam. A little steep."

"It's midsummer. Plus that includes a breakfast buffet. Food, peace, and quiet isn't cheap, dear." He leaned back and sighed. "Ah. I can hear the ocean now."

"That's the washer," Lana replied. "We'll have to plan this out, Sam. We need to call and reserve a room, make a deposit, decide what we're bringing, have someone take in the mail…"

Sam was already on the beach, watching fishermen in boats speeding by, women in bikinis jogging, and an ice cream vendor selling frozen confections. He pulled out his cell and tapped in the reservation number. Jimmy Buffett crooned about Margaritaville as he waited his turn.

"Hi, this is Suzie at the Mariner, your oceanfront home away from home."

"Hi, Suzie, I read about your Sand and Surf package. I'd like a room for two for the fifteenth—two nights." He read off his credit card information and awaited the soothing sound of approval.

He smiled at Lana. "Two days of junk food, rest, and relaxation. Just the two of us, soaking up the sun."

* * * * * *

Sam's Prius was a marvel of Japanese engineering, but it strained to hold the large suitcase, beach chairs, boxes of food and drink, and other shore necessities. He shoved and wedged the items, then slammed the trunk lid shut, hoping everything traveled in harmony. "All ready, Lana. Now, off for two days of carefree living."

Lana sighed, donned her sunglasses and floppy hat, and slid into the passenger seat. Sam took the wheel and they headed from their South Jersey home to Rehoboth Beach, Delaware.

On the hundred-mile drive, they passed through blood-red cranberry bogs and freshwater marshland dotted with cattails. Sam rolled down the window and sniffed the salt air. "I'm glad we did this, Lana. Close enough to drive, yet far away from our daily dose of screaming kids, tobacco smoke from that crazy neighbor, Mrs. Shultz, and lawn mowers revving up at 6 a.m."

They pulled onto the causeway leading to the "Nation's Summer Capital." Seagulls swooped low as families embarked on morning whale and dolphin watches. Sam tapped an odd Morse code into the steering wheel. "Man, I gotta pee. Find us somewhere, Lana."

She scanned the horizon of bait shops, breakfast joints, and gas stations. "Oh, there's the tourist information center on the right, about a quarter mile ahead."

Sam weaved through traffic and tapped his horn to signal urgency. He pulled into the lot, tossed the keys to Lana, and speed-walked to the entrance.

"Welcome to Rehoboth," a pleasant hostess said.

He spotted the men's room, smiled, waved, and made a beeline toward it. "My wife needs directions," he called out. "She'll be right in."

Lana opened the screen door outlined in seashells and small wooden birds and walked in. The woman motioned her to the counter, a city map opened and at the ready. "Your husband said you needed directions."

Lana sighed. "Sorry...Berta is it? He had to, uh, *go*."

The door opened and five boys ran in. They pushed past Sam as he left the men's room. A weary mom entered with a husband holding a Schlitz. "I'm sorry, sir, no alcohol allowed in here," Berta called out.

The man waved and turned to walk out. "Get those guys back in the car, Angie. I want to make it to the Mariner before everyone else arrives."

Sam and Lana returned to their car and drove toward the hotel. Sam frowned as he stopped at a red light. "I got a bad feeling about this. They'll probably be right down the hall from us."

"It's a large enough hotel, Sam. Maybe they're staying in a different section."

The signal switched to green. Before Sam could hit the pedal, a horn blared behind them, two couples pointing to the traffic light. He waved and drove on as the car darted past them. The man in back flicked a cigar ash from his open window, and it landed on Sam's windshield. "And those idiots will be right next to them."

* * * * * *

As he pulled into the hotel lot, Sam looked at his watch: 10 a.m. "I hope they let us check in early," he said as they left the car, gasping as the hot and humid air enveloped them. They walked toward check-in, avoiding laundry carts and kids on bikes rolling by.

"Welcome to the Mariner," said the desk clerk. "How can I help you?"

Lana smiled, glancing at the clerk's name tag. "That's a wonderful accent, Shamara. Where are you from?"

"Thank you. I'm from Jamaica." She leaned closer. "By way of Smyrna."

"We're Sam and Lana Redman," Sam announced. "We'd like to check in."

Shamara peered at the screen and requested Sam's credit card. After running the number and having Sam sign the credit voucher, she looked at the screen again. "Nothing ready yet, sir." She handed him a parking voucher. "Let me have your cell number and we'll text you when a room's ready."

They left by the front entrance and scanned the beach. Umbrellas dotted the shore. "It was worth a try," Sam said to Lana. "Let's find some breakfast." He rubbed his stomach and slapped it once for good measure. "I'm thinking peach pancakes."

They joined the wave of vacationers trekking toward Rehoboth Avenue. Lana studied the cast of characters as Sam rotated like a lighthouse, hoping to spot signs of gastronomic life. He stepped on the heel of an elderly woman, dislodging her shoe. "So sorry, ma'am. I didn't see you slow down."

The woman sneered at Sam, then steadied herself with one hand on his shoulder as she slid the shoe back on her foot with the other hand. "Not a problem, young man. Just watch your way. There's a lot of people."

Sam nodded and turned to Lana. "What a nice lady."

Lana smiled. "I think she just muttered 'numbskull' to her friend."

* * * * * *

Uncle Mike's Pancakes appeared out of nowhere. Assuring himself it wasn't a hunger-induced mirage, Sam pulled Lana toward the restaurant. "The promised land," he announced.

"There's quite a line, Sam."

Her husband shrugged. "These move fast."

Forty-five minutes later, the couple were led to a table, sticky from syrup and surrounded by screaming children. Sam slid into the chair and groaned as he stepped on a discarded hash brown potato. Lana pulled out her chair, examined the floor, and sat.

"A bit noisy, but I'm starving," Sam said as he waved for a waitress. "I'm gonna start with the largest cup of coffee ever served."

The coffee was strong and the pancakes were a gift from God. Sam made guttural sounds unknown in nature as he shoveled the syrup-soaked, peach-filled delights into his mouth, pausing only long enough to sip coffee—and breathe. Lana ate her poached eggs and toast and checked her cell.

"I give up," Sam announced to the waitress as he pointed to his nearly empty plate. He examined the bill, added a decent tip, and left with Lana to storm the beach.

* * * * * *

Having put on their swimsuits before they left home, they simply removed their outer street clothes; grabbed towels, snacks, and chairs; and turned toward the sand. Boys on bikes sped by, causing Sam and Lana to step back to regain equilibrium. "Those are the kids from the tourist information stop," Sam said. "I hope their room isn't near ours." They heard a beer can pop open, followed by an "aah." Sam looked up and saw the father, two stories up, legs propped on the railing, downing a beer.

Sam's cell buzzed. He read the text message: "Your room is ready." They put the beach items back in the trunk and went inside.

Shamara smiled. "You're in luck. A block of rooms freed up. You and the other early arrivals can get a nice start on vacation." She handed over plastic key cards. "Enjoy your stay, folks. I hope it's nice and peaceful."

Sam dispatched Lana to the room and returned to the car to retrieve their luggage. He climbed a flight of stairs, skirted laundry carts once more, and stood on the balcony outside room 217.

An odd shadow appeared from above—feet in flip-flops. He stepped toward the balcony railing to look up as Lana joined him.

The man with the beer. His wife leaned over the railing. "Hey, it's the people from the tourist center. Howdy, neighbors."

The walkway vibrated as a luggage cart navigated the narrow strip of concrete, stopping at 218. The man who had defiled Sam's car with his cigar ash slid in front of the cart, pulled his key card, and opened the room. He saw Sam and pulled out the stogie. "How ya doon? Guess we're next-door neighbors."

* * * * * *

Sam and Lana unpacked and headed to the beach. They rented an umbrella and set up their spot for the day: not too far from the water, not too far from the waffle fries, and yards away from the nearest neighbors on the rapidly filling beachfront. Lana broke open a Harlequin and Sam put on shades and watched the shore wildlife move by. He pulled a water from the cooler and opened an enormous bag of Cheetos. Life was good.

Sam turned as a rumble of fast-approaching footsteps signaled invasion from the mainland. The boys from 317 screamed and tossed a football, which bounced off umbrellas and sunbathers alike. The mom emitted a half-hearted reprimand.

"Hey, Angie. It's the couple from below us," said the dad. He walked next to Sam and Lana, dropped his gear, and declared landfall. He shook out a large mat, anchored the ends with sneakers and flip-flops, and collapsed next to Sam.

"Hi, again, folks. I'm Jim and this is Angie. We're from South Philly."

Sam nodded, picked spilled Cheetos from his shirt, and brushed off the orange dust. Lana smiled and returned a "Sam and Lana. Turnersville. Nice day, isn't it?"

Angie waved and looked toward the water. "Now where *are* those boys?" She sat in a beach chair and opened her own romance novel.

Jim nudged Sam, causing him to palm the sand to prevent toppling from his beach chair. "Chicks and their books, huh, Sam? All *I* need is a stiff drink and the sports section." He took a pull from a drink bottle and leaned close to Sam, breathing alcohol. "Too bad all the Philly teams suck."

"So true." Sam shrugged. "How hard is it to catch a football?"

Squeaky wheels fought through the sand. "Hey, Mona, look. It's 217."

The smoker from 218 extinguished his cigar and laid an even larger mat next to Lana. The two couples unpacked their supplies, applied lotion, and lay down. "Hello, again," said the man. "I'm Larry, this is Mona, my better half, and these are our friends, Mike and Hilary. We're from Reston."

"Sam and Lana from South Jersey," Sam responded. "Nice day, isn't it?"

The couples agreed. Larry looked past Sam. "Hey, and those are the folks right above you two. Must be 317. Hi, folks," he shouted loud enough to cause Sam to spill more Cheetos.

The couple waved and introduced themselves. Jim pulled out a large metallic blue bottle, grabbed several plastic cups, and, with one knee on Sam's towel, whispered to all, "They don't allow booze on the beach, but I mixed some rum and Coke and filled this cooler. Anyone want some *Coke*?" He laughed.

Five bodies swarmed around Sam. Jim doled out the mixture to extended arms as Sam and Lana edged their chairs forward to cede space. Angie handed them cups. Lana took a sip to be civil and Sam took a wary gulp. Mostly rum, little Coke. He smiled and downed the remainder in short work. "Hey, are you going to drink the rest of that, Lana?"

Lana handed the cup to Sam, who mouthed a fistful of Cheetos and took a long sip. He then passed the bag around to all assembled.

Angie smiled. "This is like one big beach party."

* * * * * *

Sam limped as he and Lana returned to the room.

"Serves you right, playing football when you're half-drunk."

"I was open! Jim should have led me. I had his son Jimmy beat on a fly pattern." Sam landed on the bed and belched. The aroma of Cheetos and rum wafted to Lana, who fanned her face and studied her husband. Before she could respond, he snorted twice, turned on his side, and entered dreamland.

From the walkway outside, the sound of a towel slapping a wet swimsuit interrupted the moment. "Ow…Larry…stop it."

Muffled laughter drifted down from Jim and Angie, on the walkway above. "Good one, Larry. Keep her in line."

Feet scampered by outside. An object thumped Sam and Lana's window as the sound of boys laughing invaded their room. "Oh, make it go away, Lana. I need to rest," Sam mumbled.

Lana heard a rapid knock. She looked through the peephole to see one of the boys tossing the football from one hand to the other as his brothers watched. She unlatched the door.

"Can Sam come out for catch?"

Lana nodded toward her now-snoring spouse. "I'm sorry. It's nap time. Maybe tomorrow."

* * * * * *

After his snooze, Sam staggered into the shower and leaned on the wall for support. "Never again, Lana. Never again. From here on, peace and quiet."

Lana smiled, adjusted herself on the couch, and turned the page on her romance. "Sure, Sam. Hey, want any Cheetos? There's a few left."

"I *never* want to see those things again. And no more rum and Coke."

They decided on takeout. Lana returned with hoagies and waffle fries. Sam painted the fries with ketchup, channeling Jackson Pollock. He forked eight fries at once and shoveled them into his mouth.

"Mmmpppphhhh mmmpppphhhh." Lana awaited the English translation as Sam swallowed. "You know, Lana, beach waffle fries are the best. The sea air, vegetable oil, pounds of salt. You can't get these at home."

Lana found a fry only slightly defiled by ketchup and chewed it slowly. An "ummm" signaled the battle had been joined. They fought for the remainder of the potatoes and fell into each other's arms covered with grease and ketchup. "Now show me your moves, big boy."

* * * * * *

The breakfast buffet lined the longest wall of the dining room. Sam balanced a plate with sausages, an omelet, hash browns, a blueberry muffin, and fruit in one hand, as he held a large OJ in the other.

Lana stirred her coffee and marveled at Sam's end run around the surrounding tables. He sat and examined his breakfast. "I got some fruit. I have to start eating healthy."

Larry approached with Mona and slapped Sam on his shoulder. "Sam, my man, how's it going this morning?"

Sam winced and emitted a muffled "ow." The couple stepped back.

"He got a sunburn yesterday," explained Lana. "I think around the two-minute warning."

Jim, Angie, and the boys stopped by. Sam rubbed his shoulder while shoveling omelet into his mouth with the other hand. Jimmy patted Sam's other shoulder, causing an injudicious "shit" to quiet the room.

"Sorry, boys," Lana said. "Mr. Redman is on injured reserve today.

A bad case of sunburn...and a gimpy knee."

Angie leaned in toward Lana. "I think you have a cut under your ear. Looks like it's bleeding."

Lana rubbed her neck, examined the substance, shrugged, and licked it off her finger, causing Angie and Mona to swoon, and the kids to utter a coordinated "Cool!"

"It's just ketchup," Lana replied, as she and Sam laughed.

* * * * * *

They walked to the shopping district while the neighbors hit the beach. Lana bounced among antique stores, book emporiums, and clothing boutiques, while Sam sat in the shade, drinking lemonade and watching Lana accumulate plunder armed only with a MasterCard. Sam realized Lana had the tactical advantage over him. He'd be dead soon from third-degree sunburn, so the next husband would have to worry about the bill.

Spotting a newspaper on the bench, he slid toward it, moaning. He cheered up when he saw the announcement for free slot play at Dover Downs Casino.

Lana returned with a T-shirt in hand. She opened it for Sam, displaying a blue crab turning pink. "I'm burning for Rehoboth," it read. "The perfect souvenir for our trip, Sam. And just your size."

* * * * * *

When they came back to the room, Lana rubbed aloe on Sam's back and legs. He snoozed in bed as she finished her book while munching Cheetos. The neighbors returned, dragging beach chairs.

A knock. "How's our Sam doing?" Larry asked, as Lana opened the door. He saw Sam passed out on the bed, his red glow causing Larry to wince. "Man, he's a lobster."

Lana chewed on Cheetos and offered the bag to Larry. "He'll

recover, Larry. He just needs to remember that he's sixty, not eighteen." She nodded toward her husband. "He's already planning a trip to Dover Downs tomorrow, so he expects to live on."

"Well, if he's up for it, we're having drinks right outside around six. Why don't the two of you pull up chairs and help us toast the vacation? Jim, Angie, and crew will be there too."

"Thanks, Larry. I'm not sure if Sam'll be up to it, but I'll check with him when he wakes up."

* * * * * *

"Wake up, Lana. It's 9 a.m. We have to get breakfast and check out."

Lana rolled toward Sam. "What do you remember about last night?"

He studied the popcorn ceiling. "Well, we met the neighbors for drinks, and then played touch football."

"Do you remember running into the rose bush?"

Sam looked at the red scratches on his side. "Oh, that explains it. I thought you just got rough last night." He laughed, stood, and walked to the bathroom. "Ouch! Oh, God," he yelled. "What happened to me?"

"So you don't remember playing in your tighty whities?"

They walked into the dining room to the applause of all assembled. "Hey, Sam," Jim called out. "How are the family jewels?"

Sam gave a thumbs up, then sat, breathing air through his teeth.

"I'll get you something, Sam," Lana said. "Just sit and bask in your athletic glory."

He worked through his omelet, pausing to accept the praise of fans as they filed out. Jimmy walked up with his brothers, followed by Jim, Angie, Larry, Mona, Mike, and Hilary. Jimmy put a scuffed football on the table. It had been autographed by all, even Lana.

"This is for you, Mr. Redman. You're our hero."

All assembled cheered again. Jimmy patted Sam on the shoulder, causing Sam to grimace. "Oh, sorry, Mr. Redman."

Sam lifted the Spalding. "Thanks, everyone. I'll put this on my mantle."

They exchanged email addresses with their new friends and left the dining room, walking to the checkout. Sam tossed the football between his hands. "How was everything, Mr. and Mrs. Redman?" said Shamara. "I hope you enjoyed your stay and all was peaceful."

The couple looked at each other. Sam laughed, then contorted his mouth to mask the pain. "It was great, Shamara. We can't wait to come back next year."

TOM MINDER LIVES IN GLOUCESTER COUNTY, NEW JERSEY, WITH HIS WIFE, PAULA. HE IS RETIRED AND WRITES NOVELS AND SHORT FICTION. HE HAS FICTION PUBLISHED IN *COMMUTERLIT*, *FICTION ON THE WEB*, AND *101 WORDS*. HE IS A MEMBER OF THE SOUTH JERSEY WRITERS' GROUP AND THE WRITERS COFFEEHOUSE. TOM HAS ALSO WRITTEN A LITERARY NOVEL, *THE LONG HARBOR TESTAMENT*, WHICH FOCUSES ON SMALL-TOWN CRIME AND RELIGION.

JUDGE'S COMMENT

A delightful story that reminds us of how a weekend in Rehoboth can rejuvenate our energies and help us play and enjoy. Even the stuffiest person can't resist the pull of the tides. Good writing, excellent characterization of the visitors, and a humorous take on how we loosen as the sun bakes us. Framed structure around the night events works well. Strong voice.

Nudge

By Cay Cutright

Madeline sat on her screened porch and wondered why they were there. She squeezed her tea bag and stared across the sand as two men carrying stakes, twine, a roll of mesh, and a hammer trudged up the beach path and over the dune. Her one-hundred-year-old home was only steps from the beach. The small cottage had been built by the Smiths and had been inhabited by family ever since.

Madeline had lived here alone at "Cottage by the Sea" in Rehoboth for ten years. She heard the voices of her two daughters in her head: "Mom, I worry about you." "It's too isolated." "Maybe it's time to think about assisted living?" Nonsense, she thought. What could be better than spending her days with the tides, the birds, the surf? And, of course, the occasional drama—*what were those men doing?*

Madeline put down her teacup and eased out of the wicker chair. The rickety screen door slammed as she walked toward the path. Cresting the dune, Madeline saw the men stepping gingerly around an area to the right of her path. One pounded in stakes, while the other unwound twine and netting.

"Good morning," Madeline called, as she shaded her eyes from the bright sun.

"Morning," said the taller man.

"What are you doing?"

"There's a turtle nest here—loggerhead. It will be protected and watched until the little guys hatch. Part of the DNR—Department of Natural Resources—Nest Watcher's Initiative."

Later, while Madeline was watering her flowers, the same young man stopped at her gate.

"Thought you might like to read about our program," he said as he handed her a brochure.

Madeline took the flyer back to the porch, studying the text. The loggerheads seemed to be determined creatures. Apparently, females return to their birthplace decades later to make their own nests. And the hatchlings have many enemies: fox, raccoons, birds, crabs, and people—and that's just on land. In the ocean, predators abound. Madeline stared at the brochure for about an hour, then found herself on the phone.

"I would like to sign up to be a turtle nest watcher," she heard herself say. After a tedious application process with a less than enthusiastic receptionist, Madeline became a DNR volunteer.

Twelve people were assigned to Rehoboth nest #L2. They would be responsible for the well-being of the nest for one two-hour shift each night during the final weeks until the all-nighters began and the eggs hatched. The DNR would monitor the nest the rest of the time. The average incubation was eighty days.

Soon, it became Madeline's habit to look at the mesh-covered nest each morning during her stroll on the beach. After two months, it was time to start the night watches. Madeline was curious to meet the other volunteers, and she planned to greet most of them at her gate. They came two at a time at 8:00 p.m., 10:00 p.m., midnight, 2:00 a.m., 4:00 a.m., and 6:00 a.m.

Madeline and the partner she'd been assigned, Ben, had the 4:00–6:00 a.m. watch. "Perfect," Madeline said to herself, "I can't sleep past 4:00 a.m. anyway."

At 3:45 a.m. Madeline heard the truck before she saw its lights. Quickly, she pulled on her plaid jacket and started outside. A young man dressed in khaki pants and a long-sleeved shirt was walking toward the beach, carrying a knapsack and a beach chair.

She caught up to him. "You must be the turtle nest watcher. I'm

Madeline." After seeing the confusion in his eyes, she added, "your partner."

"Oh, I'm sorry. I'm Ben. I, ah, thought my partner was thirty-one years old. Ah, that's what it said on the sign-up sheet," he stammered.

Madeline laughed. "Thirty-one. Eighty-one. What's a few years?" She picked up her chair and her tote and started slowly up the path with Ben. The two men who had the shift before them stood as Madeline and Ben approached.

After Ben introduced himself, Madeline told the men they could leave their chairs and gear inside her gate or even on the screened porch. "I baked you some muffins—walnut-carrot." Reaching into her tote, she pulled out three plastic bags of muffins. "Here's one for you, Ben."

Madeline settled in as Ben devoured the muffin. The familiar stars, the timpani of the ocean, the scratch of the crabs, and even the buzzing of mosquitoes: all were comforting.

"Delicious," mumbled Ben. "Thank you so much."

During the first hour, Madeline chatted happily, gathering all of the information she could about her partner. Ben was a man of few words, but she did find out that he was a part-time construction worker and that he was waiting for a letter of acceptance to Coastal Carolina University. He wanted to major in marine biology and fulfill his lifelong dream of helping aquatic animals. Even though she hadn't planned on talking about health matters, she did mention her headaches, eye problems, dizziness, and joint pain.

A gibbous moon illuminated the ocean. "That's the path the hatchlings follow," Ben stated, as he motioned toward the moonlit water. "When I was eleven, Dad and I watched the turtle hatching at Cape Henlopen State Park out on Herring Point. It was awesome. First the sand started to churn, and then the little heads started poking out. We all had flashlights covered with red material so we could witness the event and not confuse the turtles with bright lights. The nest boiled with activity as the little loggerheads pushed and climbed out of the nest and pulled their bodies toward the ocean."

"How wonderful. Is that the reason you want to major in marine biology?"

"Yeah," Ben replied with a far-off look in his eyes, "if I'm accepted and if I can afford to go. I'm expecting to hear any day now."

After eight nights of watching, Madeline received a call from the DNR ranger, Richard Perkins. "If you can, we would like for everyone to meet tonight at 10:00 at #L2. We have some protocol to review and we would like everyone to plan to spend the next couple of nights at the site. The turtle eggs should hatch tonight, tomorrow, or the next day."

Madeline had been expecting the call. Ben had explained what was going to happen, and the news invigorated her. The girl from the market had just delivered her weekly box of groceries, and now Madeline was ready to bake. Hmmmm—apple dumplings. She rolled the dough, cored three Granny Smith apples, and filled the center with cinnamon, sugar, nutmeg, raisins, and butter. The sweet aroma filled the cheerful kitchen. As the dumplings baked, Madeline prepared for a night on the beach.

Eleven of the twelve watchers arrived, plus several additional family members, including some children, but no Ben. *How unlike him*, thought Madeline. Ranger Perkins removed the protective mesh from the nest and patiently explained what the group should expect and what they should do if any of the hatchlings went off-course.

"Don't pick up a wayward hatchling. You can gently nudge them back on track to the ocean, but they must drag themselves to the water alone. Scientists think the process imprints the Earth's magnetic field, which allows the loggerhead to navigate successfully."

Where was Ben? Was he sick? Madeline wanted to call, but personal contact between watchers was discouraged. The ranger said that he would try to reach him. There was no turtle action that night, but Madeline enjoyed chatting with all the people.

The next day, she was groggy and napped after lunch. It was late afternoon when she picked up the *Cape Gazette* from the bottom of the grocery box. On the cover was a picture of college kids looking at loggerhead turtle tracks in the sand. The students all wore matching blue T-shirts with CEOE printed in gold. What did that stand for? Madeline skimmed the article. Oh, yes, the University of Delaware's College of Earth, Ocean, and Environment right next door in Lewes.

Madeline read the article and realized Ben had been nervously awaiting more than the loggerheads. She could picture him by his mailbox, holding a very thin envelope in his hand from Coastal Carolina—a rejection. Oh, that poor young man. Would he even show up for tonight's eight-hour watch?

At 10:00, Madeline waited at her gate for Ben. Some new folks came for the night; one family brought small camping cots so their children could sleep when there was no action. After waiting for thirty minutes, Madeline headed to the nest and took her spot. She wanted to have a heart-to-heart with Ben, but she doubted she would get the chance.

About midnight, a familiar figure came over the dune. It was Ben. After quick hellos, he set his chair off to the side and shut his eyes. Later in the night, Madeline stretched her legs, switched on her special flashlight, and walked over to where Ben was dozing. The top of a letter on Coastal Carolina stationery stuck out of his knapsack pocket. Acting as though she were picking up a shell, Madeline stooped for a better look at part of the letter. She saw "Thank you" and "We regret." Ben's forehead was furrowed, and he looked as though he were carrying the weight of the world. Madeline crept back to her chair, put her head back, and stared at the stars.

Again, the sun rose with no turtle activity. Weary families trudged back to their SUVs. Madeline waited to walk back with Ben. She wanted to ask lots of questions and offer words of encouragement and wisdom; she wanted to say there are other schools; but instead she said, "I made you an apple dumpling."

"Uh, thanks."

"Wait here at the gate; I'll get it."

Inside, Madeline spooned the sweet dumpling into a container. *He has to do it by himself, but maybe a nudge,* she thought, as she placed the container inside the *Cape Gazette* and tied it with a bit of string, making sure that the article about the University of Delaware's College of Earth, Ocean, and Environment was on top. The students in the T-shirts smiled back at her. She handed Ben the dumpling, looked him in the eye, and said,

"It will be OK."

"Uh, thanks. We'll just have to wait and see."

CAY CUTRIGHT AND HUSBAND MIKE RETIRED TO OCEAN VIEW, DELAWARE, IN 2014. CAY TAUGHT MIDDLE SCHOOL IN DENTON, MARYLAND, FOR THIRTY YEARS. SHE AND HER TWO DAUGHTERS MADE MANY DAY TRIPS TO REHOBOTH BEACH DURING THE SUMMERS. CURRENTLY, CAY PERFORMS WITH OVATION THEATER AND BART (BETHANY AREA REPERTORY THEATER), PAINTS, ATTENDS FREE WRITES, AND GOES TO ADULT EDUCATION ENRICHMENT CLASSES. SHE DEDICATES HER LOVE FOR ALL AQUATIC ANIMALS, ESPECIALLY TURTLES, TO HER SIX GRANDSONS.

Partners in Crime

By Joseph Crossen

The difficult case involving the misconduct of a Department of Natural Resources employee was closed. Our small firm, Preston and Braddock Investigations, had gotten the case by a stroke of good luck. It left us financially comfortable, but physically and mentally exhausted. That's why I got a suite for us at a Victorian hotel right on the beach in Rehoboth, Delaware. What better place to decompress—excellent restaurants, ocean breezes, good jazz spots at night, and the beach to walk with no special place to go.

My name is Richard Preston. My partner is Laurence Braddock. We are partners in business and in life. Not many people who love each other could work together as smoothly as we, working as we do at the business and our relationship with equal dedication.

However, I must say Larry wasn't thrilled with the idea of a week in Rehoboth. He's a city boy. DC is where he was born, raised, attended George Washington University, and now lives and works.

"We have great biking trails and parks in the District. We have museums. Concerts. We have *action,* for heaven's sake. Rehoboth has sand!"

Nevertheless, by Friday afternoon we were in the company-owned BMW M6, with the top down, smooth jazz on the radio, and behind—I don't know—several thousand cars stopped dead on Route 301/50 heading toward the Bay Bridge.

Larry was in the full throws of an I-told-you-so rant. I reached over and gave his hand a squeeze. "Tilt your seat back and listen to the music. We'll be out of this in no time."

By 7 p.m., we had checked in, showered, and changed and were now looking more touristy and less DC as we sat at an outside table in the bar, with martinis in our hands and the calming rhythm of the Atlantic in our ears. I noticed the darkness coming on gradually, shadows from the hotel lengthening on the boardwalk.

"There," I said. "Isn't this better than work?"

Larry took a long pull on his martini, raised the empty glass toward our waiter for a refill, and nodded a grudging agreement, which I noticed was partly cover for an environmental scan. When you do what we do, you are in the habit of checking out your surroundings and the people in them. I noticed Larry was doing that, and I began checking the room, too.

The dining room seating is terraced so all the guests can have a view of the ocean. Larry bent toward me and said, "Next level up, at ten o'clock from you. Fifty-something guy and a redhead. Recognize him?"

I looked. Subtly.

"Senator Whatsit from somewhere in the Midwest? The woman I don't know."

"Right. Senator Whatsit, better known as Mark Wilson, senator from the great state of Iowa. And I know who Redhead is not."

"OK. Who isn't she?"

"She is not Mrs. Senator Mark Wilson."

"Oh," I said. "Well, what better place not to run into a fellow Hawkeye than a beach in Delaware."

"Or Mrs. Senator Mark Wilson, who's probably home watching the corn grow."

I shook my head. "So cynical. Not everyone is citified."

"More's the pity."

"So, who is Red?"

"I don't know. We should find out. Investigate it like the good investigators we are."

"No. Absolutely not. We are tourists, on vacation. No investigating.

Have another martini. Your scallops will be here soon. We'll eat and drink and watch nightfall on the beach." I picked up my own martini for the waiter to notice.

"Borrring!"

"That's why we're here—boredom and relaxation." And, the martinis were really very good.

After dinner, a good meal, and too many martinis, we went to our room and, putting our last martinis down beside our chairs, fell asleep to the ocean sounding like giant rhythmic brushes dragged across a snare drum.

The fire alarm jolted us awake at 3 a.m. We both jumped up, groggy and a bit hung over, and disoriented upon finding ourselves on a hotel balcony instead of our Georgetown condo.

"What the hell," Larry shouted.

"Fire alarm," I said. "Grab some things, and let's go."

We walked quickly down the hall, juggling iPhones and iPads, into the stairwell and, along with other bewildered guests, made our way to the ground floor, out the back of the hotel, and into the summer night. Hotel management and security staff led us across the street. I looked at the hotel floor by floor and saw no flames or smoke. The sounds of sirens announced fire trucks and police vehicles.

The hotel had an underground garage, and its large automatic door noisily rose. As soon as the door was high enough, a late-model Volkswagen Beetle, gunmetal gray with tinted windows, shot up the ramp, bounced onto the street, and sped away.

"Was that an Iowa plate?" asked Larry. "I think it said 'Black Hawk' at the bottom. I could see '8-1-K' but couldn't get the rest. Between the darkness and the tinted windows I couldn't see the driver. You?"

I hadn't. The plate had a silhouetted scene on it that I first thought was a city skyline but could have been farm buildings. Too dark to tell. What I could tell was that someone was screaming from the front of the hotel, on the boardwalk side.

Larry and I ran to the front as the fire company vehicles arrived. Several people were standing, looking up and pointing. We saw what appeared to be a lifeless man draped over a fourth-floor balcony railing, bent at the waist, arms drooping loosely.

Larry moved in front of the growing group of spectators.

"Look at me," he said, drawing their attention from the body up above. "My name is Larry Braddock and that's my partner, Richard Preston." He nodded toward me when he said it. "The police are going to want to talk to you, so Richard is going to take your names and contact info."

I fired up the iPad and started taking information, starting with the people nearest the front, figuring they were among the first to notice the body.

Larry continued: "This is important: what did you see?"

Several people started talking at once. A woman holding a minuscule dog in her arms said she thought she saw a flash above her. When she looked up, there were more flashes, and the man came out on the balcony and drooped over the rail.

"How many flashes?"

"Four, I think," the dog lady said.

"We'll take it from here," I heard a voice to my left say. I turned to see one uniformed police officer and one suit.

"I'm Detective Sergeant Rudy Walker," the suit said. Walker was a trim six-footer, crisp shirt and knotted regimental tie, not the big-bellied, wheezing cop from central casting.

"I don't know who you two gentlemen are, but this is a police case. There's been a murder, and I am investigating."

All this with no mention of the cop beside him.

"We were just ask—" Larry began, but Walker stopped him and raised his hand.

"I appreciate it, but I'll take it from here."

"Sure, but—"

"Uh-uh. No *buts.*"

Detective Walker took our names, learned we hadn't seen the incident, and didn't care we were detectives. Walker was zoned in on the murder scene and had no interest in the car we saw speed from the hotel.

"Idiot. We could have helped," I said.

"He's an idiot who doesn't want any help," Larry said.

The death happened on our floor, so we and the other guests were offered food and drink in the dining room while the police processed the victim's room. A room full of strangers, we were bound together by a man's death. The rumor in our little late-night society was that the dead man was Senator Mark Wilson. Larry's interest was piqued.

We roamed Rehoboth the next day and had a late dinner at a little place two blocks off Rehoboth Avenue. I had kept us off the topic of the murder all day, but it couldn't last forever.

"I have an idea where we might find a better witness to the murder," Larry said, putting his strawberry daiquiri on the table.

"Not our problem. It's a police matter."

"Sure, but don't you want to hear what I think?"

"Not if it involves this crime, I don't."

The headline in the *Cape Gazette* that morning had confirmed the rumor: The man on the railing was the senator from Iowa, and he had been murdered. The cops weren't saying how he was murdered, but pretty soon they'd connect what must have been a few bullet wounds with the cause of death.

"What if—"

"No, please," I said. "No what-ifs. We are on vacation. People don't work on vacation. We are people. Therefore, we don't work on vacation."

"OK. OK. But what if the VW with what might—might, I said—be Iowa plates and might—might, mind you—have been driven in a rush by Red, the senator's dinner companion, was the killer's getaway car? And what if—just one more what-if here—what if someone had a better view of that balcony and might have more details? What about that?"

Exasperated, I relented just to get it out of the way, but I knew better. This was the end of vacation and the start of work on a case that we had been warned off.

So I said, "All right. Say that's true. Red was in the car. Red was the killer. Why?"

"I don't know. That's what we investigate."

Then I said, "I will hate myself for asking, but who had a better view of the crime?"

"I thought you'd never ask," Larry said.

I rolled my eyes and shook my head.

"Did you notice what was passing by when we got to the crowd on the boardwalk last night?"

"Nothing. It was after three in the morning."

"Ah, Watson. How many times have I tried to teach you my methods of observation?"

"Right now I could strangle you, Sherlock. What the hell passed by?"

"We see but fail to observe."

"Larry, I'm warning you."

"About a hundred yards off shore a big boat was passing by and it had writing on the side. Probably a charter of some kind. Someone on that boat could have seen something on the balcony. The point of the cruise must be to see the town at night, so—" Elbows on the table, he turned his hands palms up. "Obvious, my dear Watson. And if it was a charter, it has a schedule—and a passenger list. And if it has a passenger list, it may have a witness."

I hate it when he's right.

"So we have to find the charter boat that passed the beach in the middle of the night."

"Right. How hard can that be?"

It wasn't all that hard. We could have searched online and called around, but we chose to sit on our balcony that night to relax, watch the moon rise, and wait until the late-night charter went by again.

Around two in the morning, our bleary eyes spotted a boat. We put our binoculars on it and copied the sign on its side: Captain Wild's Charters.

The next day, we called the company and spoke to the captain, who said two passengers saw flashes coming from a hotel window and then saw a man slump over the balcony rail. A woman stood over him for a few seconds, then disappeared back into the room. They didn't report it because they saw the emergency vehicles arrive.

The woman was odds-on to be the mystery redhead having dinner with the senator. She might also have been the driver of the VW that shot out of the garage that night, and the VW might have had Iowa plates. A lot of "mights" and a lot of trouble right here in Rehoboth.

Private eyes are successful based on their connections, and it helps if some of those connections are, well, seedy and not of good moral fiber. One of our most dependable but ethically malleable connections is a computer geek whose parents named him Howard Hughes Fields. Larry called young Howard and gave him the information we had on our redhead. While HHF got to work on that, we'd take advantage of the boardwalk for another after-dinner walk in the seaside darkness.

It was close to midnight when Howard rang my cell. He had found our redhead by hacking the Iowa motor vehicle records.

"Howard," I said. "Are you slipping? It took almost four hours for you to get that information. Is Iowan computer security that tough?"

HHF assured me that he had other and better-paying jobs than ours and if I wanted to continue to irritate him, he would keep the information.

I apologized and groveled sufficiently that he gave me the name Alice Drummond of Ames, Iowa, and gave me phone numbers, both land line and cell.

Larry was delighted. "We are close to closing this case, dear partner. What time is it in Ames, Iowa?"

"Must be about ten in the evening," I said.

"I'll bet Ms. Alice Drummond is wide awake. In fact, I'll bet Ms. Alice hasn't slept in the three days since she put a couple of bullets in one sleazy United States senator. I wonder," said Larry, "if she'd like to tell us why." And he started dialing the Iowa cell number. He put the phone on speaker. We sat at the kitchen counter with the phone between us as it rang.

"Hello," said a female voice that sounded frightened, probably by the 202 area code she saw on the screen.

"Hello, Ms. Drummond," Larry said. "You are on a speaker phone with Richard Preston and me, Larry Braddock. We are partners in a private investigations agency. Please don't hang up. We want nothing from you but the truth. It will ease our minds to know if we are right or not."

"Right about—"

"Please don't be coy. We are not with the police. In fact, we have been snubbed by a rather Neanderthal detective, so we have no interest in helping him. We would just like to know why you shot Senator Wilson a few nights ago."

"Rick here," I said, jumping in. "We think we are correct that it was you, but we don't know why. If we could get the 'why' from you, we'd go back to our vacationing and not bother you. Isn't that right, Larry?"

"Exactly. So, Alice, aside from the fact that he had it coming, why shoot the senator?"

There was a long silence from Iowa.

Finally, Alice spoke. "Why wouldn't you go to the police? You kind of are police, aren't you?"

"Yes and no. In this case, we tried to help and were rebuffed. Pushed aside," Larry said.

"That's right," I said. "They don't want our help, and we think it will go into whatever file they stuff unsolved cases into. But the 'why' is bothering us, Alice."

"I don't know," Alice said. "You could be cops trying to trap me."

I was shocked when Larry told her we wouldn't go to the cops, but they did push us aside, and rudely at that, so I said to Alice, "Do you Skype or FaceTime?"

She opted for FaceTime, so I gave her my iPhone number. A few moments later, she saw Larry and me in our bathrobes, martini glasses on the table. I gave her a virtual tour of our room.

"Look like any police station you ever saw? C'mon, Alice. Why did you shoot him? Did he hit you? Blackmail you? What?"

Alice spoke, looking back at us across the virtual miles: "If you are cops, then at least this will be over and I can stop jumping at every text and phone call. My father came back from the Korean War looking for peace. He thought he would find it farming, and he did for a very long time. He and Mom bought a small farm near Ames, raised chickens and vegetables, and made a good living selling fresh eggs and produce. Dad thought he would work until he dropped. He loved the farm, and as we kids got older we were able to help.

Then a few years ago, along came developers who wanted to buy the farm and turn it into a golf course and luxury hotel. Over the years, Ames had grown out almost to meet our place.

"Dad said no. The farm was not for sale. The developers persisted. They came back, over and over.

"When they understood Dad's no was final, they went to Senator Wilson. Wilson knew where the right strings were and he pulled them. The county commissioners condemned the farm under eminent domain. When they took the farm and built a shopping mall, paving the fields and leaving nowhere to grow corn or raise cattle, it killed my father. He and Mom were left with the house and a small plot and the back of a mall for scenery where there had been crops and livestock.

"I couldn't let it go—couldn't let that bastard get away with it. I had heard about his womanizing, so last week, I went as a constituent to see Senator Wilson in DC, lured him into a weekend at the beach, and shot him. I'm not proud of it, but I would shoot him again for what he did to me and my family. So call the cops. Now that I've said it, I don't care anymore."

A defiant redhead stared back at us through the phone screen. Larry and I looked at each other and shrugged. He spoke first.

"You have yourself a good life, Alice Drummond."

Her face froze. She hadn't been expecting that.

"Thank you for telling us, Alice," I said. "If you're ever in DC again, look us up.

Her features began to soften. "But—"

"Good night," I said, and turned off the phone before she had a chance to continue.

"Well," Larry said, putting his feet on the coffee table and lifting his martini glass. "That's settled."

"A beautiful night for a walk on the beach," I said.

"Sounds about right."

And so we walked Rehoboth Beach under a quarter moon, hand in hand.

JOSEPH L. CROSSEN HAS PUBLISHED SHORT FICTION IN *THE BROADKILL REVIEW*, *THE CAPE HENLOPEN ANTHOLOGY 2015*, *THE BEACH HOUSE*, AND *THE BOARDWALK*, BOTH COLLECTIONS OF SHORT STORIES BY LOCAL WRITERS. HIS STORY "THE ARTIST'S STAIN" TOOK FIRST PLACE IN THE 2014 COMPETITION. HE HAS ALSO PUBLISHED POETRY IN *DELMARVA REVIEW*. CROSSEN IS A THREE-TIME FELLOW OF THE DELAWARE DIVISION OF THE ARTS WRITERS INSTITUTE AND AN ASSISTANT PROFESSOR IN THE COLLEGE OF EDUCATION AT WILMINGTON UNIVERSITY. HE LIVES IN DOVER, DELAWARE.

Senior Dance

By Shelley Johnson Carey

As she sat in the backseat of the 1989 pink Cadillac, motoring down the highway at precisely fifty-five miles per hour with music pouring from its open windows, Sylvia used an impeccably polished red nail to keep track of the items on her packing checklist. Bug spray? Check. Flip-flops? Check. When she got to the next item, she looked at the woman seated next to her. "Milly, did you remember to bring beach towels this time?"

"What do you mean, 'this time'?" Mildred fluffed her wavy white hair. "You're the one who forgot towels when we drove down to Key West in '99."

Trying to ignore the storm brewing behind him, Sylvia's husband, Larry, adjusted the crisp straw fedora atop his bald head and then continued tapping the steering wheel to the beat of Kool and the Gang's "Celebrate." Mildred's husband, Archie, rode shotgun, sporting a dark cowboy hat that allowed his curly silver hair to peek out from beneath it.

Sylvia and Mildred continued to compare checklists, their colorful sundresses reflecting their individual styles. Sylvia's sheath was a field of red and yellow flowers that looked so realistic that a bee had once tried to pollinate it. In contrast, Mildred wore an A-line with bold splashes of purple and gold.

"All the years I was a top Mary Kay beauty consultant," Sylvia said, "I never forgot a buyer's name or order. It's thanks to my memory that we're still riding in style." A stack of thick bangle bracelets slid down her arm with a clang.

"That's true, Silly," Mildred said calmly, "but your memory isn't quite what it used to be."

The women couldn't have been more different in appearance—Sylvia's fair skin required her to use the highest SPF possible, whereas Mildred's mahogany complexion seldom burned. Yet after surviving a frog dissection as ninth-grade biology lab partners, both women knew that theirs was a friendship that would last through the ages.

"I guess. But I know for a fact that you're the one who forgot to bring film when we went to Mexico with the Spanish Club in eleventh grade. That definitely wasn't me."

"Here we go again," Larry said under his breath.

Archie turned around and looked at the women. "Let's not get into all that right now, girls. Thanks to Sylvia, we're off on another exciting adventure to—what's the name of that beach again, Mildred?"

"I told him five times before we left," she stage-whispered to Sylvia and then turned to Archie. "Remember, sweetie? Rehoboth Beach."

Archie nodded. "Right. Rehoboth."

"*I* remembered to pack my boogie shoes," Sylvia said, putting her list away. "I hope we're *all* ready for the disco contest tomorrow."

Mildred gave her friend's hand a pat. "Wait 'til you see the getups I got for me and Archie. I even found some platform shoes in the back of the closet. We haven't looked so hip since the seventies."

Larry brought the Cadillac to a standstill, as long lines of cars, vans, and trailers queued up for Bay Bridge tollbooths that were too far away to see. "Remind me again why we're going all this way to go dancing?" he asked.

Sylvia sighed, surprised he could even ask the question. "Other than the fact that Milly and I are at our best on the dance floor?" She turned to her friend. "Do you remember when we all went to that club in Georgetown and you and Archie won a contest doing the hustle?"

"How can I forget? When balloons and glitter fell from the ceiling, it was just like *Saturday Night Fever*. We were washing sparkle out of our hair for days."

"What a night. That was classic Silly and Milly. We had the best times back then." Sylvia brushed back a nostalgic tear.

"We always have a great time together," Archie said. "Now as much as ever."

Sylvia touched her husband's shoulder. "And I'm grateful for my Larry and to have the two of you as my friends. But this weekend we're going to get our pizzazz back. All of us—I can just feel it. When I saw that article in *The Beacon* last spring about a disco contest at the beach, I knew we had to be there. And I'm sure that we're going to win because it's being held on September seventh, and nine and seven are my lucky numbers."

They talked more about the contest while the car inched along. When the tollbooths were in sight, both women dug around in their purses.

"I've got it," Sylvia said, holding up a Ziploc bag filled with quarters.

Mildred scooped up a handful of change. "The least we can do is pay for the toll. How much is it?"

Sylvia was about to answer when Larry let out a gasp.

"How did we get into the E-Z Pass lane?" Larry craned his neck to get a good look at the sign ahead of him. "I never got one of those little boxes." He grimaced. "What'll we do? We can't change lines now."

"We?" Archie said. "You're the one driving." He chuckled and settled back in his seat like a kid getting ready for a Saturday matinee. "Just go for it, man. I always knew that deep down you were a bad ass."

Larry pressed on the gas and the Cadillac continued down the E-Z Pass lane.

"I hope the cops don't pull us over," Mildred said, looking right and left as they rolled through an automated toll gate and past a red light.

Sylvia slipped on her sunglasses and gazed ahead. "I always did like bad boys," she said with a grin.

* * * * * *

"These crepes are to die for," Mildred said and licked a dab of strawberry jam off her spoon. A late summer's breeze swirled through the outdoor café. Archie and Larry, who had each ordered both sweet and savory crepes, grunted in agreement.

Sylvia took a deep breath. "That was the best night's sleep I've had in years. It must have been the salt air. And our room was so comfortable. I've got to find out what kind of mattresses they use at the Boardwalk Plaza."

"I'm with you," Mildred said. "This is the best idea you've had in ages."

Sylvia looked up and down the quaint shop-lined stretch of sidewalk for a sign with the restaurant's name. "What's this place called? Penny Lane?"

"No, that's the name of this little section of Rehoboth." Mildred looked down at a paper menu. "It's Café Papillion."

"We need to thank the front-desk clerk who suggested this place," Sylvia said, taking the last bite of her ham and cheese crepe. Then she pulled out her yellow pad. "Milly, we need to figure out the rest of the day. I want everything to be perfect for tonight."

"We'll get out of your hair," Larry said, standing. "We're going to knock around Browseabout Books and then stroll down to the beach and hang out on the benches with the other old geezers. We'd just be in your way if we stuck around here."

The men gave their wives quick pecks and took a few tentative steps away from table.

"Hold it," Sylvia called out. Larry and Archie came to an immediate halt and turned around.

"Did you remember your sunscreen, Larry? You know what the doctor said." He nodded. "I don't want you boys overdoing it." Sylvia continued. "You need your strength for tonight. And Larry—none of that caramel popcorn you're so fond of."

"Yes, ma'am," he said with a salute and gave Archie a quick wink.

With that, they about-faced and walked away quickly.

"I thought they'd never leave," Mildred said when they were out of sight. "Now we can get into some trouble of our own."

Sylvia looked at her to-do list. "I thought we'd start at Sharee's, that cute little dress shop I spotted yesterday, and then make our way around the town until it's time for our pedicure appointments at Robert Thomas Salon."

"Do you think we'll meet Robert himself?"

"Ooh la la. Wouldn't that be wonderful? And it could happen—today seems like one of those days when anything is possible. Including finding a pair of shorts that don't make me look like I have matchstick legs."

Mildred laughed. "You're so silly, Silly. Let's get out of here." They tossed their paper plates in the trash. "I see some baubles over there that need my immediate attention," she said, walking toward a jewelry store.

* * * * * *

Sylvia studied her reflection in the hotel elevator door. "You don't think this dress is too much, do you, Larry?" Silver lamé flowed from a single shoulder and stopped below her knees, cinched in the middle by a rhinestone belt. Gleaming barrettes held her hair back from her face and silver Capezio heels completed her look. "This is so much longer than anything I wore back in the day."

Larry's hand slid down her back to her bottom. "There's a little more to cover here than in the olden days," he said, "but I like it." Then he squinted to see himself in the shiny surface. "You know, I never thought I'd wear skinny silver dancing pants," he said with a shake of his head, "but there's a first time for everything."

The elevator door slid open and they spotted Mildred, wearing a brown curly wig, and Archie, whose hair had been combed up into an afro, in matching purple and pink paisley jumpsuits with wide bell-bottoms. More than a few heads turned as they strolled out of the hotel. "You'd think no one had ever seen people going dancing," Sylvia said.

The men left to get the car, and Sylvia and Mildred stood outside in the fragrant night air, just beyond the boardwalk. Crowds moved up and down the sidewalk to the soundtrack of a warm beach night—little ones in strollers asking for ice cream and French fries, teens laughing too loud, and families of all types and sizes, enjoying the evening's delights. Many who passed by seemed to find the women fascinating, with more than one person doing a double-take. A girl with purple hair and a skunk tattoo even asked to take a selfie with them.

Sylvia couldn't keep still. "Milly, can we practice our routine one more time?"

"Of course." Mildred did a few steps, Sylvia joined in, and then they both stopped and giggled.

"That's it! We're going to knock the judges' socks off!"

Once everyone was in the car, Larry asked for directions to the club.

"Where's that map?" Sylvia asked. "I circled where we're going."

"I don't see it," Archie said, flipping the map around.

Sylvia put on reading glasses and looked over his shoulder. "There it is…down Route 1. The Rusty Scrubber."

Mildred leaned over to see. "You mean the Rusty *Rudder*. It looks like the club's in Dewey Beach."

After a few wrong turns, Larry pulled into the club's parking lot. He'd barely turned off the engine when Sylvia threw open her door and sprang out of the car. Palm trees lined the path to the club and Sylvia, Larry, Mildred, and Archie followed the music to the entrance. A few couples dressed in regular clothes stopped and watched as the stylish group strode up the stairs and through the front door.

Inside, up on a platform, a thirty-something DJ in jeans and a

T-shirt pumped out music that was a cross between rock and country, with a few electronic sounds mixed in. The dance floor was nearly empty, with most patrons scattered across the rest of the club. The biggest crowd was at the bar.

"What's going on?" Mildred asked. "When do you think the contest will start?"

Sylvia looked around. "I don't get it. Where are the rest of the contestants?"

"I'll straighten this out," Larry said, and he and Archie headed toward the DJ. Sylvia and Mildred huddled together, suddenly feeling self-conscious because no one else was in disco garb. From across the floor they watched their husbands call the DJ down and talk with him for several minutes. Finally, the guys came back over and motioned for their wives to follow them outside.

Larry threw his arm around Sylvia's shoulders, supporting her like scaffolding. "It seems there's been some kind of mix-up," he said.

"What? I don't understand. It's September seventh and there's supposed to be a disco contest right here today. It said so in the paper."

"The DJ says that there *was* a disco contest here, but it was in July. On the ninth."

Mildred inhaled and then exhaled slowly. "July ninth and September seventh. Seven-nine instead of nine-seven."

"You mean we missed it?" Sylvia felt a wave of disappointment wash over her.

Archie leaned over to console her. "It's OK. We'll have a great time at the beach tomorrow."

At that moment, Sylvia wanted to be back at the hotel so she could crawl onto the bed and pull the covers over her head.

"Don't give up," Larry said, rubbing her sunken shoulders. "We may be too late for the contest but we could still have some fun. The DJ said he'd see what he can do."

"Let's get some tequila sunrises, Sylvia," Mildred suggested. "It's been eons since we had them."

Sylvia tried to muster some enthusiasm as they took drinks to an open table and sat down. They'd taken only a few sips of the orange and red concoctions when a familiar sound came over the speakers.

"Do you hear that?" Sylvia's eyes opened wide and she put down her drink. "He's playing 'YMCA'!" She hurried to the edge of the dance floor with Mildred right behind. Larry and Archie stood smiling as a strobe light illuminated the club.

"We're in for a treat," the DJ announced over the music. "Tonight we have two ladies in the house who did the hustle and the bump back when disco was king...I mean queen. Rumor has it that they were regulars at Studio 54. Let's go back in time with our own disco-dancing divas—Sylvia and Mildred, also known as Silly and Milly!"

Larry and Archie began clapping and the crowd joined in. Mildred pulled her stunned friend onto the dance floor.

Sylvia and Mildred didn't miss a step of their routine as they slid across the floor in unison. Then Larry and Archie joined them, and the four led the rest of the crowd in spelling out the familiar chorus—"Y-M-C-A, Y-M-C-A!"

"That was great!" Sylvia said when the song had ended.

Larry grabbed her by the hand. "It's not over yet." Van McCoy's "Do the Hustle" began and he whirled his wife around.

"M' lady," Archie said and pulled Mildred close.

"You still remember how this goes, right?" she whispered in his ear.

"Let's show everyone how it's done," he said.

Five songs later—after Larry had done his best John Travolta imitation to "Staying Alive" and almost everyone had gone down a Soul Train line two by two to KC and the Sunshine Band's "I'm Your Boogie Man"—the foursome sat at a table to catch their breath.

"That was awesome!" "You guys rock!" Young patrons streamed by, voicing their appreciation.

Sylvia mopped her forehead with a napkin and turned to Larry. "You have to tell me—how did you get the DJ to play those songs?"

"You know how persuasive I can be." Larry laughed. "I made him an offer he couldn't refuse—two crisp Benjamins for his wallet. That's all the encouragement he needed to turn the beat around."

"My bad boy," Sylvia said. "Thank you! I'll never forget tonight."

"Me either," Archie said. "I probably won't be able to walk tomorrow, but it will have been worth it."

"To Sylvia," Mildred said, holding a glass of ice water high. "Here's to a lifetime of adventures!"

An announcement broke into her toast. "For a finale," the DJ said, "we call Sylvia, Mildred, Larry, and Archie back to the floor to close us out with one more dance."

Donna Summer's "Last Dance" began playing and Sylvia and Mildred grabbed hands to take their place in the spotlight, with the guys close behind.

"Classic Silly and Milly!" Sylvia said, facing her friend, and Mildred nodded in total agreement.

Inspired by her own long-term relationships, Shelley Johnson Carey enjoys exploring themes of women's friendships in her writing. She is also the author of the soon-to-be-published book, *Thin Mint Memories: Scouting for Empowerment through the Girl Scout Cookie Program* (www.clearmessagemedia.org/press/thinmintmemories). Shelley, a certified Amherst Writers & Artists workshop leader, lives in Silver Spring, Maryland, with her husband and their two dogs, Daisy and Buddy. She works in educational publishing and received her BA from Hampshire College and her MFA in creative nonfiction from Goucher College. Although she has never won a disco contest, Shelley does a mean bump and is always up for an old-fashioned dance party.

Melvin and the Haunted Mansion

By Weldon Burge

I was ten back in 1972 when I saw Melvin for the first time. It would not be my last time.

My dad loved the Haunted Mansion in Rehoboth's Funland. The ride operated only at night, so I was already hesitant when we first stood in line in front of the building. "Tommy, you're going to love it," Dad said. "Trust me."

My mother objected, of course. "He'll have nightmares."

A vulture on the roof. A skeletal figure standing in a window on the second floor. A fully dressed corpse, arms extended, hanging from the wall above. I grabbed Dad's hand. He looked down at me and smiled. "It'll be OK, kiddo."

I knew I was in for an awesome experience even before the car smashed through the dark red, swinging doors at the start of the ride. On a huge white board at the entrance was written "Keep Arms & Legs Inside Car At All Times," with a severed zombie arm above it. Was there something in there that could snap off your arms and legs if you didn't heed the warning? Were there monsters? Vampires? Things with tentacles? Worse?

We went through the graveyard, where a large tombstone read "YOU," and then through ice caves filled with huge bats and a miner threatening to blow us up with dynamite, and a cool 3-D skull room with dancing skulls surrounded by mirrors. The best scene was the living room, which had an open coffin and a creepy ghoul playing a pipe organ. The mansion was filled with secret passages, skeletons, and even a Frankenstein monster. I was scared, but it was a fun scare, and my dad laughed along with me. Looking back, I think this was a rite of passage to him.

Rehoboth's haunted mansion paled in comparison to the Disney World version, but I think that attraction is way too slick, too commercial, and far too sanitized and wrapped up in its own technical aspects. The dark ride on the boardwalk had a carny feel to it—which is not a bad thing at all. Sure, it may be cheesy, but that's part of its charm. To this day, I visit the place every chance I get.

But I'm getting ahead of myself. This is about Melvin.

The first time I rode the ride was the first time I saw Melvin. He was the ride attendant, taking our tickets and ushering us into the car, which was suspended from an overhead track. I knew his name was Melvin because it was embroidered on his shirt pocket, red lettering on a white background with a red border. No last name. Just MELVIN.

He was bald, with huge ears that were disproportional to his face and a piglike nose that was broad with wide nostrils. His eyes were misaligned—one skewed to the left, the other tilted toward the ceiling. When we approached him with our tickets, my dad said, "Hi! How ya doing?" Melvin didn't respond, didn't even acknowledge our presence. When our car pulled up beside us, Melvin stepped forward to raise the bar and we seated ourselves. He lowered the bar and stepped back.

"He's just acting," my dad said, "pretending to be a zombie."

I wasn't so sure.

* * * * * *

The Haunted Mansion was a favorite beach attraction for horny teenage couples looking to cop a feel. You could get to second base if you were fast enough—the ride wasn't that long.

When I was sixteen, I managed to talk Norma Johnson into going on the ride with me. Super shy and super gorgeous, she resisted going on the ride at first, but then I pointed to the children in line, saying, "C'mon, they're little kids," and she gave in.

I hadn't visited the boardwalk for three years. The man taking our tickets was someone I'd not seen before. He looked bored to tears.

"Is Melvin still around?" I asked.

The guy looked at me like I had a venereal disease. "Don't know any Melvin," he said.

I assumed Melvin had retired or moved on. Who could afford to stay at this job for years? Who knows, maybe he died.

As the ride began and we entered the darkness, Norma trembled. I pulled her close, putting my arm around her shoulders.

"Nothing to worry about," I said. "Just remember, it's all for fun."

She nodded, then shivered.

Norma loosened up when we went past the graveyard display with the tombstone engraved with "Here Lies Jake—Hit the Gas Instead of the Brake."

"Well, that's just silly," she said, and smiled at me. That smile made my heart melt.

We kissed for the first time as the car went past the 3-D skull room. I slipped my left hand under her right breast as we arrived at the living room—and then I saw Melvin standing next to the ghoulish organist. He was dressed totally in black, and I would have missed him if I hadn't been paying attention. He blended into the scenery. Melvin didn't look directly at us as we went slowly by, but his head turned as the car moved through the room.

After all these years? Something seemed wrong. I pulled my hand away from Norma. And then our car turned a corner and Melvin was no longer in my line of vision.

"Did you see that?" I asked.

"What?"

"The man back there?"

She shook her head and then gently pulled my hand back to her chest.

* * * * * *

I went off to Clemson University in 1981 and visited Myrtle Beach a few times during the summers, but Myrtle Beach didn't have the flavor or charm of Rehoboth, and I yearned for my home beach—and to return to the Haunted Mansion. I didn't get back to the boardwalk until late in the summer of '87.

For the next few years, I went to Rehoboth several times each summer, with family or friends, and got to the mansion each time. I was strangely disappointed not to see Melvin. I wanted so much to see him there. He was part of my memory of Rehoboth.

* * * * * *

In 1990, I married my beautiful wife, Diane. We had our first child, Ben, in 1991. With a newborn and now a shared life, we didn't have much opportunity for vacation time. I worked a fifty-hour week for a publisher in Philadelphia. The commute alone was hellacious, particularly when I-95 was choked with traffic. But in the summer of '93, Diane convinced me that we needed some time off. So we went to Rehoboth for a few days of fun and relaxation.

By that time, Ben was a toddler and could handle some of the kiddie rides in Funland, so one night we went to the boardwalk. As we went from ride to ride, I kept glancing over toward the mansion only a short distance away, and Diane caught me.

"Go ahead," she said. "I know you're dying to."

"You sure?"

"Sure. I'll take Ben on the merry-go-round."

I smiled, nodded. "OK, I'll be right back."

As I stood in line for the ride, I realized the attraction needed love. The façade could use a fresh coat of paint. Inside, I noticed several of the gimmicks no longer worked. Of course, most folks wouldn't notice, but I remembered. I'd been on the ride so many times over the years, I knew every room, every monster, every ghoul.

The car then entered the mirrored room with the floating skulls. Melvin stood at the back of the room in the shadows, briefly illuminated by the dim lights. I saw his bald head, the eyes askance and unfocused, looking exactly like the zombie I remembered. As I went through the small room, his reflection could be seen in the mirrors at different angles. He didn't move, didn't watch my car slowly pass by. He seemed frozen in place, a part of the scene. As the car moved around a corner toward the next room, I turned in the seat to look back, but he was gone.

How could it be possible? It didn't make sense. How could a man I first saw at the Haunted Mansion back in 1972 still be here in 1993? Even back then, he looked to be in his fifties, maybe older. He would have to be in his seventies by now, if he was still alive.

I don't remember getting off the ride. I made my way through Funland and found Diane standing next to the fire truck ride, as Ben traveled in lazy circles, turning the steering wheel with such enthusiasm that he probably thought he controlled the truck. She turned to me with a smile, but quickly realized something was wrong.

"What?" she asked.

"I don't know. I think I just saw a ghost."

"Well, sure. It's a haunted house."

"No, I mean it. I think I saw a *ghost*."

Diane looked at me as if I'd just grown a third arm.

"I'm serious," I said. "I saw a man in there, the same man I saw at this ride when I was ten."

"Maybe he works here."

"No, I don't think so. He would be too old now. He just stood there, in the shadows."

"Maybe you're mistaken. It's probably a dummy, a prop, just part of the ride."

"Maybe," I said, and looked back at the mansion. "But I don't think so."

* * * * * *

My dad began slipping into dementia when he was seventy. Mom had died of lung cancer a decade before, and he never remarried. I knew how much he loved the beach, so we took him to Rehoboth for what would be his last time. For the most part, he was lucid, but at times he resided somewhere else, somewhere in his memories, in his other world. To be honest, I was somewhat envious. He seemed happiest when he wasn't with us; I suspect he was with Mom again in his mind.

When I took him to the Haunted Mansion, his eyes sparkled and he grinned. He was my young father again.

The management had upgraded the mansion over the past few years. The façade had a new paint job, the ride was smoother, and the gimmicks now all worked. There were a few additions (like a ghoul that appeared to be urinating), but all the familiar rooms were largely unchanged.

"You remember coming here, Dad? When I was a kid?"

He nodded. "Of course. The highlight of our summers."

"Do you want to ride it again, just for old time's sake?"

"Sure!"

Dad had a little trouble getting into the car, and the ride attendant helped me get him situated. When the ride started, he leaned forward against the bar, anticipating what was to come.

"Dad, do you remember Melvin? The guy who took our tickets when we first went on the ride?"

"You thought he was a zombie."

"I still see him in the mansion sometimes."

Dad turned to me. "Inside?"

"Yeah. Usually standing in the living room."

"With the coffin and the pipe organ?"

"Right. I'm glad you remember."

"Son, that doesn't sound right. He'd be older than I am."

"I know. I don't think it's possible. But I still see him. Not every time, but…"

Dad stared at me for a moment. Then we entered the mansion for his last time.

Dad didn't jump when things popped out at him from the shadows. Probably, like me, he'd been through the mansion so many times there were no surprises. He pointed and laughed a few times, however, clearly enjoying himself.

We passed through the graveyard, the room with the mad scientist and his monster, the hallway with the mounted heads, and the massive skull with the glowing red eyes. Dad loved it all.

But when we entered the living room, there was Melvin standing next to the fireplace, leaning against the grandfather clock in the corner. He didn't move, didn't appear to notice us at all. The car moved past the pile of skulls on the floor, the open coffin, and the ghoul at the pipe organ. I didn't look back this time. I was sure Melvin was no longer there.

"I love the pipe organ," Dad said.

"Sure, Dad. I always liked that, too."

The car went around the corner and into a dark hallway.

"Who was that man back there?" Dad asked.

"You saw a man? You saw Melvin?"

"I don't know if it was Melvin. But I saw a man back there, standing next to the fireplace."

"So, you did see him!"

"But I don't know why your mom was there. She shouldn't have been there."

"You saw Mom?"

"You didn't see her waving at us?"

"Dad, Mom has been gone for ten years now."

He turned to me with a look of confusion.

I sighed. I now had no idea what he'd seen, if he'd seen anything at all. Or maybe I was the delusional one.

* * * * * *

In the summer of 2000, when Ben was nine, he asked me to go to the Haunted Mansion. He'd taken a liking to the old horror films: *The Mummy, Frankenstein, The Werewolf, Dracula*, and *The Thing*. I figured he was ready for his initiation at the mansion.

As we traveled through the dark maze of rooms, I watched Ben, his sense of wonder, his infectious joy. I then understood why my dad had taken me on the ride so many years ago. This wasn't just the Haunted Mansion, and it wasn't just a boardwalk attraction. It was far more than that. As my dad had done with me, I relived that sense of discovery, new experience, vicariously through Ben. Even more than that, this was a shared adventure between father and son. A rite of passage. I understood now. This was just as important for Ben as it was for me. Perhaps more so.

I wasn't surprised to see Melvin standing at the back of the graveyard, beside a gnarly black tree among the tombstones. He disappeared behind the tree as soon as I noticed him.

"What was that monster back there?" Ben asked.

I turned to him. "You saw a monster?"

"The one behind the tree. Was that a vampire? I couldn't tell."

"What did it look like?"

"Maybe a man dressed in black. But I only saw him for a second."

I nodded. "Probably one of the props. There are so many monsters moving around in here."

"I know. It's great!"

So, I wasn't the only one who saw Melvin.

After Ben and I got off the ride, I asked the teenager taking the tickets, "Do you know Melvin?"

The kid stopped chewing his gum, trolling for a thought. "Nope. No idea."

Then I noticed the guy in the ticket booth motioning me over. The man was easily in his late sixties, unshaven and looking like every carny I'd seen in my life. I stepped to the open door at the back of the booth. He continued selling the tickets, but talked over his shoulder to me.

"You askin' about Melvin?"

"You've seen him?"

"Perty near every damn day. Where'd you see Melvin? I usually see him hangin' around the living room, near the organist."

"Wait, you've seen him? You've seen the ghost?"

The man turned to me, and then laughed until tears came to his eyes. "The way you go on, mister! Melvin don't work here no more, but this is his life. He never left."

"I don't understand."

"He ain't no ghost, mister."

He turned to the window to sell more tickets, but continued talking.

"Melvin was always a little slow, plus he's mute and his eyes ain't straight. He never looked folks straight in the eyes 'cause he couldn't. Not his fault, of course, but it creeped people out. And, being mute, that made life even more difficult for him."

"I was afraid of him when I first saw him," I said. "I thought he was a zombie, just part of the show, but that was decades ago."

"Back when he was a ride attendant, sure. Back in the early seventies. Thing is, he loved kids. Melvin had a good heart and a kind soul. It's sad the kids always thought he was scary. He'd never hurt a one of 'em."

"But I still don't understand. I could swear I saw him just now. How can that be?"

"Melvin always loved the mansion. Like I said, this is his life. So, we let him hang around, and he watches over the facilities. He don't work no more. He retired long ago, got that Social Security and the Medicare, so he's good. Lord, he must be in his seventies by now, maybe eighty. But this is his home, so we let him stay. He even has a cot back there, case he wants to spend the night."

"Nobody on the ride notices him?"

"I'm sure they do. But I 'spect they think he's part of the show, ya know? See, you probably have this memory of him from years ago, right?"

"Yes, back when I was a kid."

"So, you recognize him. You remember him. Most don't. And he don't bother nobody. But a ghost? Well, not in the true sense of the word, no."

* * * * * *

My grandson Justin screamed when the banshee leaped out at us, but he laughed afterward. He gripped my hand.

"That was scary, Pops!"

"But you weren't really scared, right? You know it's all make-believe."

"Sure, I know. It's just fun. Can we do it again when we're through?"

"You bet, kiddo. I've been riding this nearly every summer since I was your age."

I was happy. I'd initiated another generation into the simple joy that is the Haunted Mansion on the Rehoboth boardwalk.

As we came around a turn, I saw Melvin standing at the back of the living room. Just standing there, watching as our car went by. He looked good for a man pushing ninety. I don't think Justin noticed him. Or, if he did, he probably thought Melvin was one of the props, part of the scenery. In a way, he was.

I waved to Melvin, just a turn of the hand and a nod.

He did not return the gesture.

But he did smile.

WELDON BURGE, A NATIVE OF DELAWARE, IS A FULL-TIME EDITOR, FREELANCE WRITER, AND PUBLISHER. HIS FICTION HAS APPEARED IN MANY PUBLICATIONS, INCLUDING VARIOUS MAGAZINES AND ANTHOLOGIES (THE BEST OF THE HORROR SOCIETY 2013, PELLUCID LUNACY: AN ANTHOLOGY OF PSYCHOLOGICAL HORROR, GHOSTS AND DEMONS, JUST TO NAME A FEW). HIS STORIES HAVE ALSO BEEN ADAPTED FOR PODCAST PRESENTATION BY DRABBLECAST. WELDON IS A FREQUENT WRITER FOR SUSPENSE MAGAZINE, OFTEN WRITING AUTHOR INTERVIEWS. STARTING IN 2012, HE AND HIS WIFE, CINDY, FOUNDED SMART RHINO PUBLICATIONS (SMARTRHINO.COM), AN INDIE PUBLISHING COMPANY FOCUSING PRIMARILY ON HORROR AND SUSPENSE/THRILLER BOOKS.

The Last Day of Summer

By David Yurkovich

On the morning of September 22, as he had done for the entire season, Frank Mankowitz, proprietor of Famous Frank's Franks, unlocked the front door of the shop in which he performed fast-food magic on a daily and nightly basis, pulled it open, and stepped inside. The smell of fryer lard and tomato ketchup were all too familiar, but soon, so soon, there would be relief. "Relief beyond belief," as he was fond of saying. Frank switched on the interior lights, walked toward the back of the joint, and stepped into the prep area. He washed his hands, retrieved several onions, tomatoes, and peppers, and began dicing. His fingers bore small cuts and abrasions from a season of chopping. But none of that mattered now. It was the last day of summer. Frank smiled.

For the past fifteen years, Frank Mankowitz had made his living as a Rehoboth boardwalk restaurateur. His was a modest establishment, but centrally located just south of Funland. He kept the menu simple—franks, fries, burgers, soft drinks—and lived by the credo of low overhead, high turnover. During the peak Memorial Day–to–Labor Day run, it was easy to pull in a grand or more daily. A sunny weekend with a concert event at the bandstand would often yield twice that amount. Not that he was in it for the money. Well, of course he was, but there was more to it than that.

His brother-in-law, a respected financial advisor with the Newark-based Smith and Payne, tried on numerous occasions to convince Frank to relocate the business or open a "real" restaurant.

"You'd make a killing in Lewes," Manny explained, as they sat in the back of the Rehoboth Diner late one evening.

"Listen to me, Manny. I work five, six months a year and pull in more than most of the white-collar stiffs you work with. I got a fantastic view of the beach. I'm my own boss. Every day, I'm surrounded by thousands of people who want to be here. You understand that? No one is here because they have to be. Everyone wants to be here. Beautiful women. The smell of cotton candy, popcorn, taffy. The sun, the ocean air, the sounds of the boardwalk. Nights filled with music and life. This isn't just work; this is my home. Don't waste your breath talking to me about relocating."

Though for all the enjoyment, the work was intense for a man in his fifties: long days and long evenings spent leaning across a sizzling grill and pulling baskets from a deep fryer. By mid-August each year, his back began to ache, his feet felt pancake-flat, and his eyebrows were frizzled by the intense heat. By Labor Day, he was taking prescription-strength naproxen twice daily, knocking it back with far too much coffee. But year after year, Frank knew it was all worth it, because before long, the last day of summer would arrive.

And it had arrived.

All that morning, Frank randomly denied payment from customers, declaring, "This dog's on me." There was plenty in the vault, and besides, it was great PR. Sometimes, as he pivoted from grill to window, the ache in his arches was almost overwhelming, but the customers' smiling faces were like codeine and the pain was quickly forgotten. Periodically, when the foot traffic slowed, he stared at the hand-printed cardboard sign behind the counter that read "Thanks for a great season! See you next year!" and grew anxious with anticipation, like a kid waiting for the coming attractions to end and the movie to start. The afternoon passed quickly but not nearly quickly enough.

At 10 p.m., having fried his last fry and grilled his last dog, Frank switched off the equipment and locked the doors. Then he hung the sign. There would be other closure work to do, but it could wait. Frank spent several minutes in the restroom, wiping the grease from his face, hands, and forearms, and brushed his thinning gray hair. He switched off the lights and stepped out of the rear entrance before heading to the boards. No longer on the clock, he was free to indulge in the guilty pleasure of becoming just another face in the crowd. The ocean breeze was cool, a refreshing respite from the interior heat of the past eight hours.

He walked slowly north, past Funland and Kohr Brothers, stopping to chat with a few of the beach patrol officers who frequented his concession, and then continued toward Rehoboth Avenue. The boardwalk was only marginally crowded. He headed inland for a block and sipped espresso at the Coffee Mill, the first of many tranquil moments following a demanding season.

The sky was dark when Frank returned to the boardwalk, which now shone brightly, illuminated by countless lights of all colors, shapes, and sizes.

This was a time for celebration. And as he had done on closing day each season, Frank removed his socks and nonskid work shoes and stepped from the boardwalk to the beach. The sand bore such a welcome contrast to his footwear that he stood motionless for several minutes before continuing toward the Atlantic. He resumed walking and did not stop until he was ankle-deep in ocean water. The tide splashing against his legs seemed to be saying, "Welcome back; we've missed you." He gazed at the black and white of the sky and moon. Such a contrast to the multicolored boardwalk just a few hundred feet distant. It was so quiet here. Just the sound of the waves gently crashing upon each other.

Frank stepped back and sat atop the sand. He retrieved a

Camacho Corojo from his shirt pocket—another annual, albeit guilty, tradition. The tobacco was smooth and savory, and he was more than willing to risk the fine (it had been a very profitable year).

He relaxed and let the minutes drift by. There was no need to rush. Frank smiled, gazing back at his city, his home, knowing that for the next seven months, Rehoboth was *his* oyster.

DAVID YURKOVICH IS A WRITER, EDITOR, AND GRAPHIC NOVELIST WHOSE PUBLISHED WORKS INCLUDE *LESS THAN HEROES, DEATH BY CHOCOLATE: REDUX, BANANA SEAT SUMMER,* AND *GLASS ONION.* HE ALSO PUBLISHES ORIGINAL ONLINE CONTENT VIA HIS WEBSITE (SLEEPINGGIANTCREATIONS. COM). DAVID RESIDES IN MILTON, DELAWARE, WITH HIS WIFE, DIANNE, THEIR DAUGHTER, SOPHIE, AND A HORDE OF FOUR-LEGGED CRITTERS.

Salt Air Evenings

By Mady Wechsler Segal

As Ronnie entered her late mother's Rehoboth Beach cottage, she was assaulted by the smell of cleaning fluids. She had asked a friend, a year-round resident who ran a cleaning service, to pack all the contents of the twin home into boxes and scrub the house. Ronnie couldn't face her mother's belongings right away because of the feelings they would elicit. She also knew that the small cottage would be a mess, with every surface full of dusty knickknacks, old magazines, and empty vodka bottles.

Ronnie rushed to open windows and let in the late-spring salty evening air. She lingered in the tiny bedroom at the back of the house that had been hers until she escaped at age seventeen to go to college in Maryland. Brushing a tear from her eye, she nearly stumbled down the stairs from the porch to her car.

Carrying up the first of many loads, Ronnie was annoyed to see lights on in the other side of the duplex cottage. She didn't want to share the porch with others. She reveled in sitting in a rocker in the dark, watching people walk by without seeing her. She resented her loss of privacy when the owners of the other side of the house were there. She loved that they didn't come often and didn't rent out to others. As a teenager, she envied their financial ability to do that. The car in the driveway on the other side of the house had a Maryland license plate, though the owners were from Virginia. This didn't dampen her resentment, but it awakened her curiosity, even more so when she saw the interlopers lower the shades. *That's a good sign,* she thought, *people who'll stick to themselves.* Then she worried that they had something to hide, maybe even something awful like heroin or pedophilia.

When she had finished lugging the rest of her stuff into the house, Ronnie plunked down on the coffee-stained sofa and cried. It was the first time she had cried for her mother since the funeral. She planned to spend the summer here, ostensibly to settle financial matters following her mother's death, but she was also eager to escape the reminders of her late husband, Jack, in the house they had shared for nineteen years. Her mother had died less than a month ago and it was not quite a year since her beloved had succumbed to a heart attack.

Ronnie had cried herself to sleep every night from Jack's death until his funeral. But her grief paled in comparison to her anger at her mother for her smug "I told you so" at his funeral. Her mother had never accepted Jack or his family. The comment was so mean that Ronnie had refused to see her mother until she got an emergency call that her mother was in the hospital with liver failure. Now Ronnie was wracked with guilt because she hadn't made it to the hospital before her mother died. She was still angry at her mother, but also felt sorry for her. She had had a difficult life, both psychologically and financially.

After a long crying jag, Ronnie wanted to walk to the boardwalk, where she had spent every early summer evening playing games in the arcades (especially Skee-Ball in Funland) and then sitting on a bench watching people go by. She relished her privacy but loved observing the diversity of the strolling characters. She envied the big happy families and the hand-holding couples (both gay and straight). She watched older couples with awe, especially those who seemed to have been together for years and still smiled at each other. In her memory, she could almost taste the Thrasher fries, shaved ices, incredible flavors at The Ice Cream Store, Dolle's salt water taffy and caramel corn, and Candy Kitchen treats, especially her favorite, dark chocolate almond bark.

But Ronnie wasn't ready to be around people. Instead of heading to the boardwalk, she unpacked the food she had brought with her, ate a snack, and took her latest knitting project out to the porch. She wanted to sit quietly knitting in a rocker, listening to the ocean two blocks away, and breathing in the salty air. She was jolted from her reverie by the opening of her neighbor's squeaky screen door. She glared at the man who emerged.

"Hi," he said, smiling. "I thought I heard someone out here. You must be Veronica."

"I'm Ronnie. Only my mother called me Veronica."

"And apparently your next-door neighbor."

Ronnie stayed silent.

"I'm sorry, I must be disturbing you. I'm also sorry for the loss of your mother."

"Thanks."

He sat down on a rocker on his side of the porch, but the one closest to her side, which annoyed her. Ronnie knitted and rocked. Both movements soothed her. Just as she was thinking how nice it was that he was quiet, he asked, "What are you knitting?"

"A scarf. For the Red Scarf Project."

"My wife used to knit for that. It's for former foster children now in college, right?"

"Yes. Why did she stop?"

"She gave up her nursing job, knitting, and me to become a high-powered lawyer in New York."

Ronnie gasped. "I'm sorry."

"It's OK. The divorce will be final tomorrow."

"I know how loss feels. My husband died almost a year ago."

"Oh, dear, two major losses in less than a year. No wonder you seem melancholy."

Ronnie looked at him in disbelief. She couldn't decide whether she should be angry at his being presumptuous or grateful that he was perceptive.

"I'm sorry," he said. "I've offended you."

Even in the dim light she could see his startling blue eyes grow sad. "It's OK," she said. "You've described my emotional state with pinpoint accuracy. Are you a psychiatrist or something?"

"Close. I'm a clinical psychologist. I teach at the University of Maryland in College Park."

"You're kidding! I teach math there. Did my graduate work there, too—a Ph.D.—twenty-one years ago."

"That's amazing; I got my doctorate there the year before," he said.

"Interesting coincidence, but you can't get much further away in content than we are."

"Not really. I taught statistics in the Psychology Department for my first twelve years."

"And I teach statistics every other semester," Ronnie said, smiling for the first time in a long while. She stood up and walked to him with her hand out. "I'm Ronnie, a.k.a. Veronica."

"Glad to meet you. I'm Ben, a.k.a. Benjamin, but only my dad calls me that."

As Ronnie sat back down, Ben said, "I love the beach and my wife hated it, so I decided to celebrate the divorce by coming here for the summer and maybe longer."

"I fled this house, but I've missed the beach. Jack didn't like it enough to take time off from work for us to come."

"What did he do?"

"He was in construction. I met him when I filed a sexual harassment complaint against a construction firm because their workers on campus made rude comments every time I walked by their site on the way from my car to my graduate student office. The company made them stop and sent me a written apology. Plus, the owner of the company held a meeting where all the men apologized to me in person with him present. They said they hadn't realized their comments weren't funny to me. That's when I met Jack, the owner. I was wowed by the handsome boss with salt-and-pepper hair and green eyes that gleamed against his tanned face. Even more than that, I was impressed by the gracious way he handled the meeting. He was charming and calm, and he took my complaint seriously."

"So it was love at first complaint?"

Ronnie smiled. "We dated, and the more I got to know him, the more I loved him. I'm going on too much, right?"

"No, Ronnie, I think talking about the people we've loved and lost helps with grief. I'm sure to rattle on about my wife—the good, the bad, and the ugly."

"Well, the really ugly for me wasn't Jack, it was my mother's attitude toward him. She had all kinds of criticisms, especially that he was so much older than me. She said, 'Veronica, don't be a fool. Jack is more than twice your age. You're twenty-five and he's fifty-two.'"

"How did you respond to that?"

"I was snarky. I said, 'Mom, I'm a mathematician. I can do the arithmetic.' But her onslaught continued, 'He'll die and leave you a widow when you're middle-aged. Then where will you be?' I countered that he was healthy and active, played tennis three times a week, and ran on the other days. Then he went and died playing tennis."

"No one could foresee that," said Ben.

"My mother also warned that his children would resent me, that they would assume I was marrying him for his money and would worry they would lose their inheritance to our children. They did think that until I told them that Jack and I planned not to have children together. Mom also argued that Jack and I had nothing in common because I was about to get a Ph.D. and he was in construction. I called her a snob and fired back that she was jealous because I had a knight in shining armor and her boyfriend left her when she told him she was pregnant with me."

"How did she respond to that?"

"I didn't give her time to respond. I ran out the door, mad that my mother always saw the bad in everything I wanted. I headed for the beach but didn't get far because the wind was whipping around and tears were freezing on my cheeks. I came back and found my mother slugging down vodka. Remembering what I had learned in Alateen and Al-Anon, I said nothing about the drinking. Instead, I said, 'I'm sorry I said something hurtful. I know you have my best interests at heart. I'm going to marry Jack. I hope you'll try to be happy for us.' Her response was, 'I'll be happy until disaster strikes.' Then at Jack's funeral, my mother said, 'I told you so.'"

"That was cruel," Ben said.

"Yes, it was, and I never forgave her."

"That clearly was an upsetting experience for you. And returning here now has brought it back to you."

"You are correct, Dr. Ben. But now I feel guilty that I didn't see her before she died. She had a hard life and I said mean things to her. I believed my mother was jealous, but perhaps she had a right to be, struggling as she did to raise a child on her own with meager resources." Tears flowed down Ronnie's cheeks.

Ben went to her, put a hand on her shoulder for a few seconds, and then sat back down.

"Thanks," Ronnie said. "Now tell me about your wife."

"There's not much to tell now. I loved her because she was beautiful inside and out. I especially admired how she nurtured and cared for others. But she changed after she decided that earning lots of money was more important than helping others. Her increasing interest in chasing the big bucks appalled me and she started seeing me as too soft and not ambitious enough. I'd rather do things that matter than make lots of money."

"What kind of things matter to you?"

"I've always loved teaching, but lately I'm disenchanted with the way universities are headed. I want to have more personal interaction with students, not teach large classes or, worse, online classes. I started talking about teaching at a community college and having a small clinical practice. That was the clincher for my wife."

"Wow. I've been considering teaching at Delaware Tech. They don't pay much, but Jack left me enough money that I could afford the pay cut."

"I actually have a job interview there next week. I'm thinking I could be a psychology instructor and start a clinical practice in addiction counseling. Heroin has become a huge problem, including here."

"Can you support yourself on the pay?"

"I can manage. If I get the job, I'll sell my house in Maryland. Then I can invest the sale proceeds. My mom came from a wealthy family and left me money when she died, so I already have more than enough to buy this beach house."

"Lucky you. I didn't know the owners wanted to sell their half."

"They gave me a rental contract for the summer with an option to buy. By the way, I haven't spent any of my inheritance. My will specifies charities to receive what's left."

"Oh," said Ronnie, sorry she had been jealous and sarcastic.

Ronnie and Ben talked until they both started to yawn, then they called it a night.

While lying in bed and trying to sleep, Ronnie was amazed at her own openness about her feelings. For some reason, she trusted Ben. And he was candid with her, too. They had much in common, despite their different backgrounds. She wasn't happy about the loss of privacy, but she doubted that Ben would be much trouble.

* * * * * *

Ronnie spent the next few days going through her mother's belongings, one box at a time. She separated items into giveaways, throwaways, and keepers. It was hard deciding what to keep. She focused on saving what brought back sweet memories. She expected very few of these, but when she came upon a photo of herself and her mother on the beach, she began to think back. Digging deeper into forgotten stories, she realized that not all of her times with her mother were sad. They loved going to the beach together and swimming in the ocean, as long as the waves weren't rough. She remembered how happy her mommy was when they splashed into the water and swam out beyond the breaking waves. Ronnie worried about getting back to shore without being tumbled, but Mommy reassured her and led the way. Ronnie couldn't tell what now made her cry more, the disturbing memories or the joyful ones.

Every evening that week, Ronnie and Ben sat on the porch rocking and talking (and Ronnie knitting) until the wee hours. They discussed the state of higher education, what they hoped to accomplish in their teaching, and the kind of life they wanted. Ben expressed delight in Rehoboth's atmosphere, especially people's friendliness. Ronnie warned him that it would change when high season set in and vacationers arrived, bringing traffic jams, excessive drinking, and people feeding the noisy seagulls on crowded beaches. Despite this, she felt a renewal of her love for the beach, the boardwalk, and the year-round community. She even looked forward to the excitement the summer people brought.

On the third night, Ben suggested he cook dinner for them the next day, but Ronnie demurred, saying she needed some time alone.

She told him that being on her own during the day and reminiscing was helping her grief and her guilt about neglecting her mother. Ben seemed to understand.

The routine of sharing the porch in the evenings soothed her. She could move on from the day's tasks and thoughts and begin to process where they were leading her. It was uncanny how much she and Ben had in common, despite their different fields of work. Knowing she would have his companionship, his wisdom, and his humor every evening comforted her. She found herself missing him during the day; she longed to tell him right away about things she saw or did. She wanted to share with him insights she had about the past and the future. *It's only because he's such a good listener,* she told herself. *It's that clinical psychologist manner.* But then she realized he also talked a lot and she liked listening to him.

At the end of the week, Ben said, "Ronnie, I've got a multiple-choice test for you. Which of these would you like to do with me tomorrow? A: Have dinner that I cook for us. B: Have dinner out, my treat. C: Go to the beach in the morning. D: Go to the beach in the afternoon. E: None of the above. And E is an incorrect answer."

Despite her laugh, Ronnie's first reaction was to decline. But, overachiever that she was, she didn't want to fail a test. She thought about it and said, "Running the risk of getting a wrong answer, I choose D and then B, but we split the dinner check."

It was Ben's turn to laugh. "You fail the test but pass the course on the strength of your creativity—and for making me a happy man." He looked directly into her eyes and said nothing else.

"You know, this is just two new friends going to the beach and dinner, right?"

"Right. Who said anything more?" This time he winked at her.

The wink scared her. Or was that excitement she felt? "Vell, Herr Doctor Ben, ve both know zat vun can say something vit no speaking."

"Ronnie, did anyone tell you that you have a terrible Viennese accent?"

"No, because that's the first time I ever tried it. And likely the last."

They laughed and the tension eased as they renewed their usual chatter, along with moments of quiet when they just enjoyed the salt air, the distant sound of the ocean, the scent of lilacs, and the occasional bird chirp.

In bed that night, Ronnie felt the pleasant anticipation of a deep and confiding friendship. She sensed a new and powerful force in her life. For the first time in a long time, a strange contentment mixed with exhilaration swept over her. She had made appointments with the chairs of the math departments at both Delaware Technical Community College and Sussex Technical High School. The future felt promising to her, especially the thought of staying in her childhood home, letting go of painful memories, enjoying the Rehoboth beach community, and being able to teach local residents.

Ronnie thrilled at the prospect of introducing Ben to her favorite haunts and activities: the sweet treats on the boardwalk, the concerts at the bandstand, and building sand castles. She smiled as she planned to go to Kitschy Stitch, the newest yarn shop in town, to get yarn for a new project and meet other knitters.

As she fell asleep, Ronnie felt the warm presence of her mother in the room. She dreamed of clean salt air, and of Jack waving good-bye to her.

MADY WECHSLER SEGAL IS PROFESSOR EMERITA OF SOCIOLOGY AND DISTINGUISHED SCHOLAR TEACHER AT THE UNIVERSITY OF MARYLAND, COLLEGE PARK. THOUGH RETIRED FROM TEACHING, SHE IS STILL ACTIVE AS A SOCIOLOGIST. SHE STARTED WRITING FICTION AFTER TAKING WORKSHOPS AT THE WRITER'S CENTER IN BETHESDA, MARYLAND, AND IS SURPRISED BY HOW MUCH FUN IT IS. SHE TOOK TIME OUT FROM WRITING A NOVEL TO WRITE THIS STORY. MADY HAS MANY PUBLICATIONS IN SCHOLARLY JOURNALS AND BOOKS, BUT THIS IS HER FIRST PUBLISHED WORK OF FICTION. SHE IS A MEMBER OF THE REHOBOTH BEACH WRITERS' GUILD AND THE EASTERN SHORE WRITERS ASSOCIATION. MADY, HER HUSBAND, DAVID, AND THEIR DOG, LILY, DIVIDE THEIR TIME BETWEEN THEIR HOMES IN COLLEGE PARK AND BETHANY BEACH. LILY HAS WRITTEN A STORY ABOUT HER ADVENTURES, BUT IT HASN'T BEEN SUBMITTED FOR PUBLICATION YET.

JUDGE'S COMMENT

"Salt Air Evenings" is the story of a woman who puts to rest her dead mother and dead husband, and through the process, makes a new acquaintance during quiet evening conversations. This is a poignant story of setting things right and coming to terms with things lost. It is a well-written and intriguing story.

Salt Air Evenings

Finding Poe

By MaryAlice Meli

My boss, Fred, the editor of Washington, DC's *Crackdown* magazine, posts all assignments via email. For example, "Find and verify the manuscript of a newly discovered short story written by Edgar Allan Poe just before he died in 1849. Found in Rehoboth Beach. See me for more info."

My sister drove me to Fred's office. He indicated a chair and handed me a scrap of paper. I smoothed it against my knee, my right hand and arm still in a sling from injuries I suffered as a finale to my last article. The target of my investigation didn't appreciate my characterization of him as a cream-skimming crook who looted a local suburb's treasury through inflated expenses, even though I had proof to corroborate every weasely wrongdoing. I requested to be with the cops at the arrest, not considering that the shield law doesn't work against bullets. Even though the cops gave me a Kevlar vest and pushed me to the back, I still got myself shot up while the weasel got himself killed.

While recuperating, I also broke my engagement. My fiancé, a really nice guy, wanted me to quit the magazine. To pacify him, I told him I'd think about it. I did think about it and came up with several questions: Did I want to switch from excavating the truth about ne'er-do-wells to writing profiles of local celebrities and visiting dignitaries, and doing features on symphony galas? Did I really want to marry such a sweet but safe—translate boring—guy? Then I cried because I really did like the guy. Just not enough. He took it well when I returned his ring, even gave me a hug and whispered, "Let me know if you change your mind." I nodded but knew I wouldn't.

I read aloud the note Fred gave me: "Interested in reading or buying what may be the last story Edgar Allan Poe wrote before his death, contact Geoffrey Ruskin, president of the Poe-Etics, a Rehoboth Poe fan club. The handwriting in the manuscript has been verified as Poe's by a certified expert." My nose detected a smell and it wasn't the vanilla-scented smoke from Fred's e-cigarette.

"So, whaddya think, Sophie? This is right down your alley. But even better, you can dig into this without getting your other arm shot up."

"The note's not signed. We don't know who wrote this or where it comes from. I should go to Delaware for what is probably a big scam? Are you nuts or just trying to get rid of me?"

Fred inhaled as the start of a laugh but choked instead as he always did. He pounded his chest then his desk in what passed for overwhelming hilarity.

"I called this Ruskin guy," he said. "A woman supposedly found this long-lost story in an attic and claims she's Poe's way, way distant cousin." He pulled up a Post-it note from an otherwise clear desktop.

"Her name's Marlene Arnold. You can check her out when you get there. Ruskin says Arnold is a Poe family name." He peeled off another Post-it with Ruskin's information.

"The name doesn't mean it's hers or that she's related," I said. "*Crackdown* focuses on local issues and people. What does this have to do with anything in the District?"

"OK, OK. You got me. Corporate insisted I give you time off with expenses. I knew you wouldn't take it without an assignment. So, you'll be able to work this in a snap or junk it while basking on the beach. How about it?"

"You stingy bugger. I would definitely have accepted corporate's offer." Then again, after weeks of television and books my sister hauled home from the library, I was bored. "Well, at least we won't face crowds now that it's the start of October, but still warm enough for sun and sand. I'll have to take my sister Angie along." He gave a no-problem wave.

"Go crazy, girl. You're corporate's own wounded girl reporter. They got national coverage with your piece."

"If the Arnold woman sent this message to other media, I should probably leave right away, yes?" Angie loved to drive. She'd be up for this.

"Sounds good to me." Fred the Ed stood, hiked his suspenders over his gaunt frame, and held the door for me. "No more fireworks, OK?"

"I'm not the one looking for trouble."

As I walked out and headed down the hall, I heard Fred inhale and then start coughing and pounding his desk. Didn't take much string to fly his kite.

* * * * * *

"Road trip!" Angie shrieked as she raced in from the garage. "I'll pack us for two weeks. Will that be enough? Where are we staying?"

"Should be more than enough. Fred made reservations for us at the Boardwalk Plaza," I said. "I think the whole thing's a scam. We'll likely spend the whole time on the beach or shopping."

"And eating out every night—aww, such a hard life!" She sprinted upstairs to begin packing. "I'll pack some books on Poe." Angie teaches American literature at a northern Virginia high school. She took a half-year sabbatical to help me.

I called Geoffrey Ruskin in Rehoboth. I wanted to schedule a meet when we got there. Maybe he'd let me read the alleged lost work of Eddy Poe. The phone was ringing. I counted four rings, not a good sign. Voicemail picked up and a smooth, deep baritone announced, "This is Geoffrey Ruskin, president of the Rehoboth Poe-Etics, a premier coastal society supporting the work of Edgar

Allan Poe. Check our website for information on meetings and upcoming events commemorating the anniversary of Poe's death in 1849. To leave a message for me or Mrs. Ruskin, wait for the tone."

Self-important little rascal. I left my name and number and asked for a return call regarding E.A. Poe.

Angie threw two books in my lap on her way to dump a bag with jeans and T-shirts in the car. "We can leave tomorrow after rush hour."

The paperbacks included the complete short works of E.A.P. and a biography/study of "a troubled genius," or so it stated in a caption under Poe's portrait on the book cover. Dramatic. High forehead and dark, curling hair, a droopy moustache softening the grim line of tightly pressed lips, deep-set dark eyes conveying an image of either a sad or a surly troubled soul. Maybe both. Staring at those eyes, I crooned, "Once upon a midnight dreary, while I pondered weak and weary..." A loud clap of thunder interrupted me mid-"Raven." The predicted storm from what I hoped would be the last hurricane of the season was gearing up. *Oh, yeah, a stormy night just for you, Eddy baby.*

My phone rang as Angie tromped through with tote bags of underwear, pajamas, and toiletries.

"Rain or shine, we're hittin' the road again," she sang.

I answered the phone and hurried to the kitchen out of Angie's way.

"Sophie Lovejoy?" said the smooth baritone I recognized from the Poe-Etics voicemail. "Geoffrey Ruskin here."

"Mr. Ruskin. Thanks for returning my call. I'm a reporter from *Crackdown* magazine. We are interested in the Poe discovery."

"Well, Ms. Lovejoy, the Poe family told me they will discuss the manuscript with several interested parties today. But I must alert you, the family insists on a $1,000 deposit just to read it, even for media."

Ah, now the steak starts to sizzle.

"My sister and I will be in Rehoboth tomorrow morning."

After he indicated that would be acceptable, I clicked off and yelled to Angie our departure time was now before rush hour, not after, given the mess on I-95.

She responded with a muffled, "Wheee-hah." I curled up with the Poe biography and my notebook to compile questions for my interview.

* * * * * *

Angie headed to the beach while I and my notebook walked down to the Ruskin home on Philadelphia near Bayard. A trim, sandy-haired man was standing on the wide, screened porch, knocking on the door. He held a narrow-page notebook I recognized as part of a reporter's gear. It matched the one in my hand. The front door opened as I walked up the steps of the porch.

A tall, smiling woman patted the man's arm. "Glad you could make it, Tim. How's your mom getting along?"

"She's much better, Maggie, and thanks for the delicious chicken and dumplings."

The woman's silver hair gleamed in the sun as she turned to Sophie. "I'm Maggie Ruskin, and you're from the DC magazine? We've been waiting for you. What happened to your arm?"

"Long story." Sophie shrugged the question away. "I'm Sophie Lovejoy from *Crackdown*. Is your husband available?"

"Oh, indeed he is. Come in. Geoffi's on the phone right now." She led us down a short hall to a kitchen with coffee and cookies on the table. I could overhear Geoffrey saying, "Many versions of Poe's death have circulated through the decades. The one that sounds reasonable to me is that he was beaten to death in a Baltimore alley outside a bar, Gunner's Hall, on the night of October 7, 1849." He lowered his voice to a deep rumble. "His demise and the circumstances surrounding it have never been satisfactorily resolved."

"Mrs. Ruskin, have you read this newly found story?" I asked.

"Good Lord, no. And call me Maggie, dear," she said. Then at the look of surprise on my face, she added, "I'm not a Poe-Etic. Stories like that give me the creeps. Let me have a good cozy: Agatha Christie, Dorothy Sayers, or Victoria Thompson. I just go along with the Poe-Etics to help my husband. Besides, a $1,000 fee just to read it is pretty steep."

On that cue, Geoffrey Ruskin appeared. A head shorter than Maggie, he seemed to be trying to stretch himself on his tippy-toes to maximum height. He had cultivated a luxuriant gray handle-bar moustache.

I got up to shake his hand. "I'm Sophie, Mr. Ruskin."

"Just Geoffi, dear. Now what would you like to know? Oh, Timmy, I'm sorry. You can ask whatever you want, too." He turned to me. "Timmy's our main *Cape Gazette* reporter."

The *Cape Gazette* reporter looked at me, a smile on his lips, his blue polo shirt making his baby blues seem bigger and his shoulders broader. "Thanks, Geoffi," he said. "I'll just watch and listen, maybe learn something from a celebrity journalist who may win a Pulitzer this year."

So he'd read my article. And knew why I wore a sling.

Ignoring *Timmy*, I said, "Geoffi, do you have the handwriting verification from your expert along with his credentials? Proof that this really is the work of Poe, and that the paper and ink are from the mid-nineteenth century?"

"Miss Arnold did not have that documentation. She said her cousin, another Poe relative, would bring it and the story itself. The handwriting and other elements were apparently verified in Richmond, where Poe had lived."

"When will he arrive?" Tim asked.

"Late tonight," Geoffi said. "Since the seventh falls on a Thursday, we're holding our anniversary activities this weekend, with the beach night readings of Poe's work tonight. Then tomorrow at 10 p.m., we'll hold our annual séance. The public is invited to attend the readings, but only Poe-Etics members partake in the séance. The vibrations are so delicate," Geoffi said, "they must be carefully nurtured to encourage the master to appear."

"And has he appeared?" I asked, fairly certain of the answer. Tim covered his mouth with the tips of his fingers.

"Well, some group members have indicated they felt strong sensations of the poet's presence," Geoffi said, his voice now husky. "Others have heard tappings on the table or knockings in the walls, or felt sudden blasts of cold air."

"In other words, no," I said. I felt bad about showing him to be, if not a fraud, then a hard-core wishful thinker.

"From the little research I was able to do on the ride here, it seems the real reason for Poe's death may never be known," I said. "His body was autopsied then cremated the day after his death. The listed cause of death, brain congestion, left a big question mark because that was a frequent determination for death from alcoholism."

Geoffi nodded, "That's true. Eddy could not hold his liquor. Existing reports say one drink could make him woozy."

"And don't forget October 3, 1849, was an election day," Maggie said. "Bars were allowed to be open and some, like Gunner's Hall, were actual voting sites."

"You're kidding," I said. Fact really is stranger than fiction.

"Definitely," Tim said, smiling. "Not only that, they used to get the guys drunk in the bar, change their clothes, give them new IDs, and send them through to vote again. Poe was found in shabby clothes—not his own—that didn't even fit properly."

"Are you a Poe-Etics member?" I asked.

He shook his head. "I've been covering them for quite a while. It's not easy to come up with a new angle every year."

"But you do it very well," Maggie said, and I wondered if I could do that. My assignments always touched on different topics or issues. I felt respect growing for this Timmy guy.

"Come to the beach tonight for the readings," Geoffi said. "You'll see all the members in action. Afterward we'll have pizza, and the Poe family should arrive."

"One thing still confuses me," I said. "Your group has only a dozen or so members. Why would the Poe family assume you have the financial resources to pay $1,000 for a peek at the product, let alone whatever they're asking for the sale?"

Geoffi shrugged. "We can always see the bottom of our treasury so it can't be that."

"What about Phyllis?" Maggie asked. "Howard left her millions, as she's fond of letting everyone know."

* * * * * *

Pizza and Poe and Phyllis, I thought, walking home. This might turn into a fun story. I called Angie to see if she was up for the beach readings.

"Guess what, Soph?" she said. "I'm part of the show."

"What? You've gone Poe-Etic?"

"I was on the beach reading the Poe collection I gave you when a woman came along and asked me if I was in the club. She said she couldn't do the reading she'd signed up for; her grandson is in the hospital. She asked if I would read the Poe poems she was supposed to read."

"That's great. You'll be able to come to the pizza party later." Just before I went into the hotel lobby, I noticed a figure on the beach walking above the surf line. Dressed all in black except for a white shirt, he had a moustache and wore his longish, lank dark hair curled slightly behind his ears.

My arm started to hurt as it always did when I was tired and I decided I might be having hallucinations, too. Yep. I needed a nap.

* * * * * *

I was surprised at how many people showed up for the readings and at how responsive they were, oooing, giggling, applauding. Heavy dusk lent just the right degree of creepiness to the atmosphere. The readers had small lights clipped to their books and the glow reflecting upward on their faces added a gothic touch. As I walked from reader to reader down the beach, I looked for the surf-walking figure whom I thought of as a Poe impersonator. I didn't see him or anyone like him.

We poured into the Ruskin home after the readings. Everyone was excited at their success. Tables in the kitchen and dining rooms held pizzas with various toppings to cater to vegans, vegetarians, and carnivores. Surrounded by laughter and chatter, I realized I have nothing like this in my life. Just work and more work, which I love but a little of this warmth would be good, too. I glanced up to see Tim watching me. He smiled and toasted me across the table with his slice. I lifted mine back at him. Then the doorbell chimed and I hoped this meant the reason we were here had finally arrived.

Geoffi introduced a blond, plumpish woman to the group as Marlene Arnold, distant cousin of Edgar Allan Poe on his mother's side. She presented the man with her (the Poe look-alike I had seen earlier) as Arthur Herring, another distant cousin on Poe's father's side, hence, what seemed like a cultivated resemblance. He held a briefcase.

"Before I open this, I must make a few things clear," he started. "I will show the front page of the story and the certificates of authenticity but no one may handle them or read the story. I'm not interested in curiosity seekers, only genuine collectors willing to buy.

The price is $50,000. Of course, what you do with it afterward—if you want to resell it to another collector or a university or put it up for auction and get much more—that's up to you.

"If you think you could get much more, Mr. Herring, why don't you give it to Sotheby's or one of the other auction houses?" I asked.

"Now, now, let's be civilized here," Geoffi interrupted before Herring could reply.

"No, no, Geoffi, I think that's a legitimate question," Tim said. "Mr. Herring?"

Herring's face had darkened. He glared at Tim and me.

"The family—those of us who remain—have discussed this. We want this story to be preserved by those who truly appreciate our cousin, who will present this new work to scholars and then to schools for students to study. It's not all about money," he said in a low tone. Wow. Nobility oozed out of this guy's pores with gilt edges yet hadn't he just suggested that the buyer could resell it at a higher price?

Geoffi called Herring to join him in the living room, where they set up the manuscript and documents for everyone to view. I looked around for Tim but he had disappeared.

Angie and I filed in with the others. No special favors for the media, I noted. I jotted the title of the story in my notebook, "The Weary Hedonist." I didn't see a name on the verification certificate. I asked Herring who his expert was.

"All pertinent information will be provided at the time of sale," he said then turned to Geoffi. "I'm sorry, Mr. Ruskin. Interested parties in Baltimore, Richmond, and Philadelphia demand to see this work. We will leave tomorrow unless we have your decision by morning." With that, he replaced the certificates and the manuscript and snapped the briefcase shut, nodded to Marlene Arnold, and they left.

Geoffi's eyes were huge and watering. "We don't have that kind of money in our treasury."

Phyllis, who had remained silent to this point, shook her noisy bracelets and took Geoffi's arm. "Geoffi, dear, you know my Howard left me well fixed when he crossed over. I can easily cover that sale price, but I'd like to have Howard's approval."

Geoffi eyebrows reached for his hairline. Shock registered on several members' faces, whose mouths hung open that anyone could have $50,000 near to hand.

"And I think we should have a séance to contact Edgar and Howard on the beach tonight," Phyllis said, her wrists rattling as she pointed toward the ocean. The reaction from the group was immediate. People began grabbing their lawn chairs and heading toward the beach.

Tim suddenly reappeared on the porch, grabbed a couple of chairs and whispered a noirish, "Stick with me, babe."

Ordinarily, I bristle at that term but this time I laughed.

Thunder rumbled softly in the distance. A full moon shone on an angry current, dripping a ribbon of light over the waves stopping at the sand. That hurricane might kiss us yet. With the chairs in a circle, Geoffi cleared his throat. "Hold the hands of those on either side of you and ask Howard to focus with us on Edgar, his struggles, his work, his mysterious death, and this final story. Take a deep, cleansing breath, hold for a count of three and slowly exhale as you ask the poet and Howard what their wishes are. Again, breathe in, hold, breathe out." He took us through several more breaths, then paused. "We gather tonight in humility and respect to reach the author of 'The Raven.' What is your wish, sir? Shall we buy your manuscript?"

Tim's warm hand held mine firmly. The gentle pressure made meditation difficult. I heard a flapping, louder than the usual seagulls and without the annoying caw. Instead, a loud, ragged croaking tore the cool night air. In the stream of light from the full moon, I saw the largest black bird ever. Was it a crow? This bird seemed much bigger. Someone yelled in a thin voice, "It's a raven, a raven." As though orchestrated, a punishing clap of thunder made everyone jump and a few scream. I searched the sky but the bird was no longer to be seen.

A Rehoboth policeman in dark blue walked to Geoffi and whispered. Geoffi's deep baritone became a tenor. "Is he a fake? What about the manuscript?" The cop bent down again and spoke quietly. Geoffi's voice rose even higher. "It might be a forgery?" The cop nodded and walked over to Tim.

"So that's where you went?" I said to Tim, thoroughly impressed. The tall policeman removed his hat as he walked and rubbed his sandy-haired buzz cut.

"Sophie, this is my brother, Ted." Tim smiled at his brother. "Thanks, Sherlock."

"I ran Herring's license plate from the number you gave me," Ted said. The staties probably already picked him up. When the manuscript and certifications for handwriting and paper and ink authenticity prove false, we'll charge him with fraud as well as forgery. He's wanted in Florida for the same con. We'll probably turn up more places that want these two."

Later, as Angie helped me into my sweatpants and T-shirt pajamas, she said, "The poet gave his answer at the séance, you know. In sending the raven, he was telling us not to buy the manuscript: 'Nevermore.'"

I guess I could have argued the illogic of it but I liked how it fit. *Nevermore.*

MARYALICE MELI LIVES IN STEELERS/PIRATES/PENGUINS COUNTRY, AKA PITTSBURGH, PENNSYLVANIA, AND HAS WRITTEN NONFICTION IN PAST CAREERS IN EDUCATION AND JOURNALISM. SHE EARNED A MASTER'S DEGREE IN WRITING POPULAR FICTION AT SETON HILL UNIVERSITY. NOW RETIRED, SHE WRITES SHORT AND FLASH FICTION, CHILDREN'S STORIES, AND MIDDLE-GRADE MYSTERIES, AND GNASHES HER TEETH OVER HAVING TO DOWNSIZE FROM HOUSE TO APARTMENT WITHOUT THROWING ANYTHING AWAY. SHE PLACED THIRD FOR SHORT FICTION IN THE 2014 PENNWRITERS ANNUAL WRITING CONTEST AND WAS PUBLISHED IN THE REHOBOTH BEACH READS 2015 ANTHOLOGY, *BEACH DAYS*. SHE'S ALSO BEEN PUBLISHED ONLINE IN *EVERY DAY FICTION*, *INFECTIVEINK* AND *UNTIED SHOELACES OF THE MIND*.

Storm Surge

By Terri Clifton

Great black clouds sailed like ships and loomed like mountains over the Atlantic, dwarfing the towns that peppered the peninsula from the tip of Cape Charles to Cape Henlopen. On they went, past the soldiers in the watch towers, past the breakwater, into the bay, and over the curved shore that nestled the historic town of Lewes, while the radio carried warnings and tales of destruction from Florida to the Carolinas. As the heavy skies covered the Delaware coast, darkening the bayside towns of Broadkill, Prime Hook, and Slaughter Beach, people scrambled to batten hatches or find higher ground as the Great Hurricane of 1944 pushed the water and roared northward, just out to sea.

Teddy stood atop the dune and watched the clouds build and the whitecaps appear on the water. A gust of wind knocked him backward and whipped sand against his face and legs. He ran all the way home, his heart racing to match the wind.

Darkness came early, even though summer hadn't quite ended. It began to rain, big drops against the windows and the metal roof of the porch. When the lights blinked, a lantern was lit. When the electric went out completely, they ate a cold supper in the lantern's glow. His mother and uncle talked softly. His brothers were quiet. Teddy stayed quiet too, hoping the storm wouldn't notice their little house nestled on the coast.

When it was time for bed he gladly followed his mother up the stairs. He could see the worry on her face; the light from the candle in her hand had etched deeper the wrinkles around her eyes. She tucked him in her bed and told him everything would be fine.

She blew out the candle, but Teddy could see her in the flashes of lightning. He wished his father were still alive so she could feel safe, the way she used to.

Until a year ago, Teddy had shared one of the upstairs bedrooms with his brother David. Then Uncle Edgar arrived, and David moved across the hall with their older brothers, Clarence and Tom. Teddy was given a room off the kitchen, a made-over space that had once been a pantry, and its one window faced the bay. In the daytime it was all right, with shelves for his treasures, but he didn't like sleeping there. He wasn't afraid of the dark, and he wasn't afraid of the water, but he didn't like the water at night when it merged with the sky, becoming even more deep and endless. He'd wake in total darkness sometimes and the sound of the waves breaking just over the dunes would terrify him. He'd be sure they were getting closer, that the sea was inching toward the house to snatch him. So when the storm came and his mother made him come back upstairs, he was pretty sure he'd been right to worry.

His old room had a tree outside the window, and it was on the west side of the house, so he'd almost never heard the waves when he was trying to sleep. Tonight, the sound of the storm reached every part of the house and no one slept. Teddy heard, too, the creak of the stairs as Uncle Edgar went up and down, the whispers of his brothers in the next room, the startled gasp of his mother when shingles broke free from the roof. When the wind became a steady howl under the eaves, she took the Bible out of her nightstand and sat with it on her lap. Teddy pulled the covers high and kept his eyes closed. He was too old to cry. Eight years last week.

Outside, in the dangerous night, nature was battling itself, the powerful hurricane pitting the wind and water against the land. Huge waves beat relentlessly against the shoreline, overtopping dunes in places, completely breaching in others. The sand rearranged itself.

Daylight would reveal a changed landscape up and down the seaboard, but the darkness only gave up the sounds.

"The wind is shifting." Uncle Edgar's voice came up the stairwell, hours into his patrol of the house. "The worst might be over."

Teddy listened. The wind *was* changing, coming against the other side of the house now. His mother was saying a prayer, softly. He soon slept, without dreaming.

What had been a crashing and breaking sound in the dark, the light revealed to be several missing fishing shacks to the south, and two cottages could be seen washed far out into the marsh. Sand covered everything, starting with the porch. The roof of the chicken coop was gone, but the house and the small barn were still standing, minus some shingles and a screen door.

While Teddy's mother was lighting the stove, he slipped outside. He grabbed a long stick of driftwood and used it to poke at the debris all about. He had found four good shells and a cobalt bottle before he heard his name being called for breakfast.

He was crossing a flattened dune when he saw what looked like a giant ball of fishing net, but then he saw an eye. Venturing closer, he discovered it was a sea turtle, a big one, and it was completely trapped, net wrapped tightly around its shell and flippers. He knelt beside it and tugged at the tangle. "You're gonna need help."

His mother called him again.

"I'll be back." Teddy patted the net ball. The turtle just stared.

In the kitchen, Teddy's brothers were jostling for eggs and toast. His mother was pouring coffee into Uncle Edgar's cup. He thought they wouldn't be interested in his finding the turtle but he was wrong, and he was soon sorry he had told them.

"I could make a nice batch of soup, if it's as big as you say. People could use that right now. If it's alive." His mother sat the coffeepot back on the stove.

"Old Toadie at the bait shop might buy it either way," said Clarence, reaching for the jam.

"It might not have been a turtle at all," said Teddy. "I didn't get much of a look." He was quiet then and only ate enough eggs to be excused from the table.

While they had been lucky with the storm, too many of their neighbors had not. Clarence, Dave, and Tom were all older and bigger than Teddy and were sent out to help, soon followed by their mother, with a basket of food in her arms. It was the escape Teddy was looking for.

Sitting in the sand, he pondered the turtle. It had to be old because it was so big. It was almost as long as he was tall. It had fathomless jet-black eyes. Teddy couldn't help but wonder what those eyes had seen. "I'll get you out of this," he promised, not knowing how. He'd need to cut through a lot of net to set it free. Someone would see him sitting out here long before that, and then it would be the soup pot.

Teddy apologized to the creature as he moved it the only way he could, by rolling it. As slowly as he dared, and as gently as he could manage, he used the rounded shape of the tangle to move it. It was a struggle, and he puffed and sweated and sometimes had to stop for a minute. He tried to soothe the animal by talking to it, telling it what he was trying to do. He never mentioned soup.

Because the wind had pushed sand over the porch steps all the way to the kitchen door, Teddy was able to roll the ball right inside and into his room. He only had a small pen knife. The task was harder than he'd thought, but still he sawed and sawed until the first strand gave way. Now he only had to do that several dozen more times. He was so focused on the task that he didn't hear anyone, but he felt a presence and looked up. Uncle Edgar was older than Teddy's mother by several years. His face had weathered into hard lines, and he was frowning down at Teddy around an unlit pipe.

"Why are you doing that in here?"

Teddy wasn't sure his uncle had ever addressed him directly in the time he'd been here. He had nothing but the truth. "I just can't let them kill him."

Uncle Edgar said nothing, just grabbed the butcher knife from the kitchen and started cutting too.

Soon the animal started to emerge. One flipper freed, then two. On the third, the cords had cut deep and had to be eased out of the flesh. Teddy was surprised at the gentleness in his uncle's rough hands.

Liquid black eyes watched them, but the turtle never struggled. No sooner had the last of the net been cut away than they heard voices. Teddy ran to the front room and saw his brothers through the window, standing by the front gate, talking. He raced back to his room to find the turtle gone and his uncle closing the closet door with one long finger to his lips.

At the dinner table, his brothers talked nonstop about the storm damage. Just to the south, in Rehoboth, the SS *Thomas Tracy* had run aground. Teddy would have liked to have seen that. There were more tales of flooding, rescues, and loss of life. Some happier stories too. All of the Wilsons' ponies had been rounded up after their stable blew away. Eventually, David asked about the turtle.

Teddy shrugged, not wanting to lie. He glanced down the table. Uncle Edgar was eating his potatoes with a blank expression. "I hope he made it back to the ocean."

The subject changed and talk went on. Teddy helped with the clearing up and the dishes. For once, night couldn't come fast enough. As soon as he could, Teddy pled tiredness and went to bed.

He peeked in the closet, first thing after he put his pajamas on. The turtle was too large to lie flat. Uncle Edgar had propped him upright and cushioned him with the old net. It couldn't be comfortable, but it couldn't be helped. Teddy crawled into bed. He really was tired, but he couldn't sleep. A few times, he heard frantic swishing in the quiet, the turtle's flippers against the closet wall, and he would get out of bed, open the closet door a crack, and whisper encouragement, even though he didn't know what Uncle Edgar had planned. After what seemed forever, he heard feet on the stairs as everyone went to bed, except Uncle Edgar, who went out for a last pipe.

When the whole house was asleep, Uncle Edgar appeared in the doorway. Between them, they got the turtle out of the house with very little noise. Teddy was surprised to find a sort of sled his uncle had fashioned. Pulling together, they headed for the water. Only when they crested the dune did Teddy remember his fear. Very little light came from the stars and the tiniest sliver of moon. He felt pressure in his chest, and a little sick, but he kept pulling until they were at the water's edge.

All at once it was time to set the turtle free.

"We never even gave him a name," said Teddy.

"Wild creatures don't need our names. Just our help sometimes."

Slowly, sensing its home, the turtle pushed forward. Teddy moved alongside, wading into the cool water, the dark swirling around his knees. He put his hand on the shell. "Good luck," he said, as the turtle slipped away, going home.

They stood there even after there was nothing to see.

"Thank you," said Teddy.

Uncle Edgar nodded. The glow in his pipe bobbed in the dark. "We'd best get back," he said.

It was still hours 'til dawn, and lying in his bed, Teddy could hear the waves. He hadn't yet realized that they no longer scared him. He imagined the turtle gliding happily through the deep and remembered how peaceful it had been to stand there under the stars. He closed his eyes, no longer able to stay awake, no longer needing to, while cherry pipe smoke floated in on salt air.

TERRI CLIFTON IS A WRITER OF FICTION AND NONFICTION AND WAS AWARDED A FELLOWSHIP AS THE 2013 EMERGING PROFESSIONAL IN FICTION LITERATURE BY THE DELAWARE DIVISION OF THE ARTS. HER NONFICTION BOOK, *A RANDOM SOLDIER*, IS A MEMOIR OF HER SON, CHAD, WHO WAS KILLED IN ACTION IN IRAQ AND FULFILLS A PROMISE MADE. SHE HAS RECENTLY COMPLETED HER FIRST POETRY CHAPBOOK AND IS CURRENTLY AT WORK ON A NOVEL. TERRI'S INTERESTS INCLUDE PHOTOGRAPHY, MUSIC, AND TIME WITH NATURE AND FRIENDS. SHE IS INVOLVED WITH HER COMMUNITY AND LITERACY ISSUES AND IS THE DIRECTOR OF A FOUNDATION BENEFITING VETERANS. SHE MAKES HER HOME ON A HISTORIC FARM AT THE EDGE OF THE DELAWARE BAY WITH HER SON, RYAN, AND HUSBAND, RICHARD, AN INTERNATIONALLY KNOWN WILDLIFE ARTIST.

JUDGE'S COMMENT

This story about an eight-year-old empathizing with a sea turtle washed ashore during the Great Atlantic Hurricane of 1944 is a sweetly charming reminder of the paradox that, when the human instinct to help those in need is extended to nonhuman animals, we enlarge and affirm our humanity by acknowledging the inherent kinship of all life.

2016 REHOBOTH BEACH READS JUDGES

DENISE CAMACHO

DENISE CAMACHO IS THE PRESIDENT OF INTRIGUE PUBLISHING, LLC. MS. CAMACHO HAS BEEN IN THE PUBLISHING BUSINESS FOR MORE THAN TWELVE YEARS. HER EXPERIENCE INCLUDES VANITY PRESSES, PRINT-ON-DEMAND, AND SELF-PUBLISHING. SHE ULTIMATELY SETTLED ON PARTNERING WITH HER HUSBAND (AUSTIN S. CAMACHO) AND SANDRA BOWMAN TO START THEIR OWN SMALL PUBLISHING COMPANY IN 2012 AND HAS WORKED DILIGENTLY TO FIND GREAT BOOKS WORTHY OF INTRIGUE. MS. CAMACHO IS ALSO COMMITTED TO HELPING AUTHORS NAVIGATE THE PUBLISHING INDUSTRY. SHE REGULARLY ATTENDS SEMINARS ON WHAT IS NEW IN PUBLISHING AND ATTENDS WRITER CONFERENCES TO SHARE HER EXPERIENCES.

LAUREL MARSHFIELD

LAUREL MARSHFIELD IS A PROFESSIONAL WRITER, GHOSTWRITER, DEVELOPMENTAL EDITOR, AND BOOK COACH WHO ASSISTS AUTHORS OF NONFICTION, FICTION, MEMOIR, AND BIOGRAPHY IN PREPARING THEIR BOOK MANUSCRIPTS FOR PUBLICATION. SHE HAS HELPED MORE THAN FOUR HUNDRED AUTHORS SHAPE, DEVELOP, AND REFINE THEIR BOOK MANUSCRIPTS—BY OFFERING MANUSCRIPT EVALUATION, DEVELOPMENTAL EDITING, BOOK COACHING, GHOSTWRITING, AND CO-AUTHORSHIP THROUGH HER EDITORIAL SERVICES FOR AUTHORS BUSINESS, BLUE HORIZON COMMUNICATIONS (BLUEHORIZONCOMMUNICATIONS.COM).

JOHN A. NIEVES

JOHN A. NIEVES IS AN ASSISTANT PROFESSOR OF ENGLISH AT SALISBURY UNIVERSITY. DR. NIEVES HAS POEMS FORTHCOMING OR RECENTLY PUBLISHED IN JOURNALS SUCH AS: *SOUTHERN REVIEW, PLEIADES, CRAZYHORSE, THE LITERARY REVIEW,* AND *VERSE DAILY.* HE WON THE *INDIANA REVIEW* POETRY CONTEST AND HIS FIRST BOOK, *CURIO* (2014), WON THE ELIXIR PRESS ANNUAL POETRY AWARD JUDGE'S PRIZE. HE RECEIVED HIS M.A. FROM UNIVERSITY OF SOUTH FLORIDA AND HIS PHD FROM THE UNIVERSITY OF MISSOURI.

Mary Pauer

Mary Pauer received her MFA in creative writing from Stonecoast, at the University of Southern Maine. In 2011 she was awarded the Delaware Division of the Arts Emerging Fellow in Literature (fiction) and in 2014, the Established Fellow in Literature (fiction). Her short fiction has received awards from Delaware Press Association and the National Federation of Press Women. Her work has been published in *Southern Women's Review, The Broadkill Review, On the Rusk, Delaware Beach Life, Delaware Today, Avocet Quarterly, Avocet Weekly, Wanderings, The Delmarva Review* and *Currents,* an anthology of Delaware writers. She is the author of two collections of short fiction. Ms. Pauer is on staff at New Rivers Press and reads for the American Fiction Prize. She has judged writing contests in Maine and Delaware and works with private writing clients from varied disciplines.

Judith Reveal

Judy Reveal is a freelance editor, book indexer, book reviewer, and published author. She has taught creative writing classes at Chesapeake College as well as at arts councils across the Delmarva Peninsula. She presents workshops at various organizations including the Bay To Ocean (BTO) Writers Conference, Harford County Library Writers Conference, and Lewes Creative Writers' Conference. She is the coordinator for the BTO Writers Conference. She writes book reviews for *New York Journal of Books,* and has indexed more than fifty books during her career. Her most recent book, *The Four Elements of Fiction,* offers nonfiction guidance to the newer writer. Her historical fiction, *The Brownstone,* finished as a quarterfinalist in the top 100 of the 2013 Amazon Breakthrough Novel Contest.

BILLIE TRAVALINI

BILLIE TRAVALINI, A RECIPIENT OF A 2014 GOVERNOR'S AWARD FOR THE ARTS, HAS RECEIVED DELAWARE DIVISION OF THE ARTS PROFESSIONAL FELLOWSHIPS IN FICTION, NONFICTION, AND POETRY. HER RECENT PUBLICATIONS INCLUDE "ON HEARING MY SON IS SOCRATES AND MY HUSBAND FRANK SINATRA" *(THE MOTH)*, "RUSH LIMBAUGH AND THE FRENCH APPLE PIE" (EAST CHINA NORMAL UNIVERSITY), "RULES TO SURVIVE CHILDHOOD," ENGLISH AND CHINESE, (EAST CHINA NORMAL UNIVERSITY), AND "NEVER AGAIN," *(LAKEVIEW INTERNATIONAL JOURNAL OF LITERATURE AND ART)*. HER EDITED WORKS INCLUDE, *ON THE MASON DIXON LINE: AN ANTHOLOGY OF CONTEMPORARY DELAWARE WRITERS*, *TEACHING TROUBLED YOUTH: A PRACTICAL PEDAGOGICAL APPROACH*, AND *NO PLACE LIKE HERE: AN ANTHOLOGY OF SOUTHERN DELAWARE POETRY AND PROSE*. IN JULY 2016, SHE WAS A GUEST READER AND PANELIST AT THE 14TH INTERNATIONAL CONFERENCE OF THE SHORT STORY IN SHANGHAI, CHINA. SHE CO-FOUNDED AND COORDINATES THE LEWES CREATIVE WRITERS' CONFERENCE AND TEACHES CREATIVE WRITING AT WILMINGTON UNIVERSITY. A GRADUATE OF THE UNIVERSITY OF DELAWARE AND TEMPLE, SHE IS BUSY AT WORK ON *RUSH LIMBAUGH AND THE FRENCH APPLE PIE AND OTHER STORIES* AND *RULES TO SURVIVE CHILDHOOD*, A SEQUEL TO *BLOOD SISTERS*.

Also from Cat & Mouse Press

The Beach House

There is something for everyone here, from romance, history, and intrigue to jilted brides, NASCAR drivers, outlaws, and even a ghost or two.

The Boardwalk

A fortune-telling machine with a mind of its own, professional killers hanging out by the hotel pool, granny run amok in Funland…what's happened to Rehoboth?

Beach Days

Meet a researcher whose romance project includes an unexpected variable, a man who gets postcards seemingly from his dead wife, and a couple of elderly ladies who break out of the old-age home.

The Sea Sprite Inn

Jillian has lived through more than her share of tough times, but leaps at a chance to reinvent herself when she inherits the responsibility for a dilapidated family beach house.

Fun with Dick and James

Follow the escapades of Dick and James (and their basset hound, Otis) as they navigate the shifting sands of Rehoboth Beach, facing one crazy conundrum after another.

Sandy Shorts

Bad men + bad dogs + bad luck = great beach reads. The characters in these stories ride the ferry, barhop in Dewey, stroll through Bethany, and run wild in Rehoboth.

Resources for Writers

Online Newspaper

Jam-packed with articles on the craft of writing, editing, self-publishing, marketing, and submitting. Free. Writingisashorething.com

How To Write Winning Short Stories

A concise guide to writing short stories that includes preparation, theme and premise, title, characters, dialogue, setting, and more.

Come play with us!

www.catandmousepress.com
www.facebook.com/catandmousepress

CPSIA information can be obtained
at www.ICGtesting.com
Printed in the USA
BVOW07s2345071016

464310BV00007B/5/P